GOBY the Goblin

By S.A. Ellis

All illustrations by S.A. Ellis

ISBNs:
Print: 978-1-914078-64-4
eBook: 978-1-914078-65-1

Published by PublishingPush.com

Goby the goblin is dedicated to Bianca Cesarano, my daughter, she loved the stories I told her of Goby and his adventures when she was very young. I could not afford to buy books at the time, so I would make up stories to tell her. She has urged me for many years to write these stories down on paper, so here we are.

Tony Day my rock and partner, without his encouragement and support I do not think the book would have been completed.

Finally, Marie Ellis, my beautiful mum who is so gentle and kind, the nicest person I know x.

Contents

MAP OF THE THREE REALMS-GOBLINS

GRACKINIUM
GNARKULL

CALDER SEA

hardcastle

THIRD REALM

shriekal

SHRIK
VOLCANO

IMPBAHS

hootahn city

MOUNT
hoot

hanomide
MOUNTAINS

SECOND REALM

(MORZARhS)

harridan
MOUNTAIN

witches

BOGS

quazboo
(NANTAH)

CRIMSTONE RIVER

CLANDIL

LAKES

CLANOMIDE MOUNTAINS

(GIANTS)

MASSDUMOOR

CRUENS

GOBBANAM

CRUENS

TREE

MOUNTAINS

GALAMIDE MOUNTAIN
CAVE

PUMPLE
MOUNTAIN

GRAVEN TREE

(WOOLVACS)

KLEWOOD

(OWLS)

TREACLEWOOD

KRACKLEWOOD

(FARIES)

FIRST REALM

Cruel

Chapter One

The Great Avalanche

In a mystical place, filled with enchantment and magic, there stood a little mountain called Pumple. It was neatly tucked away deep within the magnificent and majestic Galamide mountain range, the First Realm of the Goblins.

It is a misconception to say that all goblins are bad. This belief simply isn't true, and not all goblins are ugly, gnarled, nasty little creatures that only want to cause trouble and misery.

Within the mountain lived a clan of goblins who were busy about their lives, living in a huge cave half way down the side of Pumple Mountain.

The cave had many little natural pockets in its walls that provided cosy homes for the goblins, as well as a handful of other little creatures.

They all lived happily together tucked away in this safe haven, living in harmony.

The goblins of Pumple Mountain were quite comical with dumpy little bodies, long legs and rather large feet.

Their ears were longer than average for goblins and they had large eyes, sat under heavy brows.

This gave them a misleading look of sadness; they were in fact quite jolly!

You could also tell a Pumple goblin by their distinctive markings; these consisted of dark circles all over their body.

They looked like little puddles on their bright green, wrinkly skin.

The goblins were generally of good heart and respected their fellow kin. They did not think an animal was a tasty feast for the table and they showed much respect for their natural habitat.

The goblins would pick berries, mushrooms and vegetables to make stews and many delicious meals. And, of course, the ever so popular berry wines which went down a treat and caused much laughter and merriment.

There were many threats outside the cave on Pumple Mountain. Beasts of all descriptions would make light work of devouring a little goblin in one go, so living in the cave grouped together worked as a good deterrent, to stop any wild beasts venturing in for a tasty snack!

All was well within Pumple Mountain until that dreadful day of the almighty avalanche, which sent huge boulders crashing down the mountainside, killing many goblins and other creatures in its path.

This was such a terrible tragedy it changed the course of life for the goblins forever!

The avalanche was caused by huge beasts called cruens.

These beasts lived on the mountain tops. They stood on two legs with huge feet and had very long muscular arms, with huge hands that could take out a goblin with one swipe!

They looked like massive gorillas but with the grandeur of a buffalo, and they had long white hair that cascaded down their bulbous backs.

Their skin had a blue chalky tinge to it that was wrinkled and tough.

They couldn't run very fast because of their short legs but they made up for this with their powerful fists that could pummel stone to ash with one swipe.

One day a couple of cruens had a fierce fight over territory; their huge bodies shook the ground to its core as they crashed into each other in combat. Unfortunately, while fighting, a huge rock that sat precariously on top of the mountain was dislodged.

It smashed into many pieces as one of the beasts was hurled into it.

This caused an almighty avalanche. The sounds of the rocks crashing down the mountainside was deafening, and many lives were lost as the thunderous rocks (and an unfortunate cruen) crashed down the mountain side crushing all life in its path!

The goblins lucky enough to escape the tragedy were either in the cave at the time, or further away working round the other side of the mountain, mining for Pumplestone.

The stones were used to make many things, from cooking utensils to furniture, and the purest stones were sold as jewellery and weapons.

They were sold to travelling warlocks, witches and other traders in exchange for spices, herbs and many other useful things.

Once the billowing clouds of dust had settled, the devastation was clear to see; everywhere was covered in rubble.

Many trees had toppled to the ground and the area was covered in stones; it was a terrible sight to see.

The final count of goblins and other little creatures killed was in the hundreds. Bodies lay strewn across the ground, under rocks and other debris, and an eerie silence hung heavily over the scene, like a black, oppressive cloud.

The cruens had always been a threat to the goblins: now and again a stray one would venture down the mountainside looking for a special treat, sometimes they were lucky and sometimes not!

They were notoriously pugnacious creatures and often fought amongst themselves, but their fighting always took place much further up the mountain on the tops, where they lived.

The impbahs were little impish creatures with big dark brown eyes and mellow-yellow skin. In between their little pointy ears sat a tuft of hair that looked totally out of place.

The impbahs always had a few scouts positioned in surrounding trees, keeping an eye on cruen activity.

If there was a threat, they would let out a high-pitched warning scream from their oversized mouths that stretched from ear to ear.

This always made the goblins' toes curl up in fright and everyone would quickly return to the cave.

It was normally quite easy to detect whether the cruens were fighting as it was usually pack-fights, but on this occasion, the fighting was just between two of them.

It all happened so quickly and unexpectedly that the alarm was not raised in time.

After many tears and too many cremations, it was time to address this constant risk, as it was not going to go away.

Decisions had to be made and it was time to move to a safer place and set up a new home.

The goblins had lived happily in Pumple Mountain for many cenatoons (which we know as centuries) but they did not want to live under the constant threat from the cruens anymore.

They could not cope with losing any more lives; they must leave their ancestral home and move....... but to where?

The popstrells were sent out first to scour the land. They looked like little bats but had strawberry-red furry chests, their ears were larger than the average bat, and they had a bright red fringe on their wings.

The popstrells were highly valued by the Pumple goblins; they were their eyes and could see far and wide, and would let the goblins know if there was danger nearby. They had returned with a handful of places that looked promising but it was difficult to gauge from the air and needed further investigation from the ground.

So, a small group of goblins, impbahs and mambooas were selected to go and check out the popstrells' suggestions.

The mambooas were unusual creatures that had the look of a monkey but with the face of a lion, and fur that looked like tight sheep's wool.

They had orange piercing eyes set in dark-brown sockets that made them look ghoulish.

Their feet were large with three toes, one being much bigger than the other two, and that helped them run extremely fast.

They had very long arms and hands that consisted of three stubby fingers with hardened pads to help them run along quickly through any terrain.

They were very quick and agile and could outrun most of the creatures within the Three Realms.

It was important that the new location was near enough so that the goblins could still mine in the mountain, but far enough away to avoid any further avalanche and cruen activity.

After what seemed like a lifetime, with many days of worry and torment for the creatures of Pumple Mountain, the group returned and relayed their mixed feelings of hope and fear.

Some of the locations they visited were just not suitable; they were too dangerous and inhabited by many poisonous plants and goblin-eating creatures.

They had been lucky to escape by the skin of their teeth.

The only place that looked promising and could offer the sanctuary they desired, and which was near enough, was a place called Kracklewood.

The wood was not like any ordinary wood. First of all, it was much bigger, and, in fact, more like a forest.

There were many trees with huge branches and dense canopies that could house some of the creatures safely and provide a comfortable home within the gigantic trunks, but Kracklewood also had a cave deep within its centre.

On investigation, the little group had ventured inside and explored, but the tunnel seemed to go on and on forever, and after hours of walking through the darkness, the tunnel split into more tunnels. At this point, they decided to head back. It was too risky and they needed to return home.

While the little group of scouts were explaining their findings to the High Council, it suddenly jogged Mr Gravenpumple's memory.

When he had first ventured out on his travels, many moolatoons ago (which we know as decades), he had come across this cave and he remembered how deep and long it was.

He had explored the cave and wanted to see how far it went and whether the tunnel would take him through the mountain to the other side.

After many days and nights in total darkness, with only the light of his staff, he had discovered that the tunnels opened up into another land.

Mr Gravenpumple was revered by all the creatures from the First Realm. He was a very old and wise wizard goblin who held the highest rank on the goblin council, earned through many deeds of bravery and great wisdom.

It was easy to distinguish him from any other goblin by the big leathery cloak that he always wore, and his crooked pointy hat that looked like it had been beaten to death by too many adventures.

He had very thick white, woolly eyebrows that hung over his little screwed-up eyes. He also had a very long white moustache and a beard that sprouted out of his pointy chin like it had been an afterthought!

Within this strange land, there were many forests that stretched for miles and miles; some of the trees which stood in clusters throughout the valley had huge leathery leaves.

The ground was covered in a pale red mist that gave off a spooky haze, and every now and then, there was a spurt of water that would shoot up into the sky.

It scared the living nightlights out of the goblin on experiencing the first burst. The sky was a milky red, which gave a strange hue to the land, and it was one of his first journeys into the Third Realm.

Mr Gravenpumple travelled extensively throughout his life, collecting potions and learning spells from all walks of life. He would then bring them home and put them to good use in Pumple Mountain.

The wizard goblin sat mulling over the suitability of the cave, but after much deliberation, he decided it was too deep and long. Not only that but halfway through, it split into five more tunnels. It was too dangerous; the risk of adventurous and stupid goblins getting lost and other less desirable creatures getting in meant the cave would not work.

Mr Gravenpumple

Chapter Two

The Master Plan

There was just one problem with Kracklewood; the wood was known to be a favourite resting place for the woolvacs!

These fierce creatures looked like large wolves, but instead of fur, their skin was scaly and they had huge teeth. They would often venture into the wood and many a goblin or other poor defenceless creature would be their meal of the day.

They took no prisoners and sometimes would just kill for the sport!

They would eat a goblin whole with a smack of the lips while an impbah wouldn't even touch the sides.

Many creatures would not dare to venture into this wood but there was no choice; the goblins had to find another home quickly and Kracklewood was looking like the only place that could work, even with the risk of the woolvacs.

Mr Gravenpumple had been pacing up and down for nights, mulling over this dilemma, when suddenly, he had a light-bulb moment and thought of a good use for the cave. With its long tunnels that ran right through the mountain, it could be an ideal solution. They could lure the woolvacs to the cave and trap them inside, then hopefully, they would never return but would settle in another land.

Thus, the 'banishment of the woolvacs' plan was born and many discussions took place within the great council to bring the plan together.

Kracklewood had suffered terribly at the claws of the woolvacs and the wood had been stripped of much of its glory. Many trees had deep scratches and grooves on the trunks where the bark had been worn away and left to ruin. The woolvacs used the trees as places to scratch their ugly scaly backs and clean their sharp teeth. They were ruining Kracklewood and they had to be chased away to another land for good!

Mr Gravenpumple was the wisest and most knowledgeable goblin to ever live in Pumple Mountains, and there was many a story to be told of his adventures. The goblin had accumulated many spells and potions on his travels from land to land, meeting warlocks, wizards and witches alike. He learnt how to influence the weather, make objects disappear and conjured up many a trick to amuse the young goblins.

This magic is what saved many lives that dreadful day when the rocks came crashing down in the great avalanche. Mr Gravenpumple had been able to cast forth a magic barrier, just in time to shield the cave. It stopped the entrance from being totally blocked so the goblins who had not been crushed by the rocks outside could crawl out of the cave unscathed.

All the creatures were to gather together to hear the honoured goblin's idea.

It was time to stand up to these vile creatures and, hopefully, drive them out for good, and Mr Gravenpumple was going to explain how this would happen.

Mr Gravenpumple called upon all the creatures that had suffered in the great avalanche and lost loved ones, to gather for a great council meeting.

All the goblins, impbahs and mambooas attended the meeting, which was held in the Graven Chambers in Pumple Mountain. It was a cavernous cave not far away from the main cave, and used for many debates and discussions.

Mr Gravenpumple had already discussed a battle plan with the chief cabinet and wanted to put it forward to the audience that had gathered.

The creatures fell silent as the great goblin stepped up to the podium, and, having flicked back his large cloak, he rearranged his large wizard hat to make himself comfortable.

He raised his head high and surveyed the crowd. The chamber would normally be crammed for a grand meeting, but sadly, now it was only half full.

The wizard goblin swallowed hard to hold back the tears and sadness he felt in his heart, but now was not the time to show weakness. He must be strong and give hope to the creatures of Pumple Mountain.

So, he breathed in deeply and cleared his throat before he spoke in a loud and clear voice.

"I would like to extend my gratitude to you all for attending this evening. We find ourselves in difficult times and need to act quickly to find a new home."

His voice bellowed deep and clear.

"We have been forced to relocate; the cave can no longer provide a safe haven."

Everyone's eyes were focused on the mighty goblin, and he had his audience's full attention as he stared deep and sternly into the crowd.

"The cruens have become too unpredictable with their constant fighting and the recent tragedy has proven this point. We have no choice; we must find a new home!" Mr Gravenpumple took a moment to steady his breath and then continued. "We have scoured the land to try and find somewhere suitable and it has been a difficult task, but we have found somewhere and it has been decided." There was a deathly silence as everyone hung on the goblin's every word. "It has to be Kracklewood!"

With this news, there was a huge outcry and much shuffling of feet and groans of protest and dismay because the creatures knew of the dangers of Kracklewood. The woolvacs would be a constant threat, and immediately, everyone became uneasy and nervous.

Mr Gravenpumple needed to calm and settle the crowd so he laid out the plan to the doubting but eager ears; no one made a sound as the goblin explained how the plan would work.

"The woolvacs need to be lured towards the cave in Kracklewood. Once the woolvacs are near the entrance, they will be driven into the cave and then it will be blocked by felling several large trees that stand close by," he said.

The trees were rotten and diseased and needed to be felled so Mr Gravenpumple did not feel too bad about their end of life.

"Once the entrance is sealed, the woolvacs will have no choice but to run deeper into the cave and through the long and winding tunnels which will take them far away from Pumple Mountain and into another land," Mr Gravenpumple said with conviction and confidence. You see, the goblin's intention was not to kill the woolvacs, but to send them packing, with a desperate wish that they would learn a lesson and change their ways and, hopefully, they would never return.

It was then explained how the creatures of Pumple Mountain would all help to get the beasts into the cave. "Once the woolvacs are all within the clearing near the cave entrance, the popstrells must come together simultaneously and swoop down on the woolvacs, so they can round them up," he said with a quick glance at Plock, the chief bat, who was perched firmly on a tall chair nearby. He explained how scouts would be sent out first to make sure there was an accurate head count of the beasts; they could not afford for any of them to escape.

"The impbahs will scream at the woolvacs from the surrounding trees with their piercing shrill," explained Mr Gravenpumple.

He secretly feared it could make everyone's ears bleed if they all gathered together and screamed at the same time.

"This will confuse and scare the beasts, and, with the popstrells swooping down on them, it will send them crazy!" he exclaimed.

"Then the mambooas, who have the ability to run very quickly and are very nimble on their feet, will run through the woolvacs at great speed, circling around them to confuse and disorientate them," the wizard goblin said in an excited tone.

"Finally, the goblins will wield their gnarled, pointed wooden sticks and shout loudly and chase the woolvacs into the cave, prodding and poking them to make sure they are steered towards and through the cave entrance," said Mr Gravenpumple in a charged and exhilarated voice.

"With all the noise and commotion, the beasts should be sufficiently scared and confused to make the plan work." He finished with a deep intake of breath.

The plan was dangerous and fraught with peril, but, if all the creatures of Pumple Mountain came together and performed their duty to the letter, then it could work.

No one said a word; the air was still and everyone was digesting this plan. Then suddenly, a lone voice shouted out from the audience in a strong deep tone;

"Mr Gravenpumple's plan seems workable, but how are we going to amass all the woolvacs together in the first place?"

The question came from one of the bravest goblins of Pumple Mountain, Gorvust. He had saved many lives and bore many scars from previous battles, too many to be told today, but suffice to say, he had won the respect and honour of all the creatures who lived in the mountain.

Mr Gravenpumple cast his eyes towards Gorvust, nodded his head slowly in a gesture of great respect and winked at him before setting about explaining how he would initially lure the woolvacs into the area near the cave with an enchantment spell.

"I will create a strong, pungent smell of cruen to entice and intrigue the beasts' curiosity," he answered confidently.

"I will use the golly berry from the Repeller bush which grows on the side of the mountain. As you all know, it is a very clever bush and produces berries that give off many different scents in order to protect itself," he said.

Dependent on what was trying to eat the berries, it would create a smell that was repugnant to that particular creature to keep it away.

"Using my able assistant, my son, Grumplepumple, we shall gather as many golly berries as possible, to use in the potion." The wizard goblin turned to get an acknowledgement from his son, who was stood nearby to show support.

The berries were dark green, lumpy and very smelly, and they were not easy to pick as they would squirt their horrible, smelly goo at you. So, they would have to distract the bushes with a little magic and create some fairy dust.

Grumplepumple would sprinkle the dust into the air over the bush and the twinkly particles would fly around in circles to dazzle and distract the bush while the berries were picked.

Grumplepumple had spent many an hour with his father picking up little nuggets of wisdom and some very interesting and useful spells, and he had mastered the art of producing fairy dust, with the permission, of course, of the chief fairy!

This plan seemed to instil a sense of encouragement and excitement in the crowd and the chatter and noise were immense as Mr Gravenpumple left the auditorium.

Everyone knew their place and what was expected of them, and, after a successful show of hands, the plan was agreed.

The attack on the woolvacs had to happen quickly, so the popstrell scouts were sent out the very next night to scour Pumple Mountain and count every woolvac there was. It was so important that all the beasts were gathered together and contained outside the cave; they could ill afford to miscount and have any stray woolvacs left behind.

The popstrell scouts worked hard over the next couple of nights to make sure all the woolvacs were accounted for. The total came to fifty-two, which was more than first estimated. Two were nearly missed as they were hiding behind a tree waiting to pounce on their next poor unfortunate victim.

Armed with the correct head count, the woolvacs could be counted into the area near the cave. They normally travelled in packs so, hopefully, they would enter in groups.

After weeks of letting the potion ferment and mixing in some magic spells, Mr Gravenpumple conjured up his potent goo. It was such an intensified smell of cruen, and so strong that he had to keep it sealed in a large pot with heavy leather straps tightly bound round the pot to stop any leakage.

The smell should lure all the woolvacs together and quickly: it was so important to get all of them together at the same time.

There was, of course, a real cruen available to use as bait. It had lost the fight on top of the mountain and came tumbling down amongst the rocks, killing many creatures in its path. If the woolvacs saw the beast, it would confirm the smell was not some trickery and would keep the beasts' attention.

The cruen had landed at the foot of the mountain. Its huge body lay battered and bruised and very still. A couple of brave mambooas had run round the body and inflicted a couple of nudges and heavy prods to check that the beast was no longer alive; there was no movement. However, to make doubly sure, a couple of goblins pricked the beast with their pointy sticks to make sure it was no longer.

"You prick it first; you're supposed to be the bravest, or so you keep bragging!" said Garvoid to his best friend, Garvtak.

"Oh, funny how you always use that line when there's a need to commit a brave act!" replied Garvtak in a sarcastic voice.

The two goblins always poked fun at each other but clearly had a great fondness for each other too. They tiptoed gingerly around the cruen and prodded and poked until they were sure the creature had gone off to the great mountain in the sky.

The body had to be hauled all the way from the bottom of the mountain to the cave entrance at Kracklewood, undetected by any woolvac or other creature that might be roaming through the wood. It was bound in a thick coating of golly berry goo and then wrapped in huge leaves to disguise it.

The cruen had been rolled onto a large raft of twigs, then dragged to its new location at the cave entrance and covered in rocks until the time was ready for it to be used as bait.

This had proved to be a difficult task as the cruen weighed a ton, and it didn't help when one of the goblins got his foot stuck in the sticky golly berry goo which had been slathered all over the beast. It took many hands to help detach the poor goblin, who nearly fainted with the rancid smell of the cruen and the goo!

Mr Gravenpumple did not want the cruen to be eaten by the woolvacs, so it was important to make sure the attack happened straight away, as soon as the beasts were rounded together in the clearing. The cruen had caused the problem in the first place but still deserved a proper burial, so prickly thorns would be placed around the beast to keep the woolvacs at bay.

Woolvac

Chapter Three

Banishment of the Woolvacs

The time had finally come to put the plan into action and Mr Gravenpumple unravelled the large pot of stinking smelly cruen goo that had been transported to the cave entrance with the assistance of his son, Grumplepumple, and a few other goblins. The cave entrance was hidden by a large boulder that had crashed down the mountain many moolatoons ago and landed a few feet in front of the cave; it completely blocked the view of the entrance. This was perfect because the woolvacs would not realise what the creatures were trying to do and the goblins could hide behind the boulder and spring out quickly and herd the woolvacs into the cave.

The rocks and cover over the cruen had been removed and its body put in place in front of the boulder and the goblins had placed several thorny branches around the body. The smell of the potion was starting to waft up into the air and seemed to be finding its way into everyone's nostrils.

It was very smelly and really disgusting and was making everyone feel really nauseous.

"Whose bright idea was it to use the cruen? Its body stinks of your smelly armpits!" said Garvtak to Toobah, giving him a look of total disgust!

"I'll have you know my armpits smell of freshly picked flowers!" said Toobah, lifting his arms and pretending to smell himself.

The mambooa was not offended by Garvtak. He was used to the goblin's jibes; he knew they were said in jest. The two of them were the best of friends and had been on many adventures together, along with Mr Gravenpumple.

The popstrells waited nervously in the trees ready to swoop down on the woolvacs, and the impbahs had been puffing up their chests in order to be able to let out the biggest screeches they could muster, but breathing in the rancid smell so deeply had made one of the impbahs faint and it fell out of the tree with a heavy thud. It had to be revived quickly, and, with a couple of quick slaps across its face from Elphin, the chief impbah, this seemed to do the trick.

"Wake up, Squimp, you idiot of an impbah. You're breathing in too deeply!" said Elphin.

The mambooas had been having races to see who was the fastest to weave in between the woolvacs legs but the horrible smell did not make this an easy task.

"That smell is making me want to vomit. I don't want to be wasting those delicious pip cakes I had earlier!" said Booma to Toobah, who always scorned his friend for his insatiable appetite for food!

"If you just eat what's given you without asking for seconds all the time, you might not have this problem," said Toobah in a reprimanding way.

The goblins had gathered and hidden behind the large boulder that obscured the cave, waiting apprehensively for the action to begin.

It was a lighter night than usual because of a full moon that shone brightly in the inky sky and there was a heavy sprinkling of bright twinkly stars.

This was good, as it would give the creatures enough light to be able to see the woolvacs clearly as they entered the area.

The creatures of Pumple Mountain did not sleep at night; for them, it was the other way round. They would wake up at dusk and go to sleep at the break of dawn. They had excellent night vision and this was the way of the goblins of the Three Realms.

It seemed an age before any movement was detected and many of the creatures had started doubting whether the plan would work. The heady smell of cruen was starting to really take its toll. Mr Gravenpumple had wrapped his cloak over his mouth and was starting to perspire heavily.

He knew he had made the potion too strong; it was certainly having a sickly effect on everyone.

He turned to Gorun, one of his chief councillors, for reassurance, and questioned whether he was doing the right thing.

"I'm not sure this is going to work, Gorun. Do you think this was the right plan? That damn potion is so strong, I'd be surprised if we haven't attracted every predator that's out there!" he exclaimed.

"My dear friend, you are the wisest and most knowledgeable wizard goblin I know. You never get it wrong! I think we just need a little more patience. Is that not what you're always telling me, hey?" Gorun replied in a jovial tone and patted his dear friend on the back.

The night was silent and still and the creatures of Pumple Mountain were becoming restless and worried. Mr Gravenpumple was starting to doubt this whole idea. What if they didn't come? What else could they do?

The plan had to work; they had spent so much time preparing for this moment, and it must work!

Then suddenly, there was movement from a few hundred yards away and something was coming closer. Then, a loud rustle came from the undergrowth a few yards away.

The first group of woolvacs burst through the trees into the clearing near the front of the cave. The strong pungent smell had worked. The beasts had picked up the scent and it was enticing them into the trap!

Mr Gravenpumple lifted up his hand to instruct everyone to hold their position and wait for his command.

Then, with a great leap forward, another group entered the arena making a low growling sound that sounded like the rumblings of a giant's belly!

The woolvacs were coming in greater numbers now, howling loudly and crashing into each other in a frenzied attempt to get to the poor cruen first, but the thorny bushes were keeping them at bay.

The popstrells were counting the beasts in as they rushed forward: ten, twenty, thirty, forty and then fifty - but where were the last two?

Plock instructed a handful of popstrells to follow him and fly off to seek the stray beasts and fortunately, they soon found them. They were circling around a pair of silly yar yar birds that had just crashed into a tree and slumped onto the ground.

The yar yar birds got their name because of the noise they made; it sounded just like they were saying yar yar!

The birds had been gawping at the sight of the woolvacs all running together in such large numbers. It was a rare sight to see.

Yar yars were beautiful birds with dusty pink feathers like a flamingo, and a large

plume of white feathers that protruded out of their heads, making them look like palm

trees. They were very funny to look at and were not the most intelligent of species.

Plus, their navigational skills were not great and had been questioned on many occasions.

The two woolvacs needed to be brought into line quickly so Plock, who was the head of the popstrells, had flown back to call upon the mambooas to help lift the dazed birds off the floor and run with them quickly towards the clearing.

Toobah instructed Booma to join him and the two mambooas sped off to rescue the birds.

Mr Gravenpumple could see what was happening and signalled to the impbahs to come to the aid of the mambooas and grab the yar yar birds as they came by. The two woolvacs, who were circling the birds, soon became distracted by the frenzied commotion from Toobah and Booma and started to chase them back towards the cave. They were not far behind the mambooas and howling loudly. Everyone held their breath as Toobah and Booma sprang out of the bush with the two yar yar birds on their backs. It was a strange sight to see!

Elphin was waiting, dangling by his feet out of a tree and plucked the birds off the mambooas' backs quickly, grabbing one of each of the birds' legs and tossing them over to a group of nervous impbahs who were positioned in the nearby tree, ready to grab them. The yar yar birds were still dazed, which was probably good, otherwise, they would have been flapping their wings. The impbahs grabbed hold of the birds firmly and placed them in the safety of the tree.

Now that all the woolvacs had been accounted for, Mr Gravenpumple gave the signal and yelled,

"Attack, attack, attack!"

The popstrells swooped down to start weaving in between the beasts, twisting and turning quickly to disorientate them. It was not an easy task as they had to dive-bomb the beasts but be quick enough to dodge the sharp claws, and there were quite a few narrow escapes.

Then it was time for the impbahs to join in. Elphin, the chief Impbah, gave the signal and his fellow kin let out the highest-pitched, deafening screeches you could imagine. The goblins had prepared for this and had stuffed sticky buds in their ears to deaden the sound, otherwise, they would not have been able to cope with the noise.

The sudden screeching awoke the yar yar birds abruptly; they had been slumped on a large branch in the tree after they had been rescued.

They started flapping their wings to keep their balance, but it was not easy while sharing the tree with a group of screaming impbahs.

All you could hear was the screech from both parties.

"Yar yar, yar yar, Eeeekkk, eeeekkk, eeekkk!" they yelled.

The yar yar birds were not going to hang around, even though they were the nosiest creatures in the land, and they quickly took flight, disappearing back into the forest.

The woolvacs looked up in horror and started to crash into each other as the little creatures performed their duty. Now was the time for the mambooas to run in between the beasts' legs; Toobah gave the order.

"Let's make these vile creatures dizzy. There's a prize for the first one who makes one fall!" he said in a competitive tone.

The mambooas leapt forward; they were so quick and agile and ran rings around the huge beasts, sending them hurtling through the air as they smashed into each other, and rolling around on the floor in pain.

A couple of the woolvacs crashed into the tree where the impbahs had positioned themselves, dislodging one that nearly fell out of the tree, but, just in time, Jowler grabbed its foot and hauled the little impbah back up to safety.

Jowler was Elphin's right-hand impbah, his faithful and courageous friend.

The woolvacs were definitely startled by this attack; they had never experienced anything like it before and were becoming very dazed, confused and tired.

Mr Gravenpumple gave the signal and the goblins ran out from behind the large boulder wielding their gnarled pointy sticks, and they started poking the woolvacs to steer them towards the hidden cave. They needed to round them up very quickly before it was too late.

The plan was working; the goblins and mambooas had grouped together. This was a very unusual sight to see! The woolvacs had never seen anything like this before and they were panicking, but suddenly, one of the beasts raised its huge body onto its hind legs and howled loudly as if it was trying to regain some order.

Mr Gravenpumple knew immediately what it was trying to do; it wanted to regroup the pack, and the wizard goblin could not allow this to happen.

He thrust his trusty staff forward and chanted a spell.

A bright blue lightning streak zapped through the air and struck the woolvac square in the chest. The beast howled in pain and quickly stumbled back.

It realised immediately that it could not take on this magic and turned on its heels and ran towards the cave.

The others followed their leader quickly, howling and whimpering loudly. The goblins and mambooas charged forward and forced the beasts further through the cave entrance and they started to disappear into the deep, dark endless tunnel, howling loudly.

All was going so well; the woolvacs were on the run and it looked like they could see the end of the pack. There were a couple of stragglers who needed to be prodded and poked, but a couple of sparks of lightning from Grumplepumple's staff soon sorted them out.

It was nice to put his magic to good use. Having practised so many times on poor unfortunate bushes, it was great that it was now useful and he hoped his father would be proud of him.

There fell an eerie silence as the howling stopped. The impbahs had ceased screeching and the popstrells had retreated back into the trees.

Toobah was checking his tribe to make sure all were accounted for and Garvtak and Garvoid, Mr Gravenpumple's two most trusted and loyal soldiers, were checking the cave entrance to give the signal to chop the trees, when suddenly, one of the beasts came running back out of the cave!

"Good gollygummuns!" shouted Garvoid, who had to throw himself sideways so as not to be crushed by the beast.

The goblins hurled themselves out of the way and everyone screamed and yelled to try and stop the woolvac in its tracks.

A couple of the mambooas ran in circles around its legs to try and make it dizzy, but this wasn't working as the beast was totally confused and kept running in the wrong direction away from the cave.

Something had to be done quickly to change its course. All the beasts had to be deep in the cave before the trees could be chopped down to cover the entrance.

All of a sudden, there was a flash of green and one of the goblins had jumped onto the back of the woolvac and was pulling at its scales to steer it back into the cave. The beast was trying to claw the poor goblin and bite its legs but the brave goblin held on tight and managed to pull the woolvac round and back on course, and disappeared into the cave.

There was no time to spare. The trees had to be chopped quickly. They had already been partially hacked and were gingerly held in place with rope, but the final chop of the axes would sever the trunks and send the trees crashing down, sealing the cave entrance. Mr Grumplepumple had cast a spell upon the trees so that when they fell, the branches would knit together to form a solid wall that would be impenetrable for good. Garvoid was waiting for the signal.

Mr Gravenpumple had a great dilemma. He had to act quickly and make a decision, and he soon realised that he had no choice but to give the order for the trees to fall; there was no time to wait for the brave goblin to dismount the stray woolvac and run back out of the cave. Howling could be heard from the cave again; some of the woolvacs must have turned around and were making their way back and would soon be near. There was no time to waste!

"What should we do?" came the cry from the goblins. Everyone was stunned and shocked by what had just happened.

With a very large lump in his throat, Mr Gravenpumple gave the order to Garvoid, who nodded reluctantly and the huge trees crashed down, blocking any chance of escape.

The noise was deafening as the trees fell and thick plumes of dust billowed upwards from the rocks as the trees made contact with the cave. It took quite a while for the dust to settle and to see if the plan had worked. Had they been successful? Had the cave entrance been totally blocked? Were all the woolvacs in the cave? Everyone waited in silence, hoping and praying that the brave goblin had been able to escape in time, but after what seemed like a lifetime, it was obvious that this was not the case. There was no sign of the goblin, Gorvust; he had sacrificed his life to make sure the plan worked.

"You made the right decision; you had no choice," said Gorun in a sympathetic tone and patted his dear friend Mr Gravenpumple on the shoulder.

All the creatures had gathered outside the cave entrance to make sure everyone was safe and accounted for. Grumplepumple was marching through the rows of creatures, crossing them off his father's list, but when he came to the goblins, it was confirmed that one was missing!

What should have been a joyous and happy occasion was filled with great sadness and sorrow; the woolvacs had been chased away from Kracklewood but at the cost of losing one of their own.

Some of the mambooas had lucky escapes with just flesh wounds that could be healed easily over time, and several of the popstrells had suffered battered and torn wings from the swooping and diving through the beasts. Many of the impbahs could not speak for days as the screaming had taken its toll, and some of the goblins had scars of battle that would probably be displayed with pride in many a tale that would be told in the future.

The one who bore the deepest physical wound was Garvtak, who had tackled one of the woolvacs to the ground just before it was about to pounce on Mr Gravenpumple as he was chanting his spell. The beast had torn into the goblin's face and left a stark reminder of what had happened that day, and of the bravery of the creatures of Pumple Mountain.

The one who bore the deepest emotional scar was Goby, for it was on this day that he lost his father!

A very grand memorial ceremony was organised for the hero goblin, Gorvust, who saved the night. Even goblins from the Second Realm came to pay homage, which was quite an honour, and a very grand and noble statue of the goblin was chiselled out of Pumplestone, and erected at the boundary of Kracklewood to make sure this very brave and honourable goblin was never forgotten. For many a night, Goby would sit underneath the statue with a broken heart and a feeling of loneliness.

This day went down in history as one of the great battles of Kracklewood and many tales were told, with slight exaggerations and additions to the contents, of course, about the bravery of the creatures who had banished the woolvacs. The plan had worked but there was still the issue of finding a new home within Kracklewood that could safely house all the creatures from Pumple Mountain.

Mr Gravenpumple was so aggrieved at the loss of Gorvust, especially as he was one of the bravest and most trusted amongst all the goblins he knew. The two of them had shared many very memorable adventures together and that had created such a strong bond, it was unbreakable.

But circumstances beyond his control had so abruptly ended Gorvust's life,

Mr Gravenpumple's only solace was that his dear friend had left his son, and he knew what he had to do.

The wizard goblin took it upon himself to raise his dear friend's young son as one of his own; the little goblin had tragically lost his mother in the great avalanche and had now lost his father and become an orphan.

Hence, from this day forward, Mr Gravenpumple had two sons, Grumplepumple and Goby.

Fairy

Chapter Four

Kracklewood

The banishment of the woolvacs had been a major success and now made Kracklewood an ideal place to relocate to, but it was imperative that the creatures of Pumple Mountain moved quickly and soon found a suitable home within the enchanted wood. The caves within the Galamide mountain range had been the ancestral home of the goblins for many cenatoons and served as a perfect habitat.

They not only housed the goblins but, over time, other creatures had come to settle within the caves as well.

The mambooas from the Third Realm were quick and agile and good at fetching and carrying within the mines, and the impbahs from the Second Realm had excellent hearing and could scream very loudly - they were good at raising the alarm if danger was nearby.

They all became important members of the family and, of course, the popstrells had always lived amongst the goblins; they were their eyes and ears and were often sent out to deliver messages and scout the land.

All these creatures worked well together and had become accustomed to each other's ways. They all had their part to play in the safeguarding of their home, and this unity helped maintain their safety from the dangerous predators that roamed the land.

But the great avalanche caused by the cruens had made it too precarious and dangerous to stay within the caves. They had no choice; it was time to move on.

Kracklewood had been identified as the safest place to build a new home now that the biggest threat had been removed but the woolvacs had caused great damage to the wood. It was time for Kracklewood to heal, and the goblins and their friends were going to make sure this happened.

Mr Gravenpumple asked Garvtak and Garvoid to set out on foot and find a suitable place, large enough to house everyone.

In the meantime, the popstrells flew across Kracklewood searching for anywhere suitable, sweeping the wood from end to end from high above.

It was not an easy task as the wood was very large and dense.

Kracklewood had started out as a little wood, hence its name, but through the ages, it had grown substantially because within the wood was an enchanted tree.

Every moolatoon, the tree would bloom and the seeds from the flowers would disperse into the air and land on the ground. Not all of the seeds would succeed in bedding into the soil.

This was because the seeds were a delicacy and many creatures would be waiting to devour them. The story goes that if you eat one of the seeds, you will live a happy and healthy life!

So, through time, the wood became more like a forest as more and more of the enchanted trees grew.

There were no more caves in Kracklewood; they had sealed up the only one that they knew of to remove the woolvacs.

Many of the trees had been stripped of their bark and left to go to ruin by the woolvacs, but the enchanted trees seemed to survive unscathed and had large enough trunks and thick, dense canopies to house some, but not big enough to accommodate everyone, and this was the dilemma.

The goblins had no joy in finding anything suitable and the whole project was turning into a source of real frustration.

Staying together was imperative to ensure safety, but there was nowhere within Kracklewood that was suitable and would work.

Time was passing on and the creatures were becoming unsettled and restless. They lived in constant fear of the threat of more avalanche.

There had been a lot more activity from the cruens; it seemed they had become restless and a few more of these huge beasts were starting to venture down the mountainside away from their homeland.

Mr Gravenpumple had been pondering long and hard on the subject at hand and was coming up with no solution. He not only had the creatures of Pumple Mountain to consider but, closer to home, he had his two sons to protect and wanted to keep them safe from harm.

The news of more sightings of cruens had unsettled him, and, after everything that had happened and the loss of Gorvust, he did not want his friend's death to be in vain!

While sleeping one day, Mr Gravenpumple was awoken by a light tap on his nose and he opened one eye to see what had disturbed him.

Sat on his nose was the most beautiful little fairy he had ever seen.

She was so dainty and willowy and had the most enormous eyes that nearly took up the whole of her face.

Mr Gravenpumple was quite taken aback, as normally, he only saw fairies when he sought counsel with the chief fairy of Treaclewood. This was a small wood that lay at the foot of Pumple Mountain to the west, about two miles away.

The fairy was slightly nervous as she was not used to balancing on a goblin's nose, but after some reassurance from Mr Gravenpumple that she would come to no harm, she proceeded to tell him the reason for her visit.

"It has come to the chief fairy's attention that you are trying to find a new home in Kracklewood," she squeaked.

"Well, you have been a true friend and aide to the fairies for a long time, so we believe we can help you and the creatures from Pumple Mountain to find somewhere suitable."

Mr Gravenpumple was very pleased to hear this news and sat up rather too quickly with excitement, propelling the fairy across the room.

"Oh, I am sorry, little one! This is such good news and just what I have been waiting to hear!" said the wizard goblin with new hope in his heart.

She only managed to stop herself smashing into a berry pot by flapping her wings furiously.

Once she had composed herself again, she began to explain how they could help.

"We have a potion that can magnify objects and help them grow to twice their size, but the only problem is that it has never been used on anything more than a toadstool or a small bush," she said with a hint of exasperation.

"In order for you to make use of this potion, you will need to use a clump of hair from one of the giants of Massdumoor," said the fairy, giving Mr Gravenpumple a quizzical look.

The wizard goblin stared into space for a minute, his brain racing with too many thoughts, then he replied eagerly,

"So, if I obtain the giant's hair, then you're telling me that we can mix this ingredient into the magnifying potion to make it strong enough to double or even treble the size of, maybe, a tree?" he asked hopefully.

"Yes, that should work; why? Do you have a tree in mind?" she asked tentatively.

"We have identified an enchanted tree worthy of serious consideration. It stands in the centre of the wood within a big clearing," he confirmed.

Mr Gravenpumple pondered the idea for a moment and wondered if this tree could be the one. If it was given a growing potion to treble or even just double its size, would this make the perfect home? Would it be big enough to house all the creatures?

It had the right distortion within its trunk to make it hard for predators to climb and had many deep crevices and holes to make good homes, plus, its top canopy was very dense with a thick mass of branches and waxy leaves to stop flying predators landing from above.

The goblin's eyes had lit up with excitement with this idea but then suddenly, his face seemed to collapse and crumble with worry, and his shoulders slumped, for to seek out a giant you were asking for trouble.

"Giants do not like company; they live solitary lives in the mountains of Massdumoor. Giants are very unpredictable and have bad tempers, plus, a giant would have no hesitation in putting a goblin in his pot!" Mr Gravenpumple said with fear in his voice.

"But surely you have many friends that will be able to help you?" replied the fairy, whose eyes became even more enlarged with this question.

Mr Gravenpumple plunged into deep thought again. How was he to get close enough to pluck a clump of hairs?

The giant, most probably, would have to be asleep and giants went days and nights without sleeping. However, when they did sleep, it could be for days on end.

It was all about the timing, so he would have to consult with his friend, Tissamarr. He was a warlock and a dear friend of Mr Gravenpumple who lived not far from Massdumoor and he was familiar with the habits of giants.

He had bumped into a few on his travels, not always with a convivial and pleasant greeting. These meetings normally ended up in a hasty retreat.

Tissamarr had a fairly good knowledge of their routine and when it was more likely that they would be in slumber.

The fairy tried to console Mr Gravenpumple and convince the goblin that this was their best chance of creating a safe and comfortable home for all the creatures of Pumple Mountain, and, with a heavy heart, he agreed.

The fairy left the great wizard goblin deep in thought.

He began to pace back and forth across his bedroom, tapping his staff a little too firmly and ended up stabbing himself in the foot!

Mr Gravenpumple decided to speak with his council, which consisted of a handful of goblins, including his son, Grumplepumple, several mambooas and a couple of impbahs, and after much deliberation, it was agreed that the goblin would take a group of his most trusted and bravest with him, to both protect and help him in his quest.

Mr Gravenpumple would send a message to his warlock friend, Tissamarr, sending one of the popstrells with a hand-written letter explaining what he required. He summoned Plock to his chamber and explained what he required of the little bat and asked if he or any of his bats would be capable of this task.

"Plock, I have a very important mission for you. I have a letter that needs to be given to my friend, Tissamarr, but I am not sure where he is at the moment. Would you be able to locate him?" asked Mr Gravenpumple quizzically. Plock looked at his revered leader with disdain and reminded the wizard goblin of the popstrells' many talents, as the little bat squeaked loudly and puffed his chest out with pride.

"Yes, of course, my dearest friend. I don't know what came over me. How dare I challenge your competence? Forgive me, I am a little stressed at the moment," replied the wizard goblin, feeling slightly embarrassed.

He then continued to explain how he wanted to ask the warlock when would be the best time to seek out a giant, and where?

Plock acknowledged the request with another affirmative squeak, then took the letter and flew off quickly.

Mr Gravenpumple knew it would take a few nights of travel to arrive at the foot of the Massdumoor Mountain range, and then they would have the task of locating one of the giants, preferably asleep. That was the easy part.

Tissamarr replied in another letter within a couple of days, explaining that he was fairly confident that he could pinpoint the location of a giant. He had unintentionally crossed its path recently while trying to track down one of his lost pockpocs. They were annoying pesky little birds that squeaked and chattered too much.

He explained how he was ready to pounce on the pockpoc when it suddenly spurted forward and flew into a clearing and onto the giant's leg!

Fortunately, the giant seemed to be engrossed and preoccupied with a poor unfortunate creature that had the misfortune to be in the giant's hands. The giant was talking to the creature and stroking its back, but Tissamarr did not think this was an act of kindness; it was more to tease the poor thing before it went into a pot!

Tissamarr made a hasty retreat, having grabbed his pockpoc in his hand, and did not look back. However, he remembered that the giant was close to one of the biggest caves in the mountain range, in a place called Mythom.

Armed with this information, the following week, Mr Gravenpumple set off to the mountains of Massdumoor with his most trusted soldiers, Garvtak and Garvoid, and several close friends. They were laden with enough food to feed an army, and also had some very special vintage berry wine to ease the nerves and give courage for the journey.

Mr Gravenpumple had made plans to meet up with Tissamarr at the foot of the Massdumoor Mountains and they would travel together to seek out the giant.

Grumplepumple was to stay at home and look after Goby, who could not go with his father on this quest as it was too dangerous.

Mr Gravenpumple had to know that his two sons were protected and Goby was in safe hands.

There was much protest from Grumplepumple but he knew his father was right. And so, under duress, he agreed but made his father promise that the popstrells would bring back word that he was safe and all was well. Grumplepumple did not mind really as he adored his little brother and would do anything to please his father.

Tissamarr

Chapter Five

The Giant of Massdumoor

The journey was not as hard as first imagined. They did not encounter any dangerous predators. The only real threat came from the yar yar birds, who could not navigate very well and were easily distracted. A couple had been too busy gawping at the group from above; they took their eye off the ball and crashed straight into a large tree that was just in front of Mr Gravenpumple.

The two birds came crashing down and landed in a clump of feathers on top of Elphin and Jowler, the two impbahs in the group, just missing the wizard goblin.

"You stupid, big, fat birds, you nearly knocked me teeth out!" shouted Jowler.

"Yar yar, yar yar, yar, yar," screeched the birds, flapping their wings wildly.

There was so much commotion and screeching from the impbahs that Mr Gravenpumple had to bash his staff over the creatures to stop the commotion. Fortunately, everyone was alright and the only damage was to everyone's dignity and pride.

The birds were quickly untangled and calmed down with a little treat of the quinct grain that was used to make the most delicious bread, and then they were soon back up in the sky and on their way.

Tissamarr was an old acquaintance of Mr Gravenpumple's. They had crossed paths many times on their travels.

One such journey was to seek out the great white owl, Srona of Mockle Wood, to glean words of wisdom and learn of distant lands, and listen to stories and fables of old, and predictions for the future.

Another time was to attend an audience with the great master, Nantah, who came out of hiding once a Junamoon. This was a new moon that was blood orange and would light up the sky with its resplendent glory, and reinvigorate the land with new growth and life. A Junamoon happened once a yulatoon (which we know as a year).

Nantah lived within the mystical land of Quazboo, amongst the enchanted shifting forests, and it was a task to try and find the right location at any one time, but this was all part of the challenge. The great warlock would preach and pass on his teachings of wizardry and magic. This masterclass event would command a huge attendance from warlocks, witches and many other creatures from across the Three Realms who had magical talents and wanted to improve their skills and become masters of their art.

It was nearly daylight when the group reached the Massdumoor Mountain range and it was time to find a safe place to sleep for the day.

They were to meet Tissamarr at dusk at a place called Midgley which was still a couple of hours away, so they could not sleep for long.

Each day, they would find a tree large enough to accommodate everyone and Mr Gravenpumple would create a flat wooden platform within the branches with his magic, gathering some of the loose twigs from the ground and bundling them together with vine leaves so everyone could stretch out and sleep comfortably.

Some of the beds they slept in were comfier than others; it all depended on whether they could find loose feathers left by forest birds to add comfort. If not, then it was a case of using the plentiful supply of waxy leaves that grew on many of the trees.

The goblins were not accustomed to sleeping in trees and it took quite a while for them to get used to it, especially Garvoid, even though he had accompanied Mr Gravenpumple on several journeys. As he turned in his sleep, he would fall out of the tree with a big thump and now had several large bumps on his head to prove it.

"Ow! Not again! Why is it always me who seems to fall out of the blasted tree? Are you pushing me, Garvtak?" demanded Garvoid in an angry voice.

"No, you stupid goblin. It's your fat backside; it's too big for the branch!" laughed Garvtak.

This was a great source of amusement for the mambooas who had lived in trees before they settled on Pumple Mountain, so they felt right at home. The impbahs were also accustomed to moving amongst trees so it did not create a problem for them.

The little group had been travelling for several nights, and, knowing that they were nearing the location to meet Tissamarr, Mr Gravenpumple set up the sleeping platform in a large tree. They all settled down to sleep, but before they did, he tied a couple of vines around Garvoid to save him the further embarrassment of tumbling out of the tree again. Mr Gravenpumple and company had fallen into a deep sleep, and they were so tired from their journey that it was already dusk when they awoke. It was an irritating buzzing sound that woke them and it seemed to be coming from above their heads. Something was hovering over them. Then, there was a high-pitched scream which came from a very distressed impbah!

"Aggghhh! What in blazing Helia is that?" yelled Jowler.

In front of him was a very ugly fly with a huge horn on its forehead that seemed totally out of place, and wings that were scrawny but large.

It was hovering over Jowler rather too close for comfort and moving its bulbous eyes over the creature.

There was the sound of laughter from below as Tissamarr greeted his friend with a cheery hello.

"I see you have met Nitnac! She located you, so I thought I would meet you here," explained Tissamarr.

The warlock commanded Nitnac to move away and come back to him. The fly hesitated for a moment and then descended quickly and disappeared under the warlock's cloak. Mr Gravenpumple was quick to descend from the tree and greet his dear friend.

"Welcome, old-timer. It's been too long since I saw you last!" he said with glee in his voice. "Who's your little friend?" he inquired.

"Oh, Nitnac is such a useful aid for me; she helps me see things from far away and is an excellent scout. She sort of looks after me and helps me detect trouble long before I stumble across it," the warlock said with kindness in his voice.

Mr Gravenpumple and Tissamarr were locked in discussion for an age. They had so much to catch up on, and Mr Gravenpumple told his friend all about the avalanche and the woolvacs; how they herded the beasts into a cave and sealed the entrance for good. The wizard goblin was quite animated in his gestures and told a slightly exaggerated tale. Goblins had a knack of doing this; not intentionally, they just got carried away.

Tissamarr seemed quite impressed with this story and gave Mr Gravenpumple a big pat on the back.

"Well, you have been busy, my friend, so now we need to get the giant's hair for you and help you make your new home. No pressure then, hey?"

The warlock lifted one of his thick white eyebrows, which had been plaited and hung low past his ears, in a questionable manner and stared at his friend.

Then, he took a deep breath and explained where they could find the giant. "Nitnac has seen the giant again and confirmed that it was close to Mythom cave, at the foot of the Massdumoor Mountain, one of many in the foothills. We think this must be the giant's home; it has been going in and out of the cave with food," Tissamarr said with trepidation in his tone.

"I believe the giant has been feeding to get itself ready for sleep. They need to eat huge amounts of food in order to last throughout their days of slumber," stated the warlock, in a matter-of-fact way.

He explained that the giant's food consumption covered a multitude of choices, from fruit and vegetables to a variety of meats from little creatures that had the misfortune to fall into the giant's traps.

This made Mr Gravenpumple feel very uneasy and his stomach started to churn at the thought of having to confront this giant, whether it was asleep or not! He did not want anyone to fall into one of the traps.

Mythom was only a couple of hours away, so Tissamarr suggested they set off soon in the hope that, when the group arrived at the location, the giant would have fallen into a deep sleep, with a full belly, and was probably tucked up within the cave. Mr Gravenpumple hoped this would be the case - it would make it so much easier to pluck a clump of hairs from the body and then they could make a hasty retreat.

It did not take as long as they thought to get to Mythom and everything seemed fine. There were the usual sounds of the night; the owls hooting and a soft wind was whistling through the trees.

The tranquillity was suddenly interrupted, though, by a low rattling noise, with an intermittent low-pitched whistle coming from just ahead of them; it was very strange. At first, everyone thought it might be a draccadin, but the whistle dismissed that thought; plus, that was the last thing they wanted to see right now. Draccadins looked like little dragons with thick scaly skin but no wings or legs, just long winding bodies that could curl around you very quickly and squeeze the life out of you with a quick twist!

On closer inspection, they realised it was the giant snoring; they were near its cave and the giant must be sleeping. "Nitnac, my dear, would you be so kind as to confirm for me that the giant is asleep?" Tissamarr asked the fly in a manner that everyone thought was perhaps too polite.

With a buzz, Nitnac immediately flew off into the cave to check.

Plock went with a couple of popstrells and the fly, they all returned quickly to confirm that the giant was definitely asleep. Plock, the head popstrell, told Mr Gravenpumple that the noise in the cave was very loud and was shaking his head to try and shake the noise away.

Mr Gravenpumple and Tissamarr led the way and peeked into the cave first, the warlock armed with his wand and Mr Gravenpumple with his trusty gnarled staff.

"You ready, Tissamarr?" asked Mr Gravenpumple, looking for reassurance.

"No, but we have no choice, do we?" replied the warlock with a very frightened look on his face. All seemed as expected except for a very distressed little creature that was trapped in a wooden cage in the corner.

"That little critter is probably there to be the first supper for the giant when it awakes from its slumber," said Tissamarr with sadness in his eyes.

The creature had clocked the goblin and warlock and started rocking from side to side within the rickety cage, and then, very quickly, started to rattle the bars furiously!

This was very alarming as the last thing anyone wanted was to wake the giant that lay curled up on his side in a peaceful position, with arms crossed and his legs tucked up. Mr Gravenpumple thought for a large giant it looked very peaceful and, dare we say, cute. But the noise that came from the giant was definitely not cute! The snores were very loud as Plock had described, and the sound was like an old tin can with dried beans rattling around inside.

Mr Gravenpumple had swallowed hard as he caught sight of the giant; he had encountered one before, a long time ago on his travels, and it had not been a pleasant experience. He had nearly lost his arm as the giant tried to pull him away from the branch of a tree where he had been hiding. The goblin had heard the giant coming and took refuge in a nearby tree, but unfortunately, he sneezed very loudly as one of his potion salts spilled out of his pocket and blew up in his face.

This, of course, got the attention of the giant and it saw the goblin positioned just within reach above his head.

Giants are quite partial to a goblin and it saw him as a nice opportunistic treat! As the giant tried to grab the goblin's arm, which was desperately holding onto a branch, the potion salts wafted towards the giant.

As it took in a breath, the powder whooshed up his nose and made it sneeze like crazy. The giant staggered back, surprised and shocked, which gave the goblin time to slip away further up the tree and hide in a large clump of leaves.

The giant was so preoccupied with trying to stop sneezing that, when it recovered, it had forgotten what it had stopped for and continued to travel on its way to an unknown destination. Mr Gravenpumple remained in the tree for a long time, unsure whether the giant was hiding and waiting to pounce on him. But he had to pluck up the courage and continue on his way so he cautiously climbed down the tree. Fortunately, his fears were wasted as the giant was nowhere to be seen but the whole experience had left the goblin terribly shaken.

The sight of the big sleeping giant was now overwhelming. It caught him off guard but he knew that he had to show the rest of the group he was not afraid, so, he stepped forward with fake confidence, with his staff held high in his hand.

The rest of the group were not far behind the goblin and the warlock; curiosity had got the better of them as they had never seen a giant before.

Toobah pulled on Mr Gravenpumple's cloak, which made him jump, then pointed violently with his large stubby finger at the giant's back, where, in between its clothing, was a gap.

There lay a patch of hair protruding just to the right-hand side above its trousers, just the right amount required to use in the fairy potion.

Everyone remained very still and quiet except for the stricken creature that was trapped in the cage; it was now getting very agitated and looked like it was pleading with the group to release it.

The strange little creature was making some very unusual clicking noises and pressing its funny little face up against the bars. Its eyes were bulging out of their sockets; it looked very distressed!

Tissamarr moved quickly over to the cage and waved his wand, and, with a flick and a chant, silenced the creature by producing a light blue powder that he blew onto the creature's face. Immediately, its face relaxed with a wide smile and a look of serene pleasure. It slumped down into the corner of the cage and fell asleep. The warlock explained that the powder would only last for a short while so the group had to act quickly before the creature awoke and started making a loud noise again.

Mr Gravenpumple nodded to Toobah, who understood straight away what he was being instructed to do and tiptoed forward to do the deed. All the others pulled back to the entrance of the cave for a quick exit while the mambooa moved forward.

A couple of the popstrells went ahead and lifted the giant's shirt so that Toobah could get a good look. Everyone held their breath as the giant's body heaved up and down with the snoring.

This movement was going to make it difficult, but Toobah gingerly crawled onto the giant and found a clump of hairs in the middle of its back.

He grabbed hold and scrunched his eyes shut, then, with a quick tug, he pulled, but nothing came away - no hairs!

Everyone looked on in horror as they thought the giant was going to wake up but fortunately, the act had not bothered it.

Toobah took a sharp intake of breath and turned to Mr Gravenpumple for advice. The wizard goblin beckoned Toobah back with the violent waving of his hand and reluctantly, the mambooa re-joined the group, feeling hopeless and upset.

It took quite a while for his heart to stop pounding like crazy in his chest. Booma patted his dear friend on the back and tried to cheer him up but Toobah was feeling so disappointed. He felt he had let the side down, and, no matter what his friend did, it didn't help.

It was time to re-think the plan and come up with another way to pluck the hairs.

"What if we all try together at the same time? That might work," whispered Elphin.

"How many are you thinking? If there's too many of us, the giant will feel the pressure on its back and wake up, surely?" quizzed Garvtak rather too loudly.

"Shusssh! We must be quiet; if we carry on like this, we'll wake the giant up!" said Mr Gravenpumple in an agitated whisper.

The wizard goblin was desperately trying to think of a spell he could use to loosen the hairs but nothing would work on such a huge body.

Tissamarr whispered to Mr Gravenpumple, "My wand can't muster a potion big enough and concentrated enough to be of any use. It seems like there is no other choice; it will have to be a collective effort," the warlock said reluctantly.

Garvtak and Garvoid volunteered immediately along with Elphin, Jowler and, of course, Toobah, the mambooa, who was determined to redeem himself.

They tiptoed over to the giant and gathered around by the giant's back.

Yet again, the popstrells went first and lifted the giant's shirt so they could get a better view, and with a nod of the head from Garvtak, the little group leapt up onto the giant's back and tried to grab a clump of hair.

But just as they were about to grab the hair, the giant decided to turn onto its other side. This threw everyone into the air with the sudden jerk of the giant's body.

The goblins were hurled off into the corner of the cave with their bodies crashing against the rock, but Toobah, Elphin and Jowler were still holding on and ended up being pinned to the giant's body.

The giant had wrapped its arms around the little creatures like you would do with a comfort blanket.

This was becoming a very dangerous situation. Mr Gravenpumple was so agitated and worried that he nearly tripped over his cloak and stumbled into Tissamarr, who had a very distressed look on his face. It didn't help that Nitnac was buzzing around madly in front of him and he had to sternly order the fly to return to the pocket of his cloak.

Then suddenly, the giant opened one eye and peered at the little group of creatures that were crushed up within its arms. Everyone took in a sharp intake of breath and you could hear a pin drop.

Mr Gravenpumple raised his gnarled staff ready to attempt some form of magic which, of course, would be futile against the enormous giant and have very little effect, and the warlock was poised and ready with his very shaky wand in hand.

The creatures stuck in the giant's arms were so terrified that Jowler fainted and Elphin was trying to stop himself from screaming; this was a natural reaction for an impbah and their screams, of course, were very loud.

Toobah was so frightened, he just froze on the spot with his eyes so wide it looked like they were ready to pop out of his head!

The giant slowly closed its eye again and snuggled down, seemingly not having registered the uninvited company, much to the delight and relief of everyone.

Then, without any thought of the consequences, Booma lurched forward and grabbed hold of Toobah's legs, which were poking out from under the giant's arms, and started to tug. Garvtak and Garvoid quickly joined the mambooa to help with the pulling.

Toobah snapped out of his state of shock, quickly realising what was happening and grabbed hold of the impbahs, and with one more almighty tug, the creatures fell to the floor in a crumpled mess.

Jowler, who had fainted, suddenly awoke and, being startled by the sight of the giant, instinctively started to scream, with a high-pitched screech.

"Eeeekkkkkkkkkkkkkkkkk!" came the sound out of the little impbah, which sounded very loud.

This must have broken the spell that Tissamarr had put on the poor unfortunate creature in the cage because it also started making a very loud clicking noise! The sounds were deafening and, of course, woke the giant up; it jerked itself up quickly to see what was happening and surveyed the room.

The giant was feeling very groggy and wiped its sleepy eyes, and it took a moment to focus, but when it did, it looked around to see where the dreadful noise was coming from.

Looking down, it saw the strange little group of creatures staring up at him, and with a little impbah screaming at the top of its voice. It surprised the giant initially, as it tried to register what was going on.

But then the realisation kicked in that they had intruded, and were in his home and had woken him up. This made the giant very angry and it let out an almighty roar!

"Arghhhhhhhhh, Grrrrrrrrr!" was the sound coming out of the very irate giant.

They could make a lot of noise if they were cross, and this was obviously the case judging by the sounds it was making.

Giants are cumbersome creatures and generally quite plump. They have big floppy bellies and short stubby legs. They are not agile and nimble on their feet and they look quite funny when they run because of the large mop of black hair which sits quite awkwardly on the top of their heads and flaps up and down in a crazy manner.

The little group quickly turned on their heels and ran as fast as they could out of the cave.

Nitnac and the popstrells were able to fly out of the cave quickly, followed closely by the mambooas who were carrying the impbahs on their backs.

This was not out of choice but because the impbahs were too frightened and had rooted themselves to the spot and couldn't move.

It didn't help Toobah and Booma's ears with the high-pitched screams coming from the impbahs, but their speed was their advantage and they were soon out of the cave and making their way towards the forest.

Mr Gravenpumple, Tissamarr, Garvtak and Garvoid did not hesitate either and ran as quickly as possible, but the wizard goblin stopped momentarily on his way out to grab the cage with the distressed creature inside and pulled it close to his chest as he ran.

He could not bear the thought of what would happen to the poor creature if left behind, even though it had contributed to the waking of the giant.

The little creature was making a very loud clicking noise and was pawing at Mr Gravenpumple's cloak through the cage bars with what seemed like gratitude and thanks.

Because the giant was still groggy from its sleep, it took a while for it to find its feet and get moving, but then the chase was on and this giant wasn't going to give up easily, especially with the chance of a grand feast in sight. There was a thunderous sound of the giant's footsteps pounding behind them as they ran from the cave; its roar was enough to make any goblin or creature shake with fear.

"Arghhhhhhhhhhhhhh!" it yelled.

The giant was very angry, knocking everything out of its way to get to them, and it was getting uncomfortably close because it could take big strides. Seeing what was happening, the popstrells started flying around the giant's head to try and distract it, with Nitnac buzzing annoyingly in its ear.

Toobah and Booma had dropped the impbahs off behind a large tree further into the forest and had run back to help. They were darting in between the giant's feet to try and slow it down so that the goblins and the warlock had time to catch up.

Squiggle

Chapter Six

The Booquar

Mr Gravenpumple, the oldest in the group, was starting to slow down. Exhaustion was taking over and the burden of his heavy cloak and carrying the distressed creature from the cave didn't help.

The giant was gaining on him fast, despite the annoying distraction of the mambooas and popstrells.

Then suddenly, Mr Gravenpumple tripped up over a tree root and fell to the ground! The cage was propelled forward and the cage door flew open, releasing the stricken creature inside. Tissamarr stopped abruptly in front of the goblin when he heard the goblin wizard yell, and turned on his heels.

"Oh no! Come on, Tissamarr, you can do this," he mumbled as he tried to convince himself.

He lifted up his trembling hand and tried to flick his wand into action but the wand was having none of it and the warlock was in no fit state to command the wand to do anything. It was just wibbling and wobbling everywhere.

"Firetillitus, operaytotus," he tried to say in a very shaky voice.

He was stricken with fear at the sight of the giant towering over Mr Gravenpumple!

All he could manage was a pathetic dribble of a spark that spat on the ground.

The two goblins were yelling at the giant and waving their gnarled sticks but this seemed like a futile gesture as the giant was only interested in the capture of what he thought was a fat juicy goblin for tea! The giant had totally set his sights on the prize at his feet.

The impbahs were screeching at the top of their voices from the forest to try and distract the giant but this made the rest of the group cover their ears and was wasted on the giant who seemed oblivious to the mayhem.

But, just as the giant was about to grab the goblin in its huge hands, there was a high-pitched sound from above - "yar, yar, yar, yar, yar, yar!!!"

Two rather cumbersome and odd-looking birds swooped down and grabbed Mr Gravenpumple's cloak in their beaks.

The giant was caught totally off guard and took a swipe at the birds as they lifted off, but only managed to brush against the goblin's cloak. It could not grab hold in time and the birds soared high into the sky.

The giant stumbled back in total disbelief, surprised by the swift action of the yar yar birds, and roared even louder than before.

Argggggghhhhhhh!" the giant screamed.

Mr Gravenpumple held on tightly to the sleeves of his cloak as the birds made a quick ascent, and soon, he was flying high above the trees below and hoping he was being flown somewhere safe.

Seeing this strange sight unfold, Tissamarr ordered everyone to run, as quickly as possible, away from the scene and deep into the forest.

Toobah and Booma lifted Tissamarr up onto their shoulders, despite his protest, and with Garvtak and Garvoid taking up the rear, they ran at high speed.

This was not easy carrying such a heavy weight but, between them all, it was just about possible; warlocks are not light.

They could hear the frustrated roars from the giant as they fled and did not glance back once.

They had left a very angry and frustrated giant behind, who they hoped would not take his anger out on some poor unfortunate creature that ventured into its path.

Once the group felt they had reached a safe place and were out of danger, they stopped and rested by a clump of trees near the meandering River Crimstone, named after a stone from the region.

They could take shelter here while they figured out what to do next.

The whole experience had taken its toll; the group were exhausted, especially the mambooas.

It took a while for Tissamarr to catch his breath as he wasn't used to riding on the shoulders of mambooas and it wasn't easy holding on as they ran. The warlock felt like his teeth were going to fall out with the constant jerking and their speed was quite frightening!

Then, all thoughts turned to Mr Gravenpumple.

"Where do you think the yar yar birds have taken him?" Garvtak asked Tissamarr.

"Will they have taken him somewhere safe? Is he far enough away from the giant now? How can we find him?" Garvoid shot his questions off like stones being fired from a slingshot!

Plock squeaked up and explained that a couple of popstrells had tried to keep up with the yar yar birds but they soared too high into the sky and too quickly. Popstrells could not fly to great heights or for long periods. They could reach the top of a tree and flap from branch to branch, but their tiny wings only equipped them for short spurts of flight.

Tissamarr opened his cloak hoping that his faithful fly was still intact; he wanted to check that she was okay. Nitnac was curled up deep in the inner pocket of his cloak. When the warlock called her name, it was a very frightened and shaken little fly that peered out of the pocket and looked up at the warlock.

The fly gave a quiet buzz to indicate that she was okay. Tissamarr was so pleased his little friend had not been harmed with all the running and jiggling about from the mambooas. He gave the fly a little drink of sap that the warlock always carried for his friend, to rebuild her strength.

Once the fly seemed rested, Tissamarr asked Nitnac to see if she could locate Mr Gravenpumple's whereabouts. The fly was happy to oblige and was soon on her way without a pause in her flight.

It seemed a long time before Nitnac returned but she was buzzing with delight as she told Tissamarr of her findings. The yar yar birds had taken Mr Gravenpumple to a cliff edge not too far away and the goblin was sitting chatting with the birds. Nitnac explained how they seemed very frustrated at the intrusion of a fly buzzing over their heads as they had been locked in deep conservation with Mr Gravenpumple.

Apparently, he was telling a story of how he came across another species of bird, in a faraway land, which was able to swim underwater for long periods of time. The birds were mesmerized by the wizard goblin and wanted to hear more of his tales.

Mr Gravenpumple recognised Tissamarr's fly and politely asked the birds to stop wafting their feathers at it. He knew then that he would soon be reunited with his friends.

While Mr Gravenpumple waited for help, he thanked the birds for their bravery. He was so grateful but, of course, was curious as to why they were willing to take the risk and help.

"Why jeopardize your lives for me? The giant could easily have killed both of you with just the swipe of its huge hands," said the wizard goblin in amazement.

The yar yar birds explained that they were flying by and heard the roar of the giant, and, being such inquisitive creatures, they flew closer to see what was happening. When they saw the commotion below and realised that the giant was chasing the group, they wanted to help but were frightened because the giant had previously claimed one of their friends for his dinner pot!

But they recognised both Mr Gravenpumple, as he stumbled and fell, and the mambooas who had helped them previously when they were about to become the next dinner for the woolvacs.

So, they knew they had to do something and quickly, and without another thought, they swooped down to the rescue. Mr Gravenpumple thanked the birds again and said if they were ever near Pumple Mountain they must call in for tea and he would personally bake them a Pip cake.

Then suddenly, Toobah and Booma came into the clearing on the cliff top, followed closely by Garvtak and Garvoid, and they greeted Mr Gravenpumple with a joyous cheer. They wanted to thank the yar yar birds for their bravery, so Garvtak gave them some quinct grain.

The birds were so pleased with this and pranced about flicking their funny head feathers.

"Wooo Hooo Hoooo!" shouted Booma, who was a little too excited.

It was a strange sight to see the birds wafting their feathers, an old goblin waving his gnarled staff in the air and two other goblins dancing around with mambooas, jumping up and down with glee!

After saying goodbye to the birds, they made a careful descent down the mountain and the group were soon reunited.

Tissamarr and Mr Gravenpumple showed great restraint and merely shook hands and nodded at each other with respect. They secretly would have liked to hug each other but this was not the right thing between elders of high rank, so they all sat down to have some tea.

Garvtak and Garvoid set about rummaging around for firewood. They made a small fire that was built using driftwood from the shores of the nearby river and lit courtesy of Mr Gravenpumple's staff, but they kept it small as they did not want to attract any attention. The impbahs set about making hot oolong, a very popular strong tea, and handed out some Pip cake made from fruits and nuts, which made everyone feel a little better.

However, the mood was sombre and everyone was feeling such disappointment at not being able to collect the clump of hair from the giant; it was playing on everyone's mind.

The group, with long faces and shoulders slumped, sat down, pondering the grave dilemma.

"How are we going to get the giant's hairs now?" said Toobah who was so disappointed he could not grab the giant's hair the first time around.

"We have really annoyed and aggravated the giant now so it will be on its guard and definitely not be sleeping for quite a while," muttered Garvtak into his woolly beard that had collected quite a few Pip cake crumbs.

Mr Gravenpumple was rearranging his cloak after it had been torn by the beaks of the yar yar birds, when he suddenly noticed something moving in one of his inside pockets.

The wizard goblin had many pockets within his cloak that held a variety of items that he felt were useful for his magic; everything from a dried piece of rare fungus to pieces of Pumplestone.

He took off his cloak quickly and threw it to the ground and stood back, not sure what to do. Whatever was inside his pocket was wriggling about and making a strange clicking sound like a muffled cricket.

Mr Gravenpumple called to the rest of the group to gather around quickly and surround the cloak.

"Come, come, there's something wriggling about in my cloak!" shouted the wizard goblin. Tissamarr got a stick and poked the pocket gingerly to see what would happen, and all of a sudden, a little creature jumped out in front of everyone, holding something up in its hand!

"It's that creature that you saved from the giant's cave, Mr Gravenpumple," said Garvoid.

"I thought it had run away when I tripped over and the cage smashed on the ground. I saw the cage door fling open with the force of the blow," said Mr Gravenpumple with hesitation in his voice.

"But instead of escaping into the forest, it must have run into your cloak pocket and hid there," said Toobah, feeling he had redeemed himself with this assumption, as everyone nodded in agreement.

The creature had the look of a lizard but its head looked too big for its body. It looked very strange; it had two long bandy legs and two very thin arms and each of its hands had three oversized fingers.

Its tail was long and coiled up; it was a very peculiar-looking creature, but somehow, bizarrely, Mr Gravenpumple thought it looked quite cute. It was waving one of its funny hands furiously in a fist at the wizard goblin, and had a big grin on its face.

Everyone was staring at the strange little creature in bewilderment. Then, it opened one of its hands and there it was!

"Oh, my Junamoon! It's a clump of black hair. It looks too thick to belong to anything else but the giant," exclaimed Garvtak.

Tissamarr bent down to stroke the little creature's head and retrieved the hair, which was matted from being so tightly held in its hand, and everyone was surprised when the warlock started to speak to the little creature in a strange tongue.

"Clock coo, coo coo, click click coo," said Tissamarr, which sounded quite comical.

The little creature spoke back with some strange clicking noises which the warlock seemed to understand, and he nodded in acknowledgement and turned to explain to the group what the creature was saying.

"It plucked the hair from the giant's arm when the yar yar birds picked up Mr Gravenpumple by his cloak; the creature was in the wizard goblin's pocket and leaned out as far as possible to grab the hair," said the warlock with a hint of pride in his voice.

"The jerk from the birds lifting Mr Gravenpumple must have been strong enough to help pull the hair from the giant's arm," explained Tissamarr to a highly delighted audience.

Tissamarr explained how the little creature had suckers on its hands so that it could hold onto things securely.

"It held onto the hair tightly; it knew how important it was to get the hair, as it had seen what you were trying to do in the cave," he said with warmth in his tone.

Mr Gravenpumple leaned down to inspect the hair in Tissamarr's hand, and sure enough, it was indeed the very hair they required to add to the fairy potion and it looked like there was enough to make it work.

Mr Gravenpumple was beside himself with joy and fell back laughing with glee.

"Haha, this is brilliant! Our strange little friend has saved the night," the wizard goblin said while laughing at the same time.

The impbahs jumped for joy and started to squeal and the mambooas whizzed round everyone a little too quickly, ending up slumped together in a heap.

The popstrells flitted around everyone excitedly and the goblins and warlock just hugged each other; etiquette went out of the window!

The little group needed to celebrate this incredible act and thank the strange little creature, so they made a wonderful tea consisting of bread, vegetables and biscuits, and, of course, the berry wine was brought out to toast this success.

The wizard goblin made sure the giant's hair was placed safely within his cloak; he wrapped it in a large leaf and bound it with some long vines that he found nearby.

Mr Gravenpumple asked Tissamarr if he would ask the little creature what it wanted to do.

"Does our little friend have a home and family to go back to?" the wizard goblin enquired.

Tissamarr looked at Mr Gravenpumple with sadness in his eyes and explained.

"The creature is a booquar and they always come in pairs. If they are separated and out of each other's reach for longer than a day, then one of them will die," he said, shaking his head.

"The one remaining would never be able to return to its home as it is no longer complete and will be rejected by the rest of the clan," said Tissamarr, glancing back at the booquar with pity in his eyes.

"This one got separated by the giant who had eaten its twin before it went to sleep." He finished his sentence with a whisper and it looked like a little tear had appeared in the corner of his eye.

Mr Gravenpumple was so saddened by this news and felt a great need to help the booquar. He thought to himself, no wonder it wanted to escape and that's why it made such a racket when it saw the group appear in the cave. The booquar would have been the first snack of the day when the giant awoke!

The little creature had saved the day and helped achieve their mission; there must be something he could do to help.

"But the only trouble is I cannot understand the booquar; only you Tissamarr can speak its language" he stated with frustration.

"Will you ask the booquar if it would like to come and live amongst us?" he said kindly to Tissamarr.

The warlock giggled to himself when the goblin highlighted this dilemma and explained that because of many previous encounters, he had perfected a spell that helped the warlock speak its language.

"I will empower you with this magic, too, so you and the booquar can converse," said Tissamarr with a broad smile cracking his craggy old face.

When Tissamarr told the little creature of the invitation, it was so happy and threw its long bandy arms in the air, then ran ever so quickly and threw itself onto Mr Gravenpumple and squeezed his arm tightly, before it jumped into his deep inner pocket to make its new home!

The journey home was mostly uneventful except for a slight deviation to avoid a Nishmoo, which was a strange-looking beast. It looked like a cross between a big black bear and a moose, its body that of a bear, entirely covered in a mass of black hair, with huge paws and long claws, but its nose was long and rather floppy like a moose. It could sniff out a tasty goblin or mambooa from a great distance if the wind was blowing in the right direction. It had been spotted by one of the popstrells flying ahead, who quickly swooped back down to the group to raise the alarm.

When the group reached the boundary of the Massdumoor Mountains, it was time to say goodbye to Tissamarr and Nitnac.

Mr Gravenpumple was sad to be leaving his dear friend but knew they would meet up again soon enough, probably at another magic convention to be held in a place that would be announced at a later date.

There was never much warning or advertising of these special events; they were very much last minute.

"Goodbye, my dear friend. You have once again proved your friendship. I will miss you but I do not think it will be long before our paths cross again," said Mr Gravenpumple with hope in his heart.

"It might be sooner than you think. I hear from the owls that there might be a wizards' convention happening soon, though, of course, we don't know where yet!" he exclaimed, raising his heavy eyebrows in jest.

The rest of the group also said their goodbyes and Nitnac buzzed around everyone's heads, making them dizzy. The group made their way back to Pumple Mountain with the addition to the family of the booquar.

For such a little chap, the booquar had gifted Mr Gravenpumple the giant's hair and that now made it possible to make a home within Kracklewood. It was so important to make him feel welcome and loved.

He knew his two sons would make the booquar feel right at home.

The wizard goblin had asked the little creature what its name was but he couldn't pronounce it very well; it was a strange sound that you couldn't quite get your tongue around, so he decided to give him a new name.

It didn't take long to come up with one; the little booquar would wiggle about in Mr Gravenpumple's pocket, so he named him Squiggle. He thought it was quite an endearing name and the booquar seemed pleased.

The little group made their way back to Pumple Mountain, while popstrells flew on ahead to break the good news. They were to return home to a hero's welcome. Now, they had hope and could start to build a new home in Kracklewood.

Draccam.

Chapter Seven

The Draccadin

Pumple Mountain paled into insignificance against the backdrop of the majestic Galamide mountain range, which covered many miles of rough and dramatic terrain.

Kracklewood sat at the base of the mountain range and it was going to be the new home for the creatures of Pumple Mountain.

In the middle of the wood, a large tree had been identified that could house everyone but it needed to be at least twice the size it already was.

A very tired but successful group came back from their quest with the highly precious cargo needed to complete the fairies' growing potion.

They had been greeted by a welcome home party and there was a celebratory meal laid out for the heroes. All the goblins had been busy baking and cooking ever since the popstrells returned with the exciting news. There was so much food that the meal turned into a whole week of eating and celebrations, Squiggle had never seen so much food in his life and there was a particular cake with his name on it which was made from a sweet nut.

No one else was getting a piece of it; the cake was the most delicious thing he had ever eaten! The little booquar pushed it away and hid it behind a rather large piece of bread until he had the opportunity to munch into it and reduce the size to a manageable chunk that he could hide in his bed.

Mr Gravenpumple and his son Grumplepumple, along with the chief fairy, set about creating the special brew over the next few months.

Goby always wanted to come along and help his father and brother even though he was still quite young. He would play with the fairies while they worked; he thought they were the most beautiful little things he had ever seen, and they would tickle his large ears and make him giggle.

Mixing the special brew was not an easy task. Fanadon, the chief fairy, kept checking the growing potion but it was not setting; it kept separating due to the giant's hair.

This added ingredient was causing the potion to split and not blend together, so, after much deliberation with the fairy council, it was decided to add a mixing gel.

The gel was made up from the sap of the toadstools that grew in Treaclewood, where the fairies lived.

It was the sap that held the toadstool's heavy, bright red with white polka dot-spotted tops in place. However, after several attempts and many heated arguments, the fairies managed to get enough onto a large leaf and transport it to the potion.

Unfortunately, one of the fairies fell into the large leaf while they were trying to transport it and became completely submerged in the gooey sap.

"Watch where you're going with the leaf, Ickle, you dumb fairy! How many times do I have to tell you to lift your wings up?!" said Fanadon to one of his young fairy helpers.

"Your wings are dipping in the sap, and when you lift them, it's flicking the sap onto everyone," he said in a very cross voice.

Ickle glanced around at everyone with an embarrassed look on his face and then tripped over his wing and fell backwards into the sap!

All the fairies starting laughing at him and it was Goby who came to his aid.

It took many hours to wash his wings and dry them out and then Grumplepumple pegged out the fairy on the top of a large bush and his wings flapped away in the gentle breeze.

Goby thought this was so cute but the fairy was not amused.

After so many months of disappointment, Mr Gravenpumple stood at the side of the chief fairy in great anticipation, praying that the sap would do the job, and, sure enough, it started to work.

The sap blended with the potion immediately and started to soften the giant's hair enough to make it set.

To watch a rather plump fairy dance around a pot with a very excited elder goblin in his battered and worn-out cloak, accompanied by two other goblins, was hysterical, and especially with a booquar sat on the wizard's hat trying to hold on for dear life!

There was a great buzz amongst the creatures of Pumple Mountain. Everyone was very excited at the thought of moving to their new home, but it was going to be strange.

The goblins had lived in the Pumple caves for so long but the tree had the character and design to suit them, with its huge gnarled trunk and enormous branches. It had so many nooks and crannies that could be carved out to make comfortable chambers.

So, the date was set for the growing potion to be administered to the tree. It was very important to get the timing right, but with the special potion and the magical powers of a new Junamoon working together, it should be enough to make the tree grow to at least twice its current size, although three-fold would be better to house everyone comfortably.

Everyone was to gather together around the tree on the next new moon rising, which was due in a couple of months.

A new Junamoon happened once a year in the Three Realms of the goblins. It was a very special time because the Junamoon would emanate special healing powers to repair and revitalise the land with new growth. It was the deepest blood orange you could imagine and so big and spectacular that it dominated the sky; it was one of the most beautiful sights to behold.

The moon would fill the night sky with its glory and magnificence.

It was honoured by all the creatures of the land with celebratory rituals of worship to thank the new moon rising. They would organise huge feasts with dancing to songs of adventures old and new.

The night sky would be filled with flashes and forks of lightning made of many colours, provided by the wizards, warlocks and witches with their magic.

Finally, the night of the new Junamoon arrived and the huge pot holding the special potion was brought into place by the tree.

Mr Gravenpumple had organised a raft to be made of thick branches intertwined with vines on which to carry the pot. Garvtak and Garvoid, plus two other goblins, were given the responsibility to move the potion into the right position.

"Don't you go spilling that precious cargo; we'll need every drop," Garvtak said to Garvoid in a condescending way as the raft was dragged over a large tree root.

" Oh, shut up! You're like an irritating bug. You try putting your back into it for a change, you fat, lazy goblin," Garvoid snapped back.

The other two goblins raised their eyes up to the sky; they were used to Garvtak and Garvoid's continual bickering.

All the creatures were in place surrounding the tree, except a few of the popstrells who had been sent out into the night to scout for any danger.

They reported back that the coast was clear but a handful of impbahs kept guard up in the surrounding trees just in case.

The celebrations in Kracklewood would commence straight away after the potion had been applied and the tree had grown. The goblins of Pumple Mountain had organised a huge display of fireworks, which were made out of the dust of the Pumplestone mixed with the very combustible oil from the yuocca plant that grew higher up the mountainside. The two ingredients were blended together and stuffed into the leaf from the yuocca and bound very tightly.

When they were ready, the leaves were propelled into the air using slingshots and Mr Gravenpumple and Grumplepumple would zap them with their staffs. The explosions were incredible, and, for a reason no one understood, the fireworks would produce a medley of colours so bright and beautiful they would take your breath away.

The food had been prepared by the goblans, the females of the clan.

"Goblins cannot be trusted to cook. They haven't the patience or the aptitude to make anything other than trouble," Gignac would say.

Gignac was Garvoid's wife and she was head cook and could be quite bossy, but in a fair and assertive way, she got the job done; she was highly respected.

"Don't mix up those bowls, Gimmy. I need to add some root vegetables and I don't want them going into the sweet dish," she said loudly, mopping her brow and giving the poor little goblan one of her very stern looks that could make even a strong goblin wither.

Berry wine had been brewed in copious amounts and poured into huge casks; it was going to be the biggest and greatest celebration of the moolatoon. Everything rested on this potion working. So much was at stake; it had to work. So much effort had gone into this moment.

The night was filled with nervous tension but the new Junamoon rising was so splendid that it held everyone spellbound and calmed the mood.

The goblins were ready; the potion had to be poured onto the roots of the tree at the very moment the moon was at its highest peak, so as to maximise the growth.

A trench had been dug around the base to absorb the liquid quickly and the magic of the moon, combined with the potion, would make the tree sprout forth and upwards with vigorous growth.

All was going according to plan; the goblins were in position to pour the potion and awaiting the signal from Mr Gravenpumple when suddenly, there was an almighty whooshing sound from the trench at the base of the tree.

It all happened so fast! Everyone had been transfixed and mesmerised by the new Junamoon rising that they were not looking at the tree.

As they all turned to see what had made the tremendous noise, they were rooted to the spot and stunned!

"Great gollygums, what is that?" screamed Garvtak with terror in his voice.

Suddenly, there was the sound of screaming which was coming from the impbahs in the trees as they could see what was unfolding.

"Eeeekkkkkkkk sceeekkkkkkk," the impbahs screeched loudly.

The popstrells flapped their wings furiously to get out of the way and retreated further into the surrounding trees.

The goblins and mambooas stood still with jaws dropped and mouths gaping at the sight in front of them.

Something was rising up out of the thick canopy of dried leaves at the base of the tree. It was rising quickly and whipping up the leaves into a swirling mass that engulfed the creature, but then they cleared and there, in front of everyone, lay a huge draccadin!

"Oh no! This can't be... no, no, this can't be happening!" said Mr Gravenpumple shaking his head violently.

It rose up quickly with its huge body towering over the creatures, bearing its enormous fangs and flicking its long, slimy black tongue in the direction of the goblins as it hissed loudly.

"Hisssssss! Hissssssss!" The draccadin made a terrible sound that frightened everyone to the core.

This made one of the goblins faint out of sheer terror and he had to be quickly dragged away out of harm's way.

Mr Gravenpumple shouted to Grumplepumple who was stood by his father's side.

"The beast must have settled in the trench after it had been dug out, and nestled itself amongst the leaves that had gathered after that blustery wind had blown over the land last week," he said anxiously.

Draccadins could camouflage their bodies by changing the pigmentation of their skin to blend in with their surroundings.

"No one will have noticed the snake lying in the trench," replied Grumplepumple.

Unfortunately, and to everyone's horror, the snake started to curl itself around the base of the tree trunk as it recoiled from the screams from the impbahs and the yells from the goblins.

This was not good because the beast was starting to climb up the tree and you could see it was squeezing the life out of it! The mambooas were whizzing round the tree waving their arms to try and chase the snake away, but, if anything, this was making the snake coil itself tighter around the tree.

Fanadon ordered his fairies to retreat quickly behind the rest of the creatures in the circle and hide in the undergrowth.

"Quick, quick, you cannot aid this fight. The draccadin is too strong!" yelled the chief fairy and the other fairies reluctantly did as ordered, but Fanadon stayed by Mr Gravenpumple's side.

The big red toadstools of Treaclewood were home to the fairies but were also a favourite meal for the draccadin when meat was not on the menu.

On too many occasions, the fairies experienced the fatal actions of a draccadin; they were probably their worst enemy.

They often lost their homes because of this creature's fondness for their toadstools and the occasional fairy would fall victim to the snake and be devoured as well!

Mr Gravenpumple was witnessing the disaster unfolding before him. He was desperately trying to think of a spell he could use to shrink the snake so that it would not strangle the tree, but everything he tried was futile.

"Minimarcalus, smalloomugus, tinitintar!" he yelled, flicking his wand furiously at the beast.

This was an enormous draccadin. It was much bigger than normal, probably enhanced by the strength of the new moon and that could have been why nothing was working.

Blue flashes from his gnarled staff were hurtling towards the snake and goblins had to duck and dive to make sure they were not in the firing line.

But the snake just squeezed tighter and tighter round the tree's trunk as the commotion intensified.

The Junamoon was reaching its peak in the night sky and the timing was critical; if they missed this opportunity, then there would not be another chance for another yulatoon.

Grumplepumple had joined in his father's attempts to help maim the snake; he had learned and mastered a wealth of magic from his father over time and knew of many spells and potions.

Much of these had been found through trial and error, with many a poor creature being subjected to humiliation at the failings of his experiments. However, he had achieved a level to earn him the right to be called a wizard. His father had given him an honorary seat on the High Council which was the proudest night of his life.

But even with the two of them throwing everything they had at the beast, it was hopeless.

"The draccadin is too big and its skin is impenetrable!" shouted Grumplepumple.

Even Fanadon tried to cast a spell to turn the creature into a statue, but this had gone terribly wrong and ended up making the snake even more annoyed, as only its tail had turned to stone and became cumbersome and heavy. But it did stop the beast from climbing the tree and it slumped to the ground.

"Well done, Fanadon, your spell has disabled it!" shouted Mr Gravenpumple in praise.

Mr Gravenpumple knew he had to do something drastic and quickly, now that the beast was hindered, otherwise, all would be lost as they were running out of time.

So, he threw off his heavy cloak and started running towards the tree and closer to the draccadin.

This startled Squiggle and he leapt out of the goblin's deep inner pocket as the cloak hit the ground, and jumped up and attached itself onto the goblin's arm, trying to pull him back.

He knew what Mr Gravenpumple was about to do!

But still, with Squiggle tightly attached, the goblin raced forward and confronted the draccadin with a dagger in his hand.

Everyone gasped in horror at the sight in front of them and they were stunned by the action of the goblin.

It all happened in a flash - Grumplepumple was equally stunned, and as the realisation sank in, he screamed with terror and hurled himself forward to help his father. However, he was quickly dragged to the ground by a group of goblins.

The brave old wizard goblin thought that the only thing that would kill the draccadin would be the Dagger of Pumplestone; it had to be plunged deep into the beast and quickly! The dagger was made for Mr Gravenpumple in honour of his master plan to drive out the woolvacs; it had taken the goblins months of toil and hard work to chisel the dagger out of the purest red crystal Pumplestone. It was a weapon of such refinement and beauty and revered and praised by many. The workmanship required had to be so precise to make it sharp enough to pierce any creature's skin. The creatures of Pumple Mountain had wanted to thank the goblin for his continuous bravery, wisdom and kindness shown to them and hence, presented him with this honorary token of gratitude to keep him safe from harm.

The draccadin reared up its ugly dragon head and hissed loudly at Mr Gravenpumple as he approached, flicking its vile black tongue and looking ready to pounce.

The wizard goblin was shouting at Garvtak and Garvoid to pour the potion into the trench while he tried to distract the beast. He waved the Pumplestone dagger frantically in front of the beast to keep its attention.

Then suddenly, Squiggle, the little booquar, leapt up from the goblin's shoulder onto the draccadin's body and crawled up onto its face, trying to poke one of its eyes with his large suckered hands to disable it.

This would give the goblin a chance to sink the dagger into its chest as the beast shook its head vigorously in an attempt to shake off Squiggle.

Mr Gravenpumple moved forward quickly to get nearer to the draccadin's underbelly but was being blinded by the dried leaves that had swirled up around the beast. However, he persevered and pressed forward as best he could with the dagger raised high.

He needed to use all his might to plunge the dagger as deep as he could; it had to pierce through the thick armour of scales and tough skin.

Everything was going wrong; everyone was panic-stricken and it was all happening so fast!

Now that the draccadin had released its grip and moved slightly away towards Mr Gravenpumple. the goblins did as they were instructed and started to pour the potion into the trench around the tree base.

"Please be careful, Mr Gravenpumple," shouted Garvtak, followed up by Garvoid yelling,

"Don't do anything stupid, Mr Gravenpumple," as they tried to see the wizard goblin through the swirling leaves.

The Junamoon had risen to its highest peak and was now at its most powerful and Mr Gravenpumple was nowhere to be seen!

Suddenly, there was a high-pitched hissing screech and a frantic clicking noise coming from the direction of the draccadin; it was writhing about furiously and thrashing its heavy tail, even though this had turned to stone.

Then the draccadin came crashing down and collapsed with a thunderous thump that shook the ground producing a thick cloud of dust that covered everything.

The Graven Tree

Chapter Eight

The Graven Tree

The tree had started to grow and there was a huge cracking sound as it burst into life, its branches surging upwards quickly into the night sky.

Branch upon branch, twig upon twig and leaf upon leaf sprouted forth from the ever-increasing trunk as it started to swell and expand at a rapid rate. The tree was consuming everything around it so the goblins had to run away quickly before they were swallowed up too.

Grumplepumple instructed everyone to run from the clearing quickly.

"Run! Everyone, run. Quickly, before the tree consumes us all," shouted a very stricken and fearful wizard goblin. Grumplepumple was desperately searching for his father as he shouted the order, and everyone ran into the undergrowth as the ground began to shake with such an incredible force.

The sound of the tree growing was ear-splitting, and everyone cowered down in fear as it stretched up, up and up into the night sky, reaching the twinkling stars above. It looked like it was about to touch the Junamoon!

Then, as quickly as it had started, it stopped, and there before the creatures stood the biggest tree they had ever seen.

It was enormous with more branches than you could ever possibly count and a canopy on top that was so thick it blocked out the stars above it.

Everyone just stared in wonderment at this incredible sight; they had witnessed the birth of their new home!

"Oh, my pumplegumple! That is one ruddy big tree," exclaimed Garvtak, nudging Garvoid in his ribs as he gazed at the tree in awe. Grumplepumple ran forward, frantically running round the tree shouting, "But where is my father? Where is his faithful little friend, the booquar, and where is the draccadin?"

It took a while for the dust to settle and everyone could take stock of what had happened; then the realisation set in, and everyone looked at each other with horror, stricken with grief. They were frantically searching everywhere to try and find Mr Gravenpumple.

Tears were streaming down Grumplepumple's face but the oldest, wisest and bravest goblin of the land was gone. He was nowhere to be seen.

The only thing that was left was the wizard's cloak that lay dusty and crumpled up in a corner of the clearing. Grumplepumple bent down to pick it up; he wanted to hold it close to him in the hope of finding some comfort, but instead, he was confronted by a very distressed, battered, bruised and dusty little booquar that was sobbing its heart out into the sleeve of the cloak.

The young wizard knew how much Squiggle loved his father and how much his father had become attached to the little creature, so he slowly scooped Squiggle up in his hand to offer some comfort. The little booquar looked up through red, bloodshot eyes and quickly scuttled off back into Mr Gravenpumple's cloak and dug itself deep into the inner pocket. Grumplepumple picked up the cloak gently, dusted it off and put it on. It was the only solace he could find to cope with the loss of his father. It was too big for the little goblin but he didn't care, and from that night forward, he wore it all the time.

"Mr Gravenpumple must have been swallowed up by the tree as it grew and it has taken the beast with it," said Toobah to Booma. Several weeks had now passed but Booma was still wiping the continual stream of tears from his face.

"There is no other explanation; the area has been searched for many nights and we have found nothing," Toobah continued with his explanation, aimed more at himself than Booma, as they sat under the huge tree.

"Mr Grumplepumple said the booquar had been tossed off the draccadin's head as it was stabbed deeply in the stomach by the dagger and landed in the undergrowth beyond the clearing," Booma replied, again wiping away another tear.

"Squiggle was dazed and heavily bruised and had tried to find his master, but to no avail, and so he slipped back under the wizard's cloak to mourn, poor little thing," Toobah said with a sad shake of his head.

"We must make sure that Mr Gravenpumple gets the best memorial ceremony there ever was. I will miss him so much; he was my dearest friend," said Toobah with a tear in his eye.

When a goblin passes away, it is believed that the soul will enter the sacred realm of Elysiom, a place of peace and tranquillity, where a goblin will spend many yulatoons reflecting on what they had learned while in physical form. Once they have discovered the true meaning of their existence and understood and accepted their purpose in life, the soul is released to be reborn.

Their new life would bring greater wisdom and empathy to others; it was a continuous journey of learning and enrichment to lead a better life each time. After the cremation, the charred remains would be crumbled up and scattered in the sacred area within the mines of Pumple Mountain, and this helped enrich the soils that produce the beautiful red Pumplestone.

The Pumple goblins' philosophy was that to have life, you must always enrich the life that surrounds you.

There was usually a big celebration to honour the life of a goblin and rejoice in what they had achieved while living on the land.

Goblins would retell stories about the goblin and each life was entered into the great book of Galamide. The book was very precious and kept in safe-keeping by the highest-ranking goblin, who had been Mr Gravenpumple, but now it was to have his name and story inscribed into its pages by his son.

A celebration did happen to honour the great wizard but there was a great sadness as well. There was no body to offer back to the caves of Pumple Mountain so the great council decided that the best place to pay homage and perform a memorial ceremony should be by the tree that took his life.

It was felt that this was the closest they could get to Mr Gravenpumple, even though not in body, but in spirit, and his presence was felt strongest there so it felt only right to hold a ceremonial fire there.

Goblins came from far and wide to pay their last respects, and warlocks, including one of Mr Gravenpumple's closest friends, Tissamarr, attended.

Witches, and many other creatures that the wise old wizard had met on his travels, also came to pay their last respects.

Even the great white owl of Mocklewood made an appearance; it sat on a distant tree with its head cocked to one side, listening intently to the words being spoken at the ceremony.

Great fires were built to cook the feast of fresh bread, root vegetables and thick grain broths with many rich herbs and spices.

Gignac, Garvoid's wife, insisted that there be a wide selection of sweet cakes, especially Mr Gravenpumple's favourite, as they would be appreciated by Grumplepumple. Therefore, many adorned the tables and, of course, the berry wine was in plentiful supply.

The goblins had put together a wonderful musical medley of Mr Gravenpumple's favourite songs, using some very strange instruments. The bigborrahs, which looked like large sitars but with many little knobbly bits all down the side, came out. When they were twisted, pulled and flicked the bigborrah would produce a haunting sound like wind blowing through a tunnel. This musical instrument was only used when there was a funeral.

Once the food had been consumed, the berry wine had been drunk and the music had been played, Gorun stood up by the great tree and clapped his hands loudly to get everyone's attention.

Gorun was a great goblin warrior who had been by Mr Gravenpumple's side on many journeys when they were young, and who had been a very close friend to the wizard goblin. He sat on the great council and often was the voice of reason and an excellent aid to Mr Gravenpumple.

He was quite distinctive as he bore a large scar, deep and dark, down the middle of his face; he had received this wound from a fierce battle with a cruen. Everyone turned their gaze to him and listened intently to his words.

"Firstly, I would like to thank everyone for coming together, some travelling a great distance over challenging terrain and through dangerous forests to celebrate the life of our great leader," he spoke with grandeur and purpose.

Then he told his audience of the mission to seek out the giant and capture its hairs in order to help create the tree that now stood before them.

It was a colourful story and one that had been told many times since Mr Gravenpumple had returned.

It played out very well again to this very special audience of creatures who had come together to honour the wizard goblin's life. After the raucous applause, the goblin calmed the audience down, by banging a large pointed staff on the ground to create a sense of drama. Then, in a quiet and respectful tone, the goblin announced the decision of the great council.

"I would like to take this opportunity to inform you of the name of our new home." There was a great stillness in the air and all attention was on the goblin, except for a couple of impbahs, who were carrying on with their chatter, much to the annoyance of Gorun. A quick nod to Elphin, the chief impbah, and a poke in their rears soon sorted them out.

The great warrior goblin drew a deep breath and then made the announcement.

"The tree will be called The Graven Tree, in honour of our dearest and most respected leader, and we would like to ask his son to take up his father's mantle and sit in his place at the head of the great council."

Everyone clapped in unison and a great cheer resounded throughout the gathering as they all agreed with this. "Well deserved and a very good decision to let Grumplepumple step into his father's chair as the head of the council," said Garvtak to Garvoid, who nodded positively while gorging on a sweet cake. He had sneaked it into his cloak pocket to eat later, but he could not resist and was now eating it. Garvtak gave Garvoid a look of total disgust and shook his head.

There had been a great gathering of the creatures of Pumple Mountain to decide who would have the honour of stepping into the position of High Councillor, but it had been a simple and easy vote.

Grumplepumple had earned the right to take his father's place and take on the leadership of the clan. Grumplepumple was surprised but pleased with this honour and solemnly thanked the creatures for this gesture. He felt it was a very suitable way to honour his father and felt very proud.

Goby was stood by his brother's side and grabbed his hand and squeezed it; he was so proud of Grumplepumple and worshipped the ground he walked on.

The loss of Mr Gravenpumple had come as a bitter blow to his son and he had not had much time to come to terms with what was happening, but it was worse trying to explain everything to a young and innocent Goby.

The little goblin had lost another member of his family too soon, and the responsibility of this now fell on Grumplepumple's shoulders, which was both daunting and scary.

It was so important to have leadership and someone at the helm to guide and hold council, and becoming the High Wizard gave the goblin the title of Mr Grumplepumple. To gain the honour of being called "Mister" was one of the greatest achievements a goblin could attain in the First Realm, and with it came an enormous responsibility to guide, support and protect.

The ceremony brought together goblins from the First and Second Realms and strengthened the union that had weakened over time. Carboot from the Second Realm sat down with Mr Grumplepumple to secure a better bond and closer relationship for the future.

"We must never let time and circumstances come between our clans again. It is of great importance that we come together and be as one," said Carboot, patting Mr Grumplepumple's back.

Mr Gravenpumple had been the conduit for binding the realms together; he would journey far and wide to meet with his fellow kin. However, of late, with age taking its toll, the journeys had become less frequent and contact had been lost.

Mr Grumplepumple felt it was important to rekindle their friendship and build a better bridge of communication. The two goblins formed a deeper alliance and shook hands.

Everything had been overwhelming and it took the wizard goblin a long time to settle into his new role, with all the responsibilities he had to take onboard. But time was of the essence; he had no time to contemplate anything.

Mr Grumplepumple had to orchestrate the move from Pumple Mountain for all the creatures and it took all his waking hours.

He liaised with the council to relocate everyone into their new home over the next few months, organising the safest method to move everything from the caves to Kracklewood, and settling everyone within the biggest tree in the Galamide Mountains.

The newly elected High Wizard goblin was given the honour of being the first to choose where he wanted to live within the great tree and he found a nice deep nook about halfway up on the west side of the trunk - it had a great view.

He wanted to be on this side so that he could see the moon rise in the night sky and see the stars twinkling up above. He would sit with Goby by his side and ponder for many an hour about the issues of the night.

He took great comfort from his new role as he now knew that his purpose in life was to keep Goby and the rest of the clan safe from harm.

Mr Grumplepumple had many things to master, being the new High Wizard. Garvtak and Garvoid, Mr Gravenpumple's right-hand goblins, took solemn oaths to serve Mr Grumplepumple with their lives, as they had his father, and stand by his side with honour and pride.

A new Pumplestone dagger was made for the young wizard goblin in honour of his new position and to offer protection to both him and the clan. The blade took many months to perfect; it had to be the sharpest blade in the land, capable of piercing the skin of any beast that threatened. The creatures of Pumple Mountain wanted the dagger to give greater protection to Mr Grumplepumple so that he would not suffer the same fate as his father.

The dagger had killed the draccadin, but not protected Mr Gravenpumple!

Therefore, this dagger needed to be able to wield a much greater power and that could only happen if the blade was given the magic Spell of Resurrection. But there was only one warlock who could offer this protection to the blade and that was the great master, Nantah, from the enchanted forest of Quazboo, who lived in the Second Realm.

Dagger of Pumplestone

Chapter Nine

Dagger of Pumplestone

Deep within the caves of Pumple Mountain, goblins would mine for Pumplestone. Some of the stones were used to make everyday items like cooking utensils, pots, pans and plates, but the purest stones were used for more refined goods like jewellery and weapons and to make a very special item; the invaluable Dagger of Pumplestone. It was being made in honour of the newly appointed High Wizard, Mr Grumplepumple.

The last dagger made belonged to Mr Gravenpumple, who plunged it deep into a draccadin that threatened to squeeze the life out of the Graven Tree.

This dagger needed to serve its new master well and give greater protection; it had to be stronger and sharper and be able to wield a much greater power to tackle any threat that presented itself to Mr Grumplepumple and the creatures of Pumple Mountain.

After many days, that turned into weeks and then months, the weapon was finally ready and it was indeed a magnificent and glorious weapon. The blade was truly magical and as it was turned, the glint from it dazzled you with the brightest light you could ever imagine.

Mr Gravenpumple had told many stories of his travels to the other realms. One particular story told of the great warlock, Nantah, who lived in the Second Realm in a place called Quazboo.

The warlock had great powers and was revered throughout the lands. Attending lessons with him was by invitation only. He would gather his pilgrims together, comprised mainly of warlocks, witches and wizard goblins, and teach them his magic.

Mr Gravenpumple had attended several of these events and brought back new magic each time, which, of course, was used for the good of the creatures of Pumple Mountain.

Dark magic was forbidden in the Three Realms. There was no place for it and no good had ever come of it; in the past, some creatures had used the magic for their own gains and suffered the consequences.

One particular creature had dabbled with dark magic to try and persuade his fellow kin to turn against the goblins of Clanomide.

The great Nantah had to cast an enchanted spell upon an object to give it greater power and protection against this enemy.

It had helped the goblins to defeat the Morzarhs who threatened to obliterate the very existence of every goblin that lived within the Realm of Clanomide.

Garvtak and Garvoid remembered this story well. They had accompanied Mr Gravenpumple on a visit to the goblins to trade their Pumplestone for seeds to plant, and many tales had been exchanged.

On reflection, this particular story was of great interest because, if they could get the great Nantah to bestow the same Spell of Resurrection on their dagger, then it would give much greater protection to Mr Grumplepumple.

Garvtak and Garvoid retold the story to the great council, with Toobah interjecting annoyingly, now and then.

"The morzarhs are evil. They live in the swamps and threatened the very existence of the Clanomide goblins, but the great Nantah came to their rescue," explained Garvtak.

"Tell them about Baras, tell them what he did," interjected Toobah again, much to Garvtak's annoyance.

Toobah had accompanied the goblins on several journeys to the Clanomide Mountains. He was always by the old wizard goblin's side, so the council listened with great interest.

Mr Grumplepumple had accompanied his father on many travels, but not this one, and he listened with some trepidation. He questioned whether there was such a need to make this journey to seek out Nantah, now that a new home had been found that offered a safe haven from predators.

Life had settled down into a steady pace within the community and he wanted to reassure the great council that no harm would come their way.

"There is no need for this journey to seek out Nantah. We have good protection already from the Graven Tree," said Mr Grumplepumple with assurance in his voice.

However, everyone was adamant that a greater protection was required and were quite insistent on the new wizard goblin making the journey.

Mr Grumplepumple realised he wasn't going to win this argument and reluctantly agreed, but it was not his safety that worried him.

Leaving his little brother Goby again was his concern. The young goblin had become so reliant on him after Mr Gravenpumple's death and shadowed his every move.

Goby was still too young to accompany his brother on this journey; he had to be kept safe from harm so he would be left in the capable hands of Gorun, the great elder from the High Council, and his goblan wife, Gorrita.

She was already very fond of Goby and would fuss around him and overfeed him, despite Mr Grumplepumple's objections, but she was only being kind and caring.

The little group chosen to go on the expedition was made up of a handful of highly skilled warrior goblins, which included Garvtak and Garvoid, and several mambooas, headed up by Toobah. Included in the group were a couple of impbahs, who could look out for predators from the trees, and, of course, the popstrells. They would fly ahead to make sure the path was clear and safe.

The date was set and they were to wait for the next full moon before they set off on their journey, which was a handful of night times away. This would help them see clearly and give them the best chance of navigating through the Galamide Mountains.

They had mapped out a course that took them through their homeland and then into the Second Realm. They would have to travel through the Massdumoor Mountains, where the giants lived, argued vehemently by Toobah and Booma, who had endured enough of giants. They also had to be careful of the greatly feared Nishmoo, who lived in the Second Realm, as they could pick up a scent from miles away.

Once they had navigated their way through the giants' territory, they would make their way to Clandil, home to the goblins of the Clanomide Mountains. They would pay a visit and hope to pick up new provisions and meet up with their old acquaintances. Mr Grumplepumple had promised his new friend, Carboot, that when he was next in the Second Realm, he would call in.

The wizard goblin remembered being amused by the Clanomide goblins. They were a little larger than the Pumple goblins and had longer ears that flapped wildly as they ran, and their skin was yellowish-brown. They had longer noses too, and hands that looked like mallets. These goblins worked the land; their ancestors had been farmers and this tradition was passed on through the cenatoons.

Then, finally, they would make their way on to the mystical land of Quazboo which lay north of the Clanomide Mountains, and seek out the great warlock. Nantah lived deep within the mountains of Quazboo in an enchanted forest, and this could be quite problematic because the forest was a shape-changer; its form would change on a regular basis so it was difficult to locate and then navigate through.

This had been the hardest part of the task for Mr Gravenpumple when he was trying to find Nantah and attend his classes, as Garvtak and Garvoid had explained to the High Council.

Mr Grumplepumple hoped this would not cause too much of a problem for them.

The full moon had arrived and it filled the clear night sky with a bright hazy glow, making the stars look extra twinkly on this night. Mr Grumplepumple had already packed his shoulder bag ready for the journey and packed his favourite biscuits that Garvoid's wife had made for him.

They had a very distinctive taste and were not to everyone's liking; they looked like mouldy cheese but the wizard goblin loved them.

He was sad to go as he had to leave behind his little brother, Goby, who he cherished with all his heart, but he knew the little goblin was safe and protected within the Graven Tree.

The popstrells had flown on ahead to check the coast was clear and the little party set off, making their way through Kracklewood.

It didn't take too long to get to the boundary of the Galamide mountains. Once there, they could see the Massdumoor mountain range stretching out ahead; they were huge mountains with rounded peaks, covered in a white ash from previous eruptions that made them look like iced muffins.

Toobah took in a deep breath and turned to look at Garvtak and Garvoid with hesitation in his eyes; the mambooa remembered their last trip into this land and did not want to experience another meeting with a giant!

The goblins gave Toobah a wink of the eye and a gentle nudge with their fists to lift his spirits and they all soldiered on.

All was quiet as the little group tiptoed through the mountains; the popstrells were scouting the land to make sure there was no danger and regularly reported back with good news to put the group's mind at ease.

A little giant, much smaller than usual, had been spotted off to the east of where they needed to go, so their course was altered slightly to make sure the giant could not pick up their scent.

It meant going further west through a small dark and uninviting wood that sat on the banks of the great Crimstone River that meandered through the mountain range, but this was better than an encounter with a giant and was greatly welcomed by Toobah, Booma and Elphin, the chief of the impbahs.

The Gobbanam Tree

Chapter Ten

The Gobbanam Tree

Mr Grumplepumple was feeling hungry and pulled out one of his favourite biscuits to have a little nibble as his stomach was grumbling. All of a sudden, out popped the head of the little booquar.

Squiggle was also partial to the biscuits and was hoping for a little treat. The wizard goblin was just about to break off a piece of biscuit to offer his dear friend when, as quick as a flash, something flicked out from out of nowhere. Whatever it was whisked the biscuit away, along with the booquar that was still attached to it!

It happened so fast that Mr Grumplepumple was startled and let out a loud yell.

"Arghh! What in Elysiom's name was what?" said the wizard goblin in an alarmed voice.

The rest of the group stopped and turned round to see what all the commotion was about and saw a very bewildered and upset goblin.

"No, no, no! Where have you gone, my dear little friend? Where are you?" shouted Mr Grumplepumple.

Panic was starting to set in as Mr Grumplepumple realised what had happened and was looking frantically around; the only thing that was close enough was a strange-looking tree which was just on the border of the spooky wood.

The group joined the goblin and Mr Grumplepumple pointed to the tree. The mambooas quickly darted up into the tree, desperately searching for Squiggle, but could not find anything.

"There's nothing here, no Squiggle," said Toobah.

"He can't just have disappeared into thin air," added Booma.

The air was still and there were just the usual sounds of the night. The popstrells scoured the area from above to see if they could see anything but had no luck.

Mr Grumplepumple was so upset. "How could this happen? What has taken my little friend so quickly and without any warning?" he said with so much sorrow in his voice. Then suddenly, the group heard a noise that sounded like a very loud cough and looked up to where it came from.

They saw the most enormous silhouette of some kind of beast; it was perched on top of the tree and was shaking its huge head. Everyone quickly ran to safety and hid behind another tree nearby, and looked on in horror as the beast seemed to rage and fling its arms about, but strangely, without making a sound, which everyone thought was a bit peculiar.

Mr Grumplepumple suddenly thought he recognised the beast's shape and looked intently at the monster even though he was frightened. It did remind him of someone with its jagged back and long spindly arms.

It looked like the shape of his friend, the booquar, but magnified to a much bigger size.

Then suddenly, he heard the familiar sound of clicking that he knew so well.

"Click, click, coo clock," was the sound that came from the tree.

The night moon had magnified the silhouette of Squiggle and made him look so big.

Much to the horror of the rest of the group, Mr Grumplepumple jumped up and sprang forward, shouting up at the beast; the clicking got much louder as it heard its master's voice.

"Squiggle, Squiggle, is that you?" shouted the wizard goblin.

Toobah ordered one of his mambooas to climb the tree quickly and retrieve the little booquar but Squiggle had got his foot stuck within one of the twisted branches of the tree and could not free himself.

So, Garvtak took charge.

"Leave this to me. That bloomin' tree needs a good lesson in manners!" he said in a brave goblin sort of way. He climbed up the tree, and, with his axe, cut through the branch to release Squiggle's foot, and gently cupped the traumatised little booquar in his hands.

Suddenly, the tree started to shake violently as the goblin hacked at its branch, and it let out an enormous scream like a wailing banshee, as it started to sway wildly from side to side.

Whaaaaa, Whaaaaa!" it screamed.

Garvtak could not hold on and was flung off the tree into the clearing below, fortunately along with the booquar that had secured its suckered hands to the goblin's arm and wasn't letting go!

Everyone ran quickly away from the tree. Garvoid helped his best friend up and put his arm round him to aid his retreat.

"Come on, old-timer. I'll help you escape. You always need my help, don't you?" Garvoid said in a condescending way.

"Only this time, you ugly wart," replied Garvtak, shaking his head in denial.

For quite some time, they could still hear the screaming behind them as they ran, and they didn't stop until they were clear of the wood.

They finally stopped by a cluster of rocks to catch their breath and decided to make a bed for the day as it seemed safe enough. So, the goblins brewed up some much-welcomed oolong tea and vegetable stew.

Squiggle relayed his experience to Mr Grumplepumple in a loud series of clicking noises which got so loud at one point that the wizard goblin had to calm the little booquar down.

"There, there, my little friend. Here's a piece of that biscuit you were after," he said in a calm and quiet voice.

He listened to the tale and then told the story to everyone else who was waiting eagerly to find out what had happened.

"The tree is obviously enchanted and has an enormous tongue that whipped up the biscuit from my hand along with Squiggle, and thrust them down the top of its trunk, where there was a gaping mouth that the tongue was attached to," said Mr Grumplepumple in a dramatic tone.

"It was trying to swallow the biscuit but did not realise Squiggle was attached and it was having difficulty trying to swallow the two together," he surmised.

"Everything had gone dark and Squiggle said he could feel a tremendous pressure as the tree was trying to digest the food," he said in a kind of statement.

Then Mr Grumplepumple explained that Squiggle had somehow managed to reach out one of his hands and secure it firmly against the side of the tree's mouth. This made the tree start to choke as it couldn't swallow, and it spat Squiggle out, and that is how he ended up at the top of the tree!

Squiggle said he was covered in goo from head to toe and was frantically trying to free himself but got his foot stuck within one of the tree's thick, twisted branches.

The group had never encountered a tree with a mouth before and noticed, on reflection, that it was quite different from the rest of the trees.

It had a yellow tinge to it that gave it a sallow and sinister look. Mr Grumplepumple checked his book of knowledge, which he always kept with him.

It was one of the most precious things that he had of his father's; it was an encyclopaedia of information that had all Mr Gravenpumple's notes in it from his extensive travels.

He came to a page that had a picture of a similar tree that his father had drawn, and under the sketch, the name, The Gobbanam Tree, had been written.

Well, the name certainly suited the tree because it had the most enormous mouth. Mr Grumplepumple chuckled to himself and wondered if his father had named the tree or was it the tree's official name?

It was duly noted in his diary as a tree to avoid at all costs in the future!

The group had a fitful sleep and they each took it in turns to keep guard until dusk arrived. Then, they pressed on with haste to reach their destination and the welcome of the Clanomide goblins.

The group travelled on through the Massdumoor Mountains with no further encounters, except for a couple of moomars that had got tangled up in a golly-berry bush and were covered in thick smelly goo.

They had the look of a squirrel with bright yellow eyes that turned green when they were frightened.

It took quite a while to prise the creatures out of the goo and clean up their long black fur.

The moomars were incredibly grateful and nearly squeezed the goblins to death with hugs and kisses.

Morzarhs

Chapter Eleven

The Morzarhs

Finally, Mr Grumplepumple and his friends reached the welcome sight of the Clanomide peak, which stood much taller than any other peak in the mountain range.

Its majestic grandeur took their breath away, and, with the full moon behind it, you could not help but look in wonder at its glory. The popstrells had flown on ahead to notify the Clanomide goblins of their arrival and they were greeted by the great wizard goblin, Carboot, and a couple of representatives from the council.

"This is a most pleasant surprise; I was not expecting to see you for at least another yulatoon," said Carboot in a jovial tone.

Garvtak and Garvoid and the other goblins gave Carboot the honorary salute by crossing both arms across the chest and bowing the head down to the knees and Mr Grumplepumple followed suit.

"We come to seek your counsel, Carboot. We are in need of finding Nantah," said the wizard goblin tentatively, trying to gauge the goblin's reaction.

"Well, that will be a task in itself. You know the great warlock does not like guests," said Carboot with a warning glance at the group.

"We know, but it is of great importance and I shall explain on our way to Clandil," said Mr Grumplepumple assertively.

Carboot nodded his head in acceptance and asked everyone to follow him.

The mambooas and impbahs stood behind to show respect and then everyone followed the goblins to their home city of Clandil, in the lowlands at the foot of the mountain.

The goblins of Clanomide were farmers and tended their crops on the flat plains between the mountains. They grew everything imaginable from huge root vegetables that looked like massive pumpkins, to nuts and fruit of every description. But the most prized crop was the quinct grain that was sold throughout the Three Realms as a staple diet; it had a nutty taste on the initial bite, then a sweetness that burst through to leave you happy and fulfilled.

Mr Grumplepumple was enthralled with the goblins of Clanomide; he found them both fascinating and amusing. They were, of course, related to the goblins of Pumple Mountain from the distant past but they seemed so different in many ways, and looked different physically. They were generally taller and had distinctive ears that were bigger and floppier, which was highly amusing when they ran, as they would flap about energetically. Their feet were longer and their eyes were smaller, like the button eyes you would find on a bear, kind of cute in a goblin sort of way!

Mr Grumplepumple and his Pumple goblins sat amongst the members of the great Clanomide council and discussed current issues of the night and swapped stories of bravery and courage about how they overcame the predators who threatened the very fabric of their existence

This was accompanied by a feast of food, too vast to be consumed within one night – well, for most, but not for Garvoid who stuffed cakes and biscuits in his cloak for a treat later.

"You greedy fat goblin! You're going to burst if you carry on like this," Garvtak muttered under his breath but loud enough for his dear friend to hear.

Even Squiggle slipped out of Mr Grumplepumple's pocket on a regular basis to replenish his stock.

Then suddenly, Carboot stood up and surveyed his audience and banged his fist on the table to get everyone's attention. It was time to be serious and let the goblins of Pumplestone Mountain know what they were letting themselves in for by travelling to seek out the great Nantah.

Carboot told the story of the morzarhs, and how Nantah, the great warlock, had helped them defeat these terrible creatures. All eyes were fixed on Carboot as the room fell still and very quiet.

"The morzarhs live north of the Clanomide Mountains in a vast area of swampland; many creatures call them the bog monsters as they live within the swamps in the water but can also walk on land," he said in a deep tone.

"Their scaly black skins are like that of snakes, but their bodies are a similar shape to a beaver," he said, as he surveyed his audience to make sure he had everyone's attention.

"They have piercing neon-green eyes with jet black slit-shaped pupils that dilate when they know their prey is frightened," he said in a dramatic manner that frightened everyone.

Carboot then continued to explain that the morzarhs had always looked on with envy on the lowlands of Clanomide. The ground was firmer and rich with minerals, and it had beautiful lakes with cascading waterfalls and, of course, the great Crimstone river.

It was nothing like their swampland with stinking bogs and bubbling mud and a permanent oppressive mist that hung over them.

They wanted to take the land for themselves; especially one of the morzarhs who had great hatred for the goblins.

"Hence the great battle!" Carboot shouted to intensify the moment.

He then continued to tell the tale. "Envy and jealously had consumed a morzarh called Baras; he was very adventurous and had travelled to see our fair land for himself.

He swam in the beautiful lakes, played in the challenging waterfalls and fed off the natural vegetation that was on offer.

Baras felt he had arrived in paradise and wanted to stay; he did not care for his homeland anymore or miss any of his family and friends, and had no burning desire or yearning to return.

But, because of his evil nature, he would terrify any stray goblin that he met by threatening to kill them and tie them to his wooden rafts and send them down the waterfalls.

Baras found this to be a great source of amusement as they screamed with horror and, unfortunately, on too many occasions, the goblin did not survive!"

The whole room was silent and hanging on Carboot's every word.

"He would often sneak out in the middle of the day while the goblins slept and steal their crops, but would stupidly leave a trail of half-eaten vegetables that led right back to his den," he said, shaking his head.

"We needed to drive him away and back to his homeland; he had become a real threat with his greedy nature and malicious tricks." Carboot banged his fist on the table and everyone jumped with shock.

Then, he continued again to explain what action they took.

"A group of our bravest goblins got together and attacked Baras in his den, and captured him and tied him up. We threatened to throw him down the waterfall with his body tied to a large branch with heavy chains if he didn't leave," he said.

"Of course, Baras was not going to say no and packed himself off to his homeland with a promise never to return. But we goblins gave Baras a little reminder of what would happen if he did ever return; we made him drink the juice of a Carronip (which looks like a pumpkin) that turned his skin permanently orange. He looked ridiculous as he ran away, much to our amusement!" Carboot chuckled and the rest of the council joined in.

Carboot then continued to explain what happened next, using his arms to dramatize the story.

He said how this had left the morzarh bitter and enraged, and the anger festered, consuming his every waking hour until it became unbearable and he wanted revenge. Baras craved the land for himself and wanted to destroy the goblins of Clanomide!

So, the morzarhs were fed many lies and told stories of how cruel the goblins were and how they wanted to attack and take over the swamplands for themselves. Baras used dark magic to cast a spell upon the morzarhs, so they believed everything he said without question.

He told them that the goblins would use the mud from the bogs as fertiliser to feed their crops; they didn't care about the morzarhs at all and wanted to banish them from their homeland.

"Using the dark magic, these tales were convincing enough to raise an army and lead the morzarhs into battle against us," he said.

Carboot surveyed the room, everyone was silent, hanging on his every word.

So, he continued to tell the story.

"It was a bitter war and many lives were lost on both sides, but Nantah, the great warlock, friend to the goblins of Clanomide, came to the rescue. He could not bear to see this tragedy continue." The goblin shook his head as if to acknowledge the sorrow.

Carboot explained how normally, warlocks were not allowed to intervene with the balance of nature but this battle was brutal; he could not allow such cruelty to carry on. He must help put an end to the carnage.

"So, he set up a secret meeting with me and offered me a gnarled staff which did not look like it had anything of importance about it. But Nantah had cast a magical spell upon the stick which gave it great powers. He entrusted me with the weapon because he knew I would use it wisely and with compassion."

Carboot explained how he was given strict instructions on how to use the staff, and, with this new-found weapon, he knew what he had to do.

"I had to seek out the wicked morzarh who had led his army into battle; I had to disable Baras. It was not easy to find the evil, cowardly creature as he had hidden himself deep behind the front line, but I gathered a small group of my best trackers and crept over and behind the enemy using a secret pass that cut through the mountain to where the morzarhs had set up camp.

We found Baras gorging his face on food, leaning against a rock with no one else in sight. It was easy to recognise him with his orange scaly skin. So, seizing the opportunity, we quickly surrounded him, much to his horror.

Baras quickly rose to his feet and stared at me with his evil neon-green eyes that went completely black when he realized we were nervous.

There was a moment of silence that seemed to last forever, then Baras suddenly let out a piercingly shrill scream, but I was quick and struck the creature with the staff." Carboot was shaking his head, reliving the experience.

"Suddenly, there was a dazzling white light that was blinding for a second, and when we could see again, it was apparent that the morzarh had been turned into a little rat!" shouted Carboot, his face wearing a broad smile.

"It shrieked with horror and started to dart in every direction in confusion, and then quickly ran away with a pitiful whimpering cry!" He finished his sentence by raising his arms up high into the air and the goblin council cheered and clapped.

"All the commotion had made some of the morzarhs rush to see what was happening, and as they watched the action unfold, they panicked. They were completely lost without the evil, manipulative Baras feeding them instructions. They were fearful that they, too, would be turned into rats.

So, without any hesitation, they quickly turned on their heels and fled back to the swamplands, never to return!" Carboot said with a heavy sigh.

Everyone in the room was silent as Carboot finished his tale. Garvoid then piped up and asked why Baras had been turned into a rat and not any other creature? The High Wizard goblin chuckled, and then turned to Garvoid to explain.

"Nantah told me that the staff would turn Baras into another creature of my choosing, but I had to tell Nantah which creature in order for him to cast the spell onto the staff."

Carboot shook his head then continued, "I had to choose one that would not do more harm but I wanted Baras to be humiliated, hence, a rat was most suitable!"

With this, everyone laughed and the room was alive with chatter as everyone started to talk amongst themselves.

Mr Grumplepumple thanked the goblin for the tale as Carboot sat down next to him and asked in a quizzical manner, "Does the magical staff still exist?"

The great wizard goblin turned and smiled at Mr Grumplepumple and told him how the weapon had crumbled into dust once it had struck the morzarh.

"If it fell into the wrong hands, it could be used as a weapon of destruction and would always cause trouble for the goblins of Clanomide," he said with a cunning smile.

"The decision had been made that it had to be destroyed once it had served its purpose," he ended, staring intently at the wizard goblin.

Carboot narrowed his eyes; he seemed to be deep in thought and trying to work something out. Then, he leant over and whispered something in his ear. The goblin listened intently and then nodded his head in acknowledgement, before sitting back slowly.

Elphin ~ Impbah

Chapter Twelve

Migney

When the great Nantah held court and offered his teachings of great wizardry and magic, the first difficulty was getting to where they took place; it was never an easy task to find the location.

The second difficulty was avoiding the Morzarhs and other predators and reach the event unscathed.

Nantah had decided to make Quazboo his home as he could keep an eye on the morzarhs and make sure they behaved themselves; plus, he liked the enchanted shifting forests.

They provided a safe haven; he was not easy to find and was left alone to perfect his magic.

Nantah was a very old and wise warlock who lived a solitary life by choice. His past experiences had left him scarred and much less in need of company.

Nantah told his stories of old to his pilgrims in the hope that lessons would be learnt and the terrible mistakes of the past would not happen again. If he could enrich the lives of his audience with his knowledge, then he hoped they would spread his teachings to heal hurts and create peace within the Three Realms, using magic for the good of all creatures.

Mr Grumplepumple and the little group were given a plentiful supply of food and drink to sustain them during their onward journey to Quazboo.

They said their goodbyes with a little trepidation and fear in their hearts for what lay ahead, but having been fed well and keeping good company, their spirits were high.

It didn't take too long to reach the end of the mountains of Clanomide and there ahead lay the swamplands of the morzarhs.

Carboot had given Mr Grumplepumple a map to help steer the group away from the bogs, and they could see the mountains of Quazboo to the northwest. The path they had to take would steer them up onto higher ground with a steep climb through the woods that lay strewn across the next mountain range.

Mr Grumplepumple remembered what Carboot had said about the particular wood they sought; it was set higher than all of the others. That was the only way you could possibly locate it; the fact that it changed shape on a regular basis did not help.

It was not easy to see, let alone navigate, through the mists near the swamplands. But once they were through and halfway up the mountain, everything became clearer and the view was different from anything they had seen before. They had entered the region of Quazboo.

As they looked back down the mountain, they could see the vast land of the morzarhs. The mists hid most of the bogs but an occasional spurt of mud would rise above the mist so that it looked like a huge pan of boiling water.

"You can understand why the morzarhs wanted to move away from this land," said Toobah.

"They need the mud; it helps to keep their bodies in good condition and stops their scales from becoming brittle," Mr Grumplepumple replied. He remembered his father telling him this on one of their journeys.

"The special properties in the mud also help to keep their skin cleansed and free from parasites, which could get trapped under their scales. If they were to move away, then they would suffer the consequence of risking their health!" Mr Grumplepumple said in a matter-of-fact way.

The wizard goblin was silent for quite a while after he had given his lesson on the morzarhs. He was thinking about his father and how he had made this journey to see the great Nantah.

It must have been difficult, and a great sense of pride overwhelmed him.

He missed his father terribly and would give anything to have him back. He was so proud of everything his father had done for him, the journeys they had made, the magic he had taught him and the adventures they had experienced. He often felt his father's presence and this was a great comfort to him. He wondered when his father's reincarnation would materialise; surely it would be quicker than most because of his learnings.

And to which Realm would he be reborn?

It was also so important to Garvtak and Garvoid to make sure they found the great warlock, Nantah. They had promised the creatures back home that they would not fail and knew how important it was to have the Dagger of Pumplestone enchanted with the Spell of Resurrection.

They had made this journey once before with Mr Gravenpumple and were determined to find Nantah again.

The popstrells had been flying above and in front to try and locate the enchanted wood and kept reporting back with updated news.

It was difficult to pinpoint the right wood but there was one that continually sat above all the rest and seemed slightly smaller in size.

This must be the one, thought Toobah, who instructed one of the mambooas to join him and they ran ahead to check out the wood. Toobah had also made this journey before and was sure he would recognise the right forest.

He came back feeling positive as they had seen bright dazzling lights, like fireworks, spurting up into the sky above the trees and the mambooa thought this must be Nantah practising his spells.

Mr Grumplepumple agreed that this must be the work of Nantah experimenting with new spells, so everyone braced themselves and made their way towards the wood.

The popstrells stayed on the perimeter near the outer trees to keep watch. Plock told Mr Grumplepumple that they would keep watch for any nasty predators.

As soon as the little group were inside the dense, thick wood, it became very dark and difficult to see. Goblins, of course, were used to night light, as they had very good night vision, but not this blackness It was all-consuming and very oppressive and worrying. Mr Grumplepumple lit up his staff to guide the way and everyone followed in line, tiptoeing slowly through the wood.

"Keep close together; we don't want anyone straying off and getting lost," said the wizard goblin in a teacher-like manner.

They could hear strange noises coming from above that were unfamiliar to their ears; whooshing and popping sounds, and then there were the occasional flashes of light that exploded into the sky.

"Whizzzzzz Pop Bang, Whizzzzz Pop Bang," was the sound of the fireworks.

This made the impbahs very nervous and they scrambled onto the back of Toobah and Booma for reassurance, much to their annoyance.

They continually had to chastise the creatures for screaming in their ears when they were spooked!

"I'm so, so sorry, Booma," said Jowler who was trying to bury his head in Booma's fur.

The group followed the sounds of the fireworks until they came to a large opening, but as soon as they entered, it changed shape and turned into a narrow tunnel that seemed to have a light at the end of it.

Mr Grumplepumple had to act quickly, for to linger too long in one place in this wood could end up with the little party being separated, and that was the last thing he wanted to happen.

So, he told everyone to run as quickly as possible to reach the light before the wood changed shape again.

"Run, run quickly! There's no time to dilly-dally," he shouted.

As they approached the light, they could see a group of creatures dancing around what seemed like a fire. They were making some strange noises and waving their arms up in the air.

They were chanting a song in a tongue that no one recognised. Elphin suddenly gripped Toobah a little more tightly.

"Ouch! You are an annoying little impbah!" he cursed.

As the group approached, the chanting stopped and the strange little creatures stood and stared at the group in silence.

They were wearing colourful garlands of flowers around their necks and had strange hats on their heads which looked like they were made out of vines, twisted and braided into cones.

Everything went horribly quiet and you could cut the air with a knife, but Elphin climbed down from Toobah's back and walked forward slowly and with confidence.

One of the creatures flicked its head from side to side trying to decipher what to do for what seemed like an age and then suddenly, what appeared to be a broad smile covered its face, as it sprang forward with such speed and grabbed Elphin, giving him a massive hug, and started to kiss him all over!

This took everyone by surprise but, of course, eased the tension, and then before you could say twiddling sticks, the other two impbahs were embracing the rest of the strange little creatures.

"Oh wow, oh wow, oh, woop, hoo!" shouted the impbahs.

Mr Grumplepumple and the rest of his party were confused but relieved to see the reception the impbahs were receiving.

After an exhaustive period of hugging, Elphin turned round and put his thumb up in the air to indicate all was fine, then, after another exchange of back-patting, he walked back to the group with his new friends to explain what this was all about.

"These little creatures are related to us. They are distant cousins; we lost touch many years ago when the great Volcano of Shrik erupted in our homeland in the Second Realm," said Elphin in a raised voice.

"It was decided that the impbahs had to split up to try and survive and protect our race. I had struck up a great friendship with Migney and was devastated when we parted, so to see each other again is just so incredible," Elphin was shouting due to his level of excitement.

After everyone had calmed down and all the kisses and embracing had stopped, Elphin asked his dear friend what they were doing here in this enchanted wood. "Why are you here? This seems a strange place to settle," asked Elphin.

The strange little impbah sat down on the floor to get comfortable, making sure Elphin sat down next to him, and then began his story.

"After the great eruption, some impbahs went north to seek a safe haven, but many stayed nearer to the homeland of Shriekal. They were prepared to take the risk of living with an active volcano. Their hope was that the volcano would now stay dormant for a long period of time and all would be fine again," said Migney, trying to catch his breath as he was speaking so quickly.

The homeland of the impbahs is in the north of the Second Realm where the land is festooned with many forests, and amongst this thick vegetation stands the biggest volcano in the land.

"It soars high above any other landmark," said Migney.

"You can actually see it from the boundary of the First Realm on a new Junamoon," interjected Elphin.

Migney explained that after the eruption, he could not find his dearest friend and had to travel with his family. They had decided to go south but it was difficult to keep everyone together.

Unfortunately, they ran into a pack of crocutas (wild hyenas). They knew of these beasts from tales of old told around the campfires. They came across them while travelling over open land. The beasts came out of nowhere, howling loudly, and started chasing them.

"They were very fierce and hungry and our elder members were too slow. It was horrible; we could do nothing but run for our lives," said Migney sadly.

On hearing this news, everyone hung their heads in sorrow.

"Then suddenly, there was a massive flash of brilliant white light which blinded everyone momentarily, and straight in front of us there stood a wood with a narrow clearing," said Migney in an excited voice.

"Without hesitation, we quickly ran forward to escape the beasts, not knowing what lay ahead, and as soon as we entered the wood, it closed up around us. All we could hear in the distance was the haunting laughter from the crocutas," Migney spoke in a low whisper.

"We were so frightened and stunned by what had happened, it took quite a while for us to settle down, but then suddenly, we felt a great calmness descend upon us and there, in front of us, stood the great Nantah," said Migney with his eyes wide open, trying to increase the drama of the story.

"The warlock had seen what was happening and knew of our plight and wanted to help, so he cast a spell and moved one of the enchanted woods to our location. We had reached the land of Quazboo," said Migney.

"Nantah offered us shelter and food and said we could stay for as long as we wanted. He asked where we were heading for. Our answer was, we did not know. Our thought was to travel until we came to a place that felt right," continued Migney.

"Hence, we decided to remain here in Quazboo. The great warlock showed such kindness and did not mind our company. We felt safe and secure and have become quite useful." Migney's impish face lit up with a huge smile.

"We fetch ingredients for potions and spells for the warlock and we were just celebrating the success of a new spell. Nantah was so pleased with our efforts that he gave us a feast and maybe a little too much berry juice!" Migney hiccupped.

Elphin then explained to Migney and the others how he and his tribe had managed to reach Pumple Mountain and had been so fortunate to meet the goblins who welcomed them into their homeland with open arms.

They had settled into a new way of life within the caves amongst the goblins and mambooas.

Nantah

Chapter Thirteen

The Great Nantah

Mr Grumplepumple was so pleased that Elphin had been reunited with his long-distant cousins but was eager to press on and locate the great warlock. He wanted to receive the protection for the dagger as soon as possible and then he could head back home.

He missed his little brother and felt a great urge to return to Kracklewood.

Migney explained that it was not easy to locate the warlock's home because of the ever-shifting wood; "Nantah always finds us when there is an errand to run. Normally, it is to collect ingredients for his potions. Just let me confer with my friends for a moment," he said.

Migney ushered his little group together and they huddled close in a circle and started whispering to each other, occasionally looking up at Mr Grumplepumple.

This made the wizard goblin feel slightly awkward, but by the look on Migney's face, the result of their discussion looked promising as they all seemed happy and were giggling to themselves as they separated.

Migney got himself close up to Mr Grumplepumple and whispered into his ear, "We could set off one of the special fireworks. They're kept for times of urgency when we feel there is danger nearby and we're threatened," he said.

With this, the little impbah giggled and had the most impish look on his face! Nantah had repeatedly told the little impbahs not to use the fireworks unless it was really necessary.

"The warlock must have been nearby and experimenting with some potions when we first entered the wood, as we could hear loud noises and saw flashes of bright lights," said Mr Grumplepumple.

The impbahs decided this was an extraordinary situation that called for extraordinary action.

So, one of the precious fireworks was lit and sent a huge rocket up into the sky. It soared with such ferocity that it scared the little group half to death!

Zooooommmmm!! It shot high into the air.

No sooner had the rocket exploded into the sky than the great warlock of Quazboo was stood before them.

Nantah looked sternly at Mr Grumplepumple and his little group of goblins, mambooas and impbahs and leaned heavily on his staff with a deep sigh. Then he glanced towards Migney who stood nervously, swaying from foot to foot.

Nantah was such a wise old warlock who had travelled many lands and met many creatures throughout his lifetime and gained much knowledge and wisdom. He already knew what the situation was and why the firework had been lit; he had the amazing talent of seeing the past, present and future. This had been perfected through years of study, experiments and with the help of his jewelled staff.

Garvtak and Garvoid immediately knelt in front of Nantah and started to chant a ceremonial rhythmic song in a low steady tone which the great warlock recognised immediately.

"Oh, mystic warlock, from days of old, great worship we pay to the wisdom you hold."

"Oh, mystic warlock, from days of old, great homage we pay to your courage, so bold," the goblins repeated several times.

He touched both the goblins' heads gently in acknowledgement. Nantah recognised these goblins - they had attended several of his classes with Mr Gravenpumple, and reading their minds, he realised the reason for their quest. Then, the warlock turned to Mr Grumplepumple and spoke in a slow, deep tone.

"You have the presence of your father; I can feel your sincerity and empathy, two great attributes." The warlock was holding his stare on the wizard goblin and it seemed like he was trying to bore deep into his soul.

This made Mr Grumplepumple very nervous but he held his ground and knew he had to show courage and determination.

Nantah had now cast his eyes down to the goblin's cloak which was moving violently on one side. Everyone was staring at the cloak as Mr Grumplepumple became agitated, slapping the cloak down to stop the movement from inside.

Suddenly, out popped Squiggle, holding the Dagger of Pumplestone! The dagger was far too heavy for the little booquar to hold so Mr Grumplepumple grabbed it quickly before it fell to the floor. Everyone laughed at this and it broke the tension.

Nantah told the little group to follow him down a narrow tunnel that he quickly created with his staff, and he reassured his impbahs that they were not in trouble for setting off the firework, for which Migney was very relieved.

"Young Migney, I need eyes in the back of my head to keep you from trouble. There's never a dull moment when impbahs are around," he said and chuckled to himself, which put Mr Grumplepumple at ease.

The group followed the warlock through a dense wood until they finally came to a big clearing and there, in front of them, was a huge cave. They were told to wait outside while Nantah beckoned to Mr Grumplepumple.

"Come forth, young wizard, we have much to do," said Nantah in a matter-of-fact way.

The wizard goblin had seemed hesitant at first, as he had been deep in thought, but he quickly snapped out of it.

Just before he disappeared, he turned back to look at his friends with a hesitant smile, then gave a reassuring wave and he was gone.

It seemed a long time since they had gone, and the group were becoming worried and starting to fret. Garvtak and Garvoid started pacing back and forth.

"Oh, where is Mr Grumplepumple? He should have come out by now!" said Garvtak in a worried voice.

"I think you should go and have a look. You're always telling me how brave you are," replied Garvoid as he poked his friend in the ribs.

"You just can't stop yourself, can you? You're like an itch that I can't scratch, with your constant moaning and groaning. Mr Grumplepumple will come out when he's good and ready," was Garvtak's stark reply.

"Well, why are you pacing up and down with me, then?" said Garvoid mockingly.

Then suddenly, the warlock and the wizard goblin reappeared, deep in conversation.

Nantah did not hang about, but quickly bade farewell to the wizard goblin and his little group with a gentle nod and a wave of his staff, and walked back into the dark cavernous entrance of his home.

Mr Grumplepumple seemed somehow to have changed physically; he looked older, his eyes seemed sterner and his demeanour was stronger and more determined. He pulled out the Dagger of Pumplestone and raised it into the air. Everyone looked on in wonder as the dagger started to glow a crimson red. It looked like it was on fire; the intensity of colour was incredible.

Then suddenly, there was an enormous flash and everything went dark!

The next thing the little group felt was a whoosh of wind surrounding them and lifting them into the air. They were spinning around so fast, and it happened so quickly that no one had time to scream or do anything!

It was a very strange feeling as if some tremendous force was pulling them through a tunnel and they were flying, but it was total darkness and it seemed like a mighty wind had enveloped them and was whipping their bodies.

"Whoooooosh, whooooosh," was the sound of the ferocious wind.

Then, before they could catch their breath, they were dropped to the ground. They scrambled to their feet quickly, frightened and bewildered, trying to understand what had happened.

As their eyes began to focus, they looked about and recognised the familiar surroundings. It was a miracle! They were back at the boundary of the Galamide mountains.

Everyone in the group looked up in awe at Mr Grumplepumple who stood steadfast with his staff in one hand and the dagger in the other.

The weapon had returned to its pale rose Pumplestone colour and the wizard goblin quickly put it back into its holder under his cloak.

Garvtak and Garvoid congratulated Mr Grumplepumple for such a wondrous piece of magic.

"Mr Grumplepumple, that was some magic you just performed. That was incredible! I feel like I've just gone two rounds with a cruen," said Garvtak, who was trying to smooth down his matted beard.

"I've never experienced anything like that before," said Toobah, who was also trying to smooth down his fur, which now looked like it had just been whisked into a frenzy and looked all bobbly.

Everyone was beside themselves with bewilderment, but joyous to be in one piece and back on the ground.

"Nantah granted me a favour, so I asked for a safe and speedy return home for everyone. So, with the great Nantah's help, we cast a spell to whisk all of us back home through what was called the Great Vortex," Mr Grumplepumple explained.

"This form of magic can only be performed in times of need; it took much effort and will have left the warlock exhausted and weak for several days, but he wanted to grant my wish out of great respect for my father," he said.

Toobah struck up a worried face and asked what had happened to the popstrells who had been left behind at the entrance to the wood.

"Where's Plock and his crew? Have we left them behind? It's a long way for them to fly back," he said with a very concerned look.

Mr Grumplepumple looked down at the little mambooa and gave him a gentle pat on the shoulder for reassurance; he told the group that Nantah had sent them home earlier through the magic of the vortex.

"They should be back in the safety of Kracklewood; it was much easier to transport the popstrells further because of their light weight," he said.

Elphin and the other impbahs felt a deep pang of guilt and sadness; they had not been able to say a proper goodbye to Migney and his family.

It had been such a joyous reunion and they were hoping to stay a little longer, but circumstances had dictated their speedy return.

They could only hope that there would be an opportunity to meet up again in the not-too-distant future now that they knew where they lived, or maybe Migney and his kin could visit them?

The goblans of Kracklewood had been busy preparing a feast for the return of the little group.

The popstrells had returned in a flash of bright sparks on the edge of Kracklewood and startled a goblin who was collecting some berries.

The poor goblin was knocked over with the force of the flash and desperately tried to untangle itself from a Gwire bush, which was not the most pleasant of experiences as its branches were full of hairy spines that could give a goblin a nasty rash.

"What the blazing Helia was that? Ow, ow, ow, that hurts!" shouted the goblin.

The popstrells were very apologetic and helped to pluck the hairy spines out of the very distressed goblin, who could not help yelping in protest every time a spine was plucked!

"Owwww, Owwwww!" he screamed loudly.

Once the goblin was back on his feet, the popstrells flew off home to explain what had happened and how the great Nantah had sent them ahead of the group to let everyone know they were safe and would soon be returning home.

Nothing was spared in the preparation to welcome the group back; there was an abundance of food consisting of every vegetable imaginable and fruits of every description.

The goblins had harvested an early crop of golly berries to make a particularly strong batch of berry wine and many colourful flowers had been picked to decorate the tables.

Garvtak's wife had paid special attention to Mr Grumplepumple's seat and had gone a bit overboard on the flowers; there was hardly anywhere for the goblin to sit!

"Don't you think you've gone a bit over the top with the flowers, Gizzarla?" said Gignac with a wry smile on her face.

"I just want Mr Grumplepumple to know how much we care and that we are just so grateful that they are all back in one piece," Gizzarla replied with a sense of pride in her voice.

"I wonder what they get up to on these journeys they take? Sounds to me like they have too much fun. I'd love to go with them sometime," said Gignac, lifting her chin up as she started to ponder the question.

The group entered the Galamide mountain range with excitement but also a sense of something lost; the experience with Nantah had changed Mr Grumplepumple.

He seemed less youthful and carefree and had aged quite dramatically since first setting off on the quest. Garvtak and Garvoid were worried about this transition and wanted to know what had happened when Mr Grumplepumple had entered the cave with the great warlock, Nantah.

"What happened? Was there a price you had to pay for being gifted the Spell of Resurrection?" asked Garvoid in a concerned voice.

"You can ask me again later. Let's sort out the mambooas and impbahs first and send them ahead with the other goblins," said Mr Grumplepumple in a dismissive way.

Toobah and the mambooas, Elphin and Jowler, were impatient to get home and the wizard goblin could see this so he instructed them to press on ahead with Goolan and Gimtok, the other two warrior goblins, and let everyone know that all was well and the quest had been successful.

Garvtak and Garvoid stayed back with Mr Grumplepumple as instructed and set up camp at the foot of the Galamides to rest, as they were exhausted and wanted to feel refreshed for their short journey home the following night.

There was a suitable tree, large enough to set up a safe platform to make a bed, and the three goblins settled down for the day.

They ate the last of the pip cake, a rich fruit cake made from a variety of fruit pips, that were crushed down to a pulp and mixed with nuts to make a nutty but sweet taste. They washed it down with some golly berry wine.

Garvtak leaned over to Mr Grumplepumple, and, with a reassuring light squeeze of his shoulder, asked if he was alright. Both himself and Garvoid were very concerned for the wizard goblin; he was definitely not himself.

He had changed in a way that made him seem much more mature than his years. Mr Grumplepumple let out a deep gentle sigh and looked at the two goblins with kindness in his eyes; he cherished these two greatly and felt blessed to have such a deep friendship.

He proceeded to tell his friends of the sacrifice he had to make in order to keep the protective spell that Nantah had granted for the Dagger of Pumplestone.

"When we visited our friends in the Clanomide Mountains and held council with Carboot and the other honorary members, I was given a warning. Carboot whispered in my ear that if I was to accept the enchanted spell from Nantah, it came with a price," he said in a whisper.

"Carboot had accepted his weapon to defeat the morzarhs but relinquished it immediately after it had been used so that it could be destroyed. This would then release his soul which had been trapped within the staff," said Mr Grumplepumple, who seemed a little reluctant to carry on with the tale.

"But even though he had decided not to keep the weapon, it had taken its toll and Carboot had been stricken with an illness which paralysed his body and left him weak and aged before his time." The wizard goblin lowered his head as if he had a great weight on his shoulders. He then explained how Nantah could not afford to gift a spell of such magnitude to just anyone to protect a weapon. The receiver would have to use it wisely and solely to protect against a threat to life, and not be frivolous with its use, as the consequences were fatal.

The wizard goblin seemed very hesitant to continue but his companions pressed him for more information.

"When the weapon is used, the creature wielding the weapon becomes one with it and it possesses their soul. The bearer would lose years of their life depending on how many times it was used," said

Mr Grumplepumple looking furtively at Garvtak and Garvoid to gauge their reaction to this news.

"To accept the Spell of Resurrection in the first place would cost you ten years, hence my aged appearance on leaving the cave with Nantah," he finished with a heavy sigh.

Garvtak and Garvoid looked pale and shocked when they heard this news and started to shake their heads, and pleaded with Mr Grumplepumple to give the spell back.

"Nothing is worth the price of you losing years off your life and ageing too quickly. We must go back to Nantah and get this spell reversed. We must," said Garvtak loudly with a tremor in his voice and Garvoid was nodding his head vehemently in agreement.

The wizard goblin was touched by their words and he thanked them, but this was the only way the creatures of Kracklewood could protect themselves if the occasion arose and their lives were threatened.

He was willing to pay the price and emphasised that the need to wield the weapon would hopefully not arise too often.

Mr Grumplepumple asked that the goblins keep this knowledge to themselves and made them swear an oath to reveal nothing to anyone about their conversation.

They did this reluctantly and with deep sorrow; they knew Mr Grumplepumple was not for changing his mind.

The three goblins slept fretfully that day and got up early to return quickly to Kracklewood and the upcoming celebrations.

A great council was held on their return, headed by Mr Grumplepumple, who told of the journey to seek out Nantah, and the joyous reunion with the goblins of Clanomide.

It was decided that there was a need to rekindle the friendship with their fellow kin and many future visits on both sides would be organised.

Elphin explained the reunion with his long-lost cousins and described how they assisted the great Nantah in his work in Quazboo.

Secretly, the little impbah felt very disappointed that he could not say goodbye properly to his dear friend, as their meeting had been too brief.

Why did Mr Grumplepumple have to whisk them back home so quickly?

Elphin felt slightly resentful of this action, and the offer of a visit to Pumple Mountain had not been extended to the impbahs from the Second Realm. So, Elphin vowed to return himself as soon as possible to reunite with his lost long friend, Migney.

Mr Grumplepumple was very glad to be home; the journey had taken its toll and ageing ten years had put a greater strain on his physical state.

But he still had more than enough strength to pick up his little brother, Goby, in both arms and lift him up high into the air with glee, and plant a huge kiss on his face.

This delighted the little goblin who worshipped his big brother with such pride and love, for he had become his mentor and guardian. Goby had so many questions to ask his brother. He wanted to know everything that had happened in minute detail.

"What was that tree called again? How many impbahs were there? What did Nantah say when he saw you?" The questions were relentless.

The little goblin did not stop, insistently probing until Mr Grumplepumple could take no more, and with a slight feeling of guilt, cast a little sleeping spell on Goby to quieten him down.

The celebrations were supposed to last for one night but because of the new-found blanket of security and protection given by the Dagger of Pumplestone, there seemed to be even more reason to extend the festivities.

The Dagger of Pumplestone was returned for safe-keeping to its special case; this was made out of the finest wood in the land, from a tree that only grew on the top of Pumple Mountain.

The trunk was as dark as ebony and as smooth as silk, and strangely, the tree had very little foliage. In order to chop branches off these trees, the goblins had to enter the territory of the cruens and this was a perilous act.

But Garvtak and Garvoid, along with Goolan and Gimtok, had taken up the challenge and miraculously completed the task unscathed, and without having to confront the beasts.

The case was also lined with a soft fleecy cloth that was made from the thread of the Blue Spiders of Pumple Mountain, the Aranemos.

Altogether, it was a beautiful case and most worthy of the precious Dagger of Pumplestone.

Toobah~Mambooa

Chapter Fourteen

The Third Realm

Three Realms made up the magical land of the goblins. Within the First Realm, there stood the majestic Galamide mountain range, home to the Pumple goblins who had lived within Pumple Mountain before they moved to Kracklewood.

Within the Second Realm lay the Clanomide mountain range and this was home to the Gorple goblins.

The Third Realm was home to the Hebble goblins that lived in the Hanomide mountain range at the foot of Mount Hoot. This was the forgotten Realm.

The goblins from the First and Second Realms visited with each other on a frequent basis but the goblins of Hanomide had somehow faded into a distant memory.

There had been no contact with this clan for some time and it was questioned whether they still existed.

Mr Grumplepumple had discussed this issue at length with Carboot when he last visited to trade for Pumplestone to use in making new tools for farming.

The Third Realm came up in conversation now and again, when the High Council met to discuss the issues of the night, but was continually brushed aside for another night.

Life had settled down in Kracklewood and the goblins from Pumple Mountain had found peace and harmony living in the Graven Tree.

One day, while Toobah was clearing out an old trunk full of dusty books and scrolls, as requested by Mr Grumplepumple, he came across a faded picture that rekindled an old memory.

Toobah was looking at a drawing of a group of mambooas stood together; they were standing proud and smiling.

This instantly caused great pain in his heart and he sat down and a tear started to roll down his cheek. He recognised the faces within the group and there, in the centre, stood Toobah himself in his finest armour with his head held high. The mambooas were a race of creatures that were indigenous to the Hanomide mountain range in the Third Realm.

Toobah left the dusty books that he was supposed to clean and nestled down under a large branch near the top of the Graven Tree to study the picture in a better light, nearer to the twinkling stars in the sky.

He must have been staring at the picture for quite a while and lost track of time as it was late and daylight was on the horizon.

Mr Grumplepumple had been calling him for quite a while and was becoming concerned, but the mambooa had been lost in memories of old and had not heard his calls.

When the wizard goblin finally found the mambooa, he was ready to chastise the little creature but then registered the sad look on his face.

Toobah showed Mr Grumplepumple the drawing and immediately, the wizard goblin's face relaxed, and he placed his arm around his dear friend and gave him a hug.

"Oh, my dear friend, I sometimes forget you do not come from the First Realm since you have lived amongst us for so long," the wizard said with warmth in his voice.

"We feel this is our home and are forever grateful to the goblins of Pumple Mountain for accepting us into the family, but I must admit, I often wonder what has happened to the rest of my tribe," Toobah replied with great sadness in his voice.

***

124

All had been well until that terrible day when the Great Forest of Hanomide had been threatened by raging fires that swept through the mountain forest of their homeland.

It was said that the fires started after a fierce battle between two witch sisters who had fallen deeply in love with the same warlock.

There was no end to their bickering and squabbles and it finally ended in the most brutal of battles with the two witches taking to the sky on their broomsticks.

They inflicted terrible burns on each other with their wands, and sparks were flying everywhere, but they were not only hitting each other; the sparks were spraying all over the land below.

Then, one enormous spark hit a large tree and it instantly became consumed in flames which spread from tree to tree quickly within the forest where the mambooas lived.

Seeing the devastation the witches had created with their stupid envious actions, the mambooas desperately tried to put out the fire but it was too late! The fire had taken a strong hold on a large part of the forest and was threatening the lives of all the creatures that lived there.

As the fires took hold, Toobah and the other mambooa warriors gathered as many of their kin as possible and instructed them to follow them out of the forest to a safer area.

But the fires were raging out of control and everyone was fleeing for their lives, with creatures running in every direction.

Some of the mambooas decided to climb into the mountains and seek refuge in the caves up above, and other tribes made their way to the northern shores. But Toobah could see that the fire had taken a dreadful hold on the land so decided to take his party further afield to pastures new.

It was a terrible decision to have to make, to separate themselves from the rest of the tribe, but Toobah felt this action was necessary to protect his small group.

After days of travelling with a very weary troop, it was decided to rest awhile and work out the best course of action.

They found shelter in an old ruin that looked like it had once been a splendid castle of great majesty. But the ravages of time had taken their toll and the top of the castle tower had become overgrown with dense vegetation and large bushes and trees.

It made an ideal place to rest and provided safe shelter for the group. Should the mambooas stay and try to regroup with the other mambooas, or was it too late as there was no home to go back to?

It was a very difficult decision to make and one that Toobah and his fellow warriors deliberated over long and hard.

While they were sat contemplating their dilemma, a group of goblins had entered the area and were making their way through the castle grounds. Toobah was very wary of the goblins as there had not been any contact with them for quite some time and their last encounter had not been pleasant.

The goblins of Hanomide had lived in harmony with the creatures from the land for many moolatoons. But after a fierce quarrel between the prince-goblin, Harqin, and a young, arrogant warlock, the goblins ended up splitting up the harmonious unity of the creatures and drove many into the forests of Hanomide.

The prince-goblin had ordered many of the creatures who lived within the great city of Hootahn to turn their backs on the warlocks and witches who lived amongst them. Harqin wanted to banish them all from Hanomide. He had become very intolerant and harboured great hostility, and madness was starting to creep into his daily thoughts and actions.

The mambooas lived within the city walls of Hootahn in the city parks. They had a good relationship with many of the warlocks and witches.

They did not want to get embroiled in this fight and wanted to remain neutral, but it was proving to be too difficult. So, the mambooas retreated further away from the city and ended up living in the Great Forest of Hanomide at the foot of Mount Hoot.

The prince-goblin was not happy with the mambooas vacating the parks and requested a council with Toobah. The mambooa obliged and went to the city to see Harqin to explain his actions.

This did not go down well and the prince-goblin was infuriated with Toobah and wanted to punish him for his disloyalty.

The mambooa was thrown into the dungeons under the Great Hall and made to stay there until he changed his mind.

When Toobah did not return to the forest from his visit, the rest of the mambooas became worried and upset. Word soon reached them of the prince-goblin's actions and something had to be done to rescue Toobah. Some of the older mambooas gathered together to come up with a plan to rescue their leader and this is when the armour first appeared.

They had to prepare for the worst. The mambooas felt it was important to protect themselves from the sharp goblin weapons if they were to encounter any goblin soldiers.

The armour was made out of twisted bark that had been pulled and stretched to make a thick yarn.

This was then sewn together in a large disc to make a chest-plate and tied into place with heavy leather straps.

Large pieces of bark were used to create the head armour and crafted in such a way as to produce eye, nose and mouth slits and protect the rest of their faces. They looked quite fierce and menacing; the mambooas were hoping they would unnerve the goblins with their appearance.

It was only a small group that entered the city that night as dusk fell. Goblins seemed to be everywhere so it was difficult to keep out of sight, but they managed to stay hidden until they reached the city dungeons.

Suddenly, they were confronted by a group of goblins who had been returning from a local gathering in the grounds. The goblins turned the corner to be confronted by a small group of peculiar-looking creatures with very strange wooden objects attached to their bodies.

The goblins were startled and un-nerved at this sight and the confusion was sufficient to give the mambooas time to attack and disarm the goblins by circling their opponents quickly and grabbing their pointy staffs!

Enzo, one of Toobah's trusty soldiers, poked one of the goblins in the groin to show they meant business and the goblin gave out a sharp yelp and retreated quickly behind a larger goblin.

Enzo said in a stern manner, "Where are you keeping the mambooa?"

He demanded to know where Toobah was being held, and at first, the goblins were defiant and said nothing, sharing quick nervous glances

But then, Booma suddenly jumped forward right in front of the largest goblin and started chanting loudly.

"Piddily, giddily, boobar BOO, piddily, giddily, boobar BOO!"

It sounded like gobbledygook but seemed to do the trick, especially when he started waving his arms about madly!

It must have reminded them of the prince-goblin and they thought Booma was about to cast a spell.

There was no further defiance and the goblins led them quickly round the back of the Great Hall to where the dungeons were.

Enzo instructed the largest goblin to unlock the dungeon door and release their leader.

Toobah was so shocked at seeing his friends that he stood motionless for a minute, and then an overwhelming sense of pride filled his heart.

He had not realised his fellow mambooas were capable of such bravery and rushed forward and hugged each of them.

Booma instructed the goblins to step inside the dungeon cell and the goblins complied without any resistance, still totally stunned and confused by the sight of the creatures in their wooden armour, and the threat of magic.

The group left quickly, and as they were leaving the dungeon, they could hear the goblins shouting to raise the alarm.

The mambooas had to move fast and this was their advantage, as mambooas were one of the fastest creatures of the Three Realms. They were quick and agile, and therefore, very hard to catch.

The prince-goblin soon got wind of the escape. He was enraged and started to scream and shout, throwing any object he could find.

This included a poor little goblin who just so happened to be within his reach. The goblin was hurled against a table and crashed to the floor.

He was uncontrollable, shouting at everyone, and destroying objects around him, anything he could get his hands on.

He ordered the goblins who had let the mambooas escape to be left caged in the dungeon and given no food or water.

He wanted to make an example of their incompetence and leave them to die!

This was the final straw for the goblins. They realised that the prince-goblin had gone completely mad and was turning all the creatures of Hanomide against them.

Something had to be done and quickly. A secret meeting was held within the great council, led by Hatnal, the chief goblin, and it was quickly decided that the prince-goblin had to be dethroned and sedated to manage the madness that had consumed him.

But he was not going to go quietly. When they tried to arrest him, in a fit of rage, he pushed past everyone and turned on them.

He started chanting a spell that made objects start to fly around the room in a whirlwind.

"Conspiritatus, Windarlartus, Proctimartal!" he bellowed at the top of his voice.

Everyone had to duck and dive to avoid being hit; Harqin was using his ancestral magic against his own people. This was an unspeakable sin and unforgivable.

Then suddenly, he ran out of the room and into the city streets shouting at the top of his voice, swearing and cursing and saying that he was going to have his vengeance on his people for their betrayal.

He was screaming and flailing his hands wildly in the air as he shouted at the top of his voice that he was going to cast a terrible curse upon the city and bring forth the Gnarkull!

Then the Prince-goblin disappeared into the dense Great Forest of Hanomide never to be seen again, and many people think he was probably a tasty meal for one of the fierce creatures that roamed the forests.

Toobah was keeping a close eye on the goblins as they passed through the grounds of the castle and to his relief, they carried on through to the mountains beyond, oblivious to the eyes that were watching them so closely.

It was an arduous journey through dense forest and along narrow, tricky paths on the ridges of dangerous mountains. But through true grit and determination and a niggling gut feeling that there was a place of sanctuary, Toobah led this group of battered and worn-out mambooas to Galamide.

***

Mr Grumplepumple had listened intently while Toobah retold the story again and the mambooa turned to the wizard goblin with tears in his eyes.

The two of them watched the sunrise over the beautiful land of Galamide.

Mr Grumplepumple went to bed that morning filled with great sadness for Toobah, and a niggling urge to try and finally make contact again with the goblins from the Third Realm.

Did they still exist, and if so, where did they live? What were they like? So many questions to answer and he kept mulling these questions over and over in his mind. With all the upset of having to move from the caves of Pumple Mountain to seek their new home in Kracklewood, the Third Realm had been forgotten and buried in time.

Mr Grumplepumple

Chapter Fifteen

Elphin's Ticket

The very next night, Mr Grumplepumple called a meeting of the council to put forward his proposal to seek out the goblins from Hanomide, in the Third Realm. He did not mention a promise he made to Toobah to find his lost tribe of mambooas.

There were mixed feelings from the council who generally were happy to leave things as they were.

They felt they had had enough adventure for a couple of yulatoons and just wanted to be settled and content within the Graven Tree.

"I have been contemplating for some time whether we should seek out the goblins from the Third Realm. I believe it is time we unified the Realms," he said in a commanding voice, trying to show conviction and authority.

"Why, all of sudden, are you presenting this notion to us? What's prompted this?" asked Gorun, one of the most esteemed members of the council.

"I have had many discussions with Carboot from the Second Realm and he agrees, it is time we had unity and an alliance would give us greater strength against any danger that might show its hand," he continued, sweeping his audience for their reaction to his reasoning.

"I made the decision last night to do something about it," he replied, feeling slightly hot under his cloak with guilt.

He was aware that he had slightly exaggerated the timescale of his deliberation but he wanted the council to think this thought had been in his head for quite some time, and, once he got a notion in his head, that was it and there was no letting go.

He was determined to start this quest but needed the council's blessing.

Gorun asked Mr Grumplepumple, "Are you thinking of taking this journey by yourself or just wanting to send a group of warriors to seek out the goblins of Hanomide?"

Mr Grumplepumple gave Gorun one of his familiar looks, as if to say, did you really just ask me that question?

"Of course, I will be going; I need to lead this party. I have the knowledge and experience required to get everyone to the Third Realm safely," he said, in a way that could not be debated. He had automatically won and, as far as he was concerned, the decision was made.

He told the council he would ask for volunteers, rather than putting anyone on the spot. He knew this would be a journey full of uncertainty and not everyone would be comfortable with going.

The council agreed this was only right so, the very next night, Mr Grumplepumple sent out his request for volunteers to accompany him on the journey.

The first recruit was, of course, Toobah, then Enzo and Booma, followed very closely by Goby.

Mr Grumplepumple was not happy with this as Goby was his most precious and dearest brother, still very young and innocent, but Goby was not taking no for an answer. The little goblin was so eager to go on an adventure and bursting with excitement.

Over the last two yulatoons, Goby had grown up quickly and was equipped beyond his years with magical spells. Mr Grumplepumple had taught him well, and for such a little goblin, he had the drive and determination of a goblin twice his age.

Many of the other mambooas wanted to join the mission but it was felt that a small number would be best to go undetected and not attract too much attention, so, in the end, there were just three of them.

Thus, the decision was made. Mr Grumplepumple would be accompanied by Toobah and two other mambooas, plus Goby and Garvtak and Garvoid, his faithful and trusted goblin warriors.

In addition, a handful of popstrells were recruited to fly ahead and be the eyes of the group.

It was decided to make the journey on the next full moon which would give good light, and this was not due for another couple of weeks so there was plenty of time to get ready.

It was decided that the little group would enter the Third Realm of Hanomide by travelling through the Second Realm of Clanomide from the direction of Quazboo; this would be much easier than trying to climb over the top of the Galamide mountains to the west and risking a confrontation with the cruens.

The night came for the little group to make the journey. They had packed all their provisions; the goblans had provided all sorts of fruits, nuts and vegetables and biscuits, and, of course, some extra special golly-berry wine to make the mission easier.

Gignac, Garvoid's wife, asked whether she could come on the journey but Garvoid was adamant he could not cope with the stress if something happened to her.

Gignac was a feisty goblan; she sometimes accompanied her husband on short journeys to Treaclewood to visit the fairies, and a couple of times to visit the owls of Mocklewood, but to take her on this journey when they did not know what to expect? Garvoid felt it was best that she stayed home. Gignac was not happy with this decision but Garvoid hoped that when he returned, she might have mellowed.

They had a stunning setting to send them on their way. The full moon was resplendent in its glory; the light it gave seemed brighter than usual.

The Graven Tree looked magnificent and the party was feeling very positive and eager to go.

They were just about to set off when Elphin came hurtling round the corner, fully equipped with some form of back-sack that looked quite inventive, comfortable and useful.

No impbahs were invited on this trip as there did not seem a valid reason why they should be put in jeopardy.

There was no connection with the Third Realm for these creatures, but that was not going to dissuade Elphin from coming.

He knew that, if he made his real intention known, he would not have been allowed to come, but by giving out the back sacks that he had made for each party member, he thought this would buy him a ticket for the journey.

"Please, Mr Grumplepumple, these back sacks will make your journey much more comfortable. I hope this will earn me a place on the trip," Elphin explained so quickly that he was getting tongue-tied.

"And, I can climb trees and be your lookout and warn you of any danger," he said, reasoning with the wizard goblin.

Everyone was most impressed with Elphin's offering; they looked and felt really good and could be worn easily on the back.

The impbah demonstrated how to put their arms through the two large handles and all the food could be stored within the sacks.

The back sacks had been made out of the thread from the Blue Spider of Pumple Mountain, which was soft but very strong. Elphin had learnt how to weave the thread into a thickness that could be knitted together to produce the back sack.

He had come across the item on his travels with Mr Gravenpumple and knew if he could make something similar, he would impress the wizard goblin. He asked Giliboo, a young goblan, to help him and had clandestine meetings with her to learn the skill.

Mr Grumplepumple thought the idea was ingenious and would definitely help, instead of having to stuff everything in their cloaks and lugging uncomfortable bags.

How could he say no? He could not deny the little impbah's request to join the group. He had obviously gone to great lengths to impress, and of course, it was much easier to transport their provisions, so he felt he could not refuse this heartfelt request.

So, now there were eight members in the group, as well as the popstrells, who set off first to make sure no danger lay ahead. The first part of the journey was largely uneventful as they meandered through the familiar terrain. However, Goby learned a valuable lesson after he stopped to gather some golly berries from a very inviting bush. He was squirted with so much goo that Mr Grumplepumple had to dip him in a nearby stream several times to wash the goo away.

But he dangled him upside down so his head was submerged half the time!

"What's that gurgling sound I can hear?" asked Elphin.

"Just an over-excited and mischievous goblin who needs a lesson in staying put," replied Mr Grumplepumple with a jovial smile.

That would teach him a lesson and make the little goblin think twice before he ran off again, leaving the group panicking as to where he had gone.

Goby was a handful to manage at the best of times; he had his father's spirit of adventure and a very courageous streak, but he also had his mother's kindness and empathy with others.

It was hard to stay annoyed with the little goblin, plus, he had the most enormous ears, much bigger than the average goblin, which did bring some ridicule and laughter from some quarters, but in general, made him more endearing.

The first day, they found an old twisted tree with dense foliage to act as cover and keep them protected while they slept.

Goby was so excited because he had never slept away from the safety of the Graven Tree or Pumple Mountain so this was all new.

But he knew he must stay close to his brother at all times now, after his severe telling off, and secretly welcomed the embrace of Mr Grumplepumple as they snuggled down to sleep.

Toobah did not sleep well that day. He kept thinking about his lost friends and family back in Hanomide and questioned whether they would still be alive.

"Will they welcome us? Will we receive a warm greeting or will they be hostile and angry?" asked Toobah of Booma who had positioned his bed next to his best friend.

"I just hope we can find them; it has been a long time and we have heard nothing," said Booma in a solemn tone. Enzo was restless too and they were up early just as the sun was setting. They gathered together and embraced in solidarity and nodded their heads in respect when Mr Grumplepumple passed.

The wizard goblin did not sleep well either and was also up early. He started a fire to make breakfast and asked the mambooas to gather round for a discussion.

Mr Grumplepumple had not visited Hanomide before so wanted to glean as much information as possible about the land and the goblins that lived there.

"It is important to plan the quickest and safest possible route through Clanomide to get to the Third Realm without attracting too much attention to ourselves," said Mr Grumplepumple with authority.

"Should we visit the goblins of Clanomide first?" asked Toobah.

"There is no need to alert the goblins of Clanomide of our quest. If we are successful and locate your lost tribe and the goblins of Hootahn, then we can tell our story to Carboot and the other goblins on our return journey," replied the wizard goblin who was searching the mambooas' faces for agreement.

At the end of the second night, the party reached the boundary of Galamide just before Helia was making its celestial climb into the sky.

They had another fretful day's sleep and rose early to study their map.

After much discussion, they decided to go through the mountainous path of Quazboo and thus avoid the swamplands where the morzarhs lived.

If they were detected by Nantah then that would not be such a bad thing as Mr Grumplepumple would be delighted to see the great warlock again.

He could seek his counsel to ask some advice for the best approach to entering Hanomide.

They travelled for many nights, climbing and negotiating the sharp, hazardous rocks; they were so grateful for the full moon that shone brightly. But Elphin nearly fell down the side of the mountain when he was startled by a yar yar bird.

It nearly crashed into a tree while gawping at the small group as they climbed, but managed to swerve just in time and made a quick deviation, before swooping back down the mountain.

Mr Grumplepumple thought they really were silly birds with little sense of direction, and overly nosy; he was surprised they had wings to fly as they seemed to get them into trouble all the time!

They came to a large opening with a huge forest ahead. This looked familiar to the party from a previous trip but there was no natural track through; it was very dark, dense and menacing.

They could hear a strange, eerie, unfamiliar sound coming out of the forest. It sounded like a creature was in pain and producing a deep gruff sound that was intermittent, alternating with a low howling noise.

"Grumph grumph. Owww owww. Grumph Owww," came the sound from the dark forest.

Goby looked up at Mr Grumplepumple and squeezed his hand tightly for reassurance.

"What do you think that is?" Goby said in a meek and feeble voice.

The popstrells were gathered on a nearby tree looking intently at Mr Grumplepumple; they did not want to venture into the forest or fly over it. The wizard goblin squeezed his staff tightly and raised his head to listen; he did not recognise the noise.

It was not one he had encountered on any of his travels with his father, Mr Gravenpumple.

"I have never heard a noise like that before, dear brother. I am as perplexed as you," he said trying to press his ear further towards the direction of the sound.

Then suddenly, Elphin stepped forward and turned to face the great goblin. The little impbah looked so strong and defiant with his shoulders pushed back and his little arms strapped to his side.

He spoke in a low but firm voice;

"Mr Grumplepumple, it is my duty to go forth and investigate this strange and peculiar noise. I am hoping my fellow kin live within this forest, and if I am in danger, then I believe they will instantly come to my rescue".

He adjusted his back sack and straightened his cloak as if trying to look assertive and brave.

"I hope you understand now why it was so important for me to come with you on this journey as my true intention was to seek out my dear friend, Migney, again and reunite with my friends."

It had not crossed Mr Grumplepumple's mind that this was the reason why the little impbah wanted so desperately to join the mission, but now, it all made sense.

The wizard goblin looked down upon the impbah's face and heaved a big sigh, for he knew how important it was for Elphin to see his friends again, and felt disappointed that he had not thought of this when making his plans.

He extended his hand onto Elphin's shoulder and patted it gently and agreed without another thought to let the impbah enter the forest.

But he vehemently repeated the need to let them know what he found quickly and not try and be a hero.

Nishmoo

Chapter Sixteen

The Rescue

The eerie noise soon stopped once the impbah had entered the forest and everyone looked at each other with fear.

"What's happening? Has Elphin found the source of the noise?" asked Goby, who was hiding under his brother's cloak, and hoping whatever was in the forest could not see him.

Everything was strangely silent and calm. Everyone was standing rooted to the spot when suddenly, Elphin came sprinting out of the forest with a very angry Nishmoo in pursuit!

"Arghhhhhh! Arghhhhhh! Runnnnn, Runnnnn!" screamed Elphin.

The impbah was running as fast as he could, flapping his arms about and screaming at the top of his voice to the group to run!

The creature was not gaining quickly as it was limping and seemed to be in pain but its huge bear-like body was still bounding forward at a disturbing rate. Its long nose was lifted high, sniffing the air as it smelled food!

Nishmoos are not creatures you want to encounter at the best of times. They are hunters that mainly feed on little creatures of the forest but a little goblin, mambooa or impbah would be a special treat!

Everyone in the little group was willing Elphin to run faster and Mr Grumplepumple pointed his staff at the nishmoo and chanted a magical spell.

"Haltabrata. Stoparatta, Terminatrus!" he yelled.

A bright blue spark whizzed forward towards the beast but missed as the nishmoo tripped over itself and fell to the ground.

It made a loud groan but quickly recovered and carried on its pursuit.

It seemed to be possessed and made them question whether the creature was just stupid to pursue the impbah if it was in such pain, or was there another reason why it seemed so eager?

Then suddenly, as if out of nowhere, there was Nantah, closely followed by a handful of impbahs, running towards the beast from the north of the forest. Nantah seemed to be floating, and on closer inspection, you could see he was riding some strange sort of creature. It was hovering very low and nearly touching the ground. It had a huge wingspan and made the great warlock look quite small and insignificant on its back.

The impbahs were screeching loudly behind the warlock, as impbahs do.

"Eeeeekkkkk, eeeekkkk!" they screamed. This disturbed the nishmoo, which had suddenly stopped in its tracks when it noticed the other little group appear.

Elphin was so elated to see the other impbahs that he came to a sudden halt and started waving his arms so madly, you couldn't be sure if he was greeting them or warning them to stop and turn around.

"Ohhhhhh, wooooooo, whaaaaaaaa!" Elphin screamed incoherently.

All of a sudden, the popstrells starting to squeak very loudly;

"Squakkkkkkk, squakkkkkkk," they squeaked in unison. They had been perched in some trees nearby and had not wanted to enter the forest when Mr Grumplepumple had asked.

The sound was quite terrifying and unusual, as normally you would not hear a squeak out of them.

Then, with a tremendous whoosh and a very high-pitched cry, something flew out of the forest from where Elphin and the nishmoo had run out. Everyone turned to look in the direction of the noise.

"Arkkkkkkk arkkkkkkkkk arkkkkkkkkkk!" The sound was ear-piercing.

The creature was moving at a frightening speed and swooped down so fast and grabbed the bewildered and confused nishmoo quickly in its winged claws, before soaring up into the sky and off into the distance!

This all happened so fast and everyone was terribly shaken up. One minute, Elphin was running for his life, and Nantah and the impbahs were coming to the rescue, and then the threat was totally eliminated by some terrifying creature that just sprang out of the forest with such speed and took the problem away!

This was all too much for Mr Grumplepumple who had to sit down to catch his breath. Goby was jumping up and down with glee and shouting, "Victory!" Then he started running round in circles.

The strange winged creature landed nearby the wizard goblin and Nantah dismounted quickly and rushed over to check Mr Grumplepumple was alright. Elphin embraced Migney with such vigour that the poor impbah was struggling to breathe and the other impbahs were dancing around the pair.

Goby was highly delighted with this act and he quickly joined the group and started to dance amongst the impbahs too.

Then, with great urgency, Plock swooped down and perched himself on Mr Grumplepumple's shoulder and started squeaking into his ear.

"There, there, Plock; calm down. I can't understand what you're saying."

The popstrell was bobbing about so violently it was quite unnerving to watch. Then the wizard goblin jumped up quickly and turned to the group, his face ashen and his voice trembling with fear.

"We must leave this clearing immediately. The creature that took the nishmoo will be back very soon and it will take no prisoners; we must move fast!"

Nantah offered Mr Grumplepumple and the goblins a lift on the back of his winged creature and they gratefully accepted, but before the wizard goblin mounted, he quickly plucked Goby out of the impbah's embrace.

"Come on, Goby, there's no time for celebration; we need to go, and quickly," he said, grabbing his brother by the collar of his cloak.

He plopped him in front of him and wrapped his arms protectively around the little goblin. Garvtak and Garvoid gingerly climbed on board, holding onto each other.

The mambooas ran quickly behind with the impbahs in tow and they all followed Nantah to the safety of the enchanted forest where the great warlock lived.

Nantah flicked his staff a couple of times and the forest changed shape. A large clearing became visible and the winged creature aimed for it and landed in the area with relative ease.

Once the goblins had dismounted, they stared at the creature with wonderment and praised its beauty and grace.

"I've never seen anything so beautiful in my whole entire life," said Garvoid, who kept rubbing his eyes to make sure he hadn't dreamt this.

Nantah introduced his faithful friend and explained that it was an Elphabian. The creature had the look of a gazelle, with huge curved horns that protruded out of its head, but with large willowy wings and a long tail.

It had the most beautiful smooth fur that was milky orange and felt like silk to the touch.

Goby was mesmerised by the creature; even in the storybooks that his brother had read to him, there were no creatures like this.

The creature was quite a sight to see and of much interest to everyone; Goby wanted to stroke the creature, as did the mambooas and impbahs, but Nantah explained how Elphabians were solitary and shy creatures and did not want fussing.

"Elphabians live alone most of their lives and are not used to company," said Nantah in a tone that meant they must pay attention and heed his words.

The creature flew off, quickly and with ease, up into the sky, away back to its home up in the clouds above the mountain tops.

Migney and the other impbahs insisted that the little group stay and rest awhile and start off again on their journey the following night.

There was very little resistance from anyone, as the whole incident had been such a shock to them all and they were all still feeling quite nervous.

The nishmoo experience had fairly tuckered them out and they bedded down for the day within the enchanted forest.

Mr Grumplepumple took this opportunity to speak with the great Nantah about what he knew of the Third Realm and asked his advice about the best way to get there and what to expect.

The great warlock drew up a map of what he knew about the Third Realm and the lie of the land. He had not visited the place for quite a while, but he had sufficient knowledge to show a path that would lead the little group to the great Mount Hoot.

Here lay the capital city, Hootahn, at the bottom of Mount Hoot, in the heartland of Hanomide.

This was where the goblins of Hanomide lived, or at least, used to!

It was a tearful departure the next night. Elphin desperately wanted to stay and be reunited with his cousins but also wanted to help Mr Grumplepumple with his mission.

"I want to stay with you, Migney, I have found my long-lost family and I don't want to leave again so soon, but I am torn. My intention was to stay with you but I am now feeling Mr Grumplepumple may need my help," he said, shaking his head and pacing back and forth, which was making Migney dizzy.

He was so torn that Migney even suggested that he could come on the journey.

It was the unexpected wisdom of little Goby that resolved the dilemma.

Goby was becoming quite fond of Migney. He liked the way the two impbahs were so close and he also found them quite comical when they were in each other's company, which had only been for one night.

It would be fun to have the pair of them on the journey, he thought.

So, Goby asked his brother if this would be acceptable before he mentioned it to Elphin.

"I noticed Elphin pacing just before. If he's not careful, he will wear out his feet," he said, glancing at his brother to make sure he was paying attention.

"I think the poor little impbah is divided, whether to stay or come with us and continue the journey." Goby was now staring at his brother.

"Can Migney come? I think it would be good to have him with us, don't you?" he asked with a quizzical look.

Mr Grumplepumple had drummed into Goby to stop airing his ideas and suggestions in public; he must always consult with his brother first.

Too many times did Mr Grumplepumple have to usher his brother away and explain that Goby just had a very broad imagination; his ideas were too farfetched and not feasible.

He did not want to quash Goby's enthusiasm, just channel it in the right direction.

"If Migney accompanied us on the journey, then on our return, we could travel through Quazboo again and we could drop Migney off. That way, the two impbahs could get properly reacquainted and I know you would welcome the opportunity to speak with Nantah again." He finished the statement with a flick of his rather large ear.

Mr Grumplepumple could not argue and readily accepted the idea and the little group set off with an extra impbah in tow.

Harqin

Chapter Seventeen

Harqin

It took much longer than they first thought to reach the border of Clanomide. The mountainous route was difficult, with steep cliffs and very narrow paths through deep ravines and it was very loose underfoot.

Goby was having great difficulty keeping his balance on the high, narrow tracks, and once or twice, he felt so nauseous he nearly fell. Garvtak was keeping a watchful eye on the little goblin and eventually decided to wrap a rope around himself and Goby as reassurance for both of them.

Mr Grumplepumple was deep in thought, thinking about what the popstrell had whispered in his ear after they had experienced the horror of the beast that took the nishmoo.

Plock had told the wizard goblin that the creature was a gnarkull and the popstrells knew of this creature from past experience.

The gnarkull came from a land across the Calder Sea but were known to venture into the Realms on occasions.

When the popstrells went scouting, they occasionally came across the carnage these beasts had caused and the remains of what once had been a living creature.

Their trademark was sickening; they would tear their prey into little pieces. The beasts had the look of a bat, but were much bigger and stronger with huge wings and the sharpest of claws, and would tear a creature to bits with no remorse.

It was said that once it had its sights on an animal, it would never let go and would hunt it down.

The gnarkull would have returned, once it had feasted on its prey, hence the need to depart as quickly as possible from the scene.

The thought of a confrontation with this creature sent a shiver down Mr Grumplepumple's spine and he wanted to dismiss any further thoughts of this beast from his head.

He thought he would check on his faithful friend, Squiggle, the booquar.

He delved deep into the pocket of his cloak to stroke his head, but, to his horror, the little booquar wasn't there!

Then, all of a sudden, his hat started to wobble and his little friend popped his head down in front of the wizard goblin, with a big cheesy smile on his face, and waved his unusually large hands in front of him. Mr Grumplepumple laughed so loudly that his shoulders shook.

"For one moment, I thought I'd lost you, my dear little friend, but no, you'd just been busy nibbling on a berry," he said while laughing.

"Click, click coo, clock, click," replied the booquar.

"Oh, you've just plucked it off a nearby bush and needed more room to enjoy its delights, so you decided to move up into my hat and I didn't realise!" This amused Mr Grumplepumple.

As the little group climbed over the last peak, they were suddenly confronted with a vast expanse of land. It was covered in forest as far as the eye could see, except for an occasional mountain peak popping through here and there.

The land was covered in a strange, pale-red mist that hovered over the ground, and periodically, great spurts of water would shoot up through the mist into the air.

"Whoooshhh!" went the water. The first eruption made everyone crash to the ground in sheer terror at the sound and sight of the water shooting up, but after a few times of seeing this unusual activity, they became accustomed to it.

Mr Grumplepumple thought it would be a good idea to get a good day's sleep before they ventured down into this unknown land. If there were to be any surprises, then being rested and alert would definitely help their cause.

"I'll go and see if there's anywhere suitable to rest up, Mr Grumplepumple," said Garvtak, who always liked to impress the High Wizard.

"You'll need some help with that, won't you, Garvtak?" said Garvoid, not wanting to miss out on some praise.

They scoured the area to find the best place to set up camp. A little further up from where they had stopped, there was a large ledge that cut deep into the side of the mountain with a large overhang.

This would serve them well as it was high enough to see any danger down below and would be very difficult for any predator to approach from above as the ledge was on a steep cliff-edge.

Everyone welcomed the stop and settled themselves in for the day. Their back sacks were full of food to eat and golly berry wine to drink, and all was well.

The morning sun was rising from the east; it had a blue haze to it that made it look very celestial and mellow, but this was not suitable for goblins and their friends because of the sensitivity of their eyes. If the goblins had to walk the land in daylight, they would use their second eyelid, but it was not to be used too much.

It was a fragile layer of skin that could easily dry out if not kept supple and soft. The sap from a spindle bush, a very spiky and prickly bush with bright red leaves and a very tough bark, was used to moisturise their eyelids. The sap was mixed with crushed macadao nuts to make up a balm.

Mr Gravenpumple had invented this cream while making up one of his potions. He stumbled across the recipe for the creamy balm when he used the wrong ingredients from his pickle pots.

After a few tweaks, he had perfected the balm and it was used to protect the goblins from Pumple Mountain if they needed to travel by day.

The balm was also used to trade for other products from goblins and creatures of the Realms and was especially favoured by witches for their wrinkly skin.

After a fitful day's sleep, Mr Grumplepumple awoke to a strange sound, one he had heard before but was not connecting in his head because of where they were.

"Weeee Ha ha ha, weeeeeee ha ha, hee hee!" came the sound from down below.

It sounded like a gleeful happy laugh, a chuckling sound interspersed with bursts of raucous laughter and high-pitched squealing.

The noise woke everyone up abruptly and the group peered over the ledge, curious to see what it was.

A burst of water that periodically spurted up through the pale-red mist seemed to have something pivoting on top. It wasn't easy to make out what it was, but the creature was making a very loud noise and really seemed to be enjoying itself with much laughter and frivolity!

"Whoooo Haaaaa, weeeee ha ha," came the sound again.

Goby was so curious to know what it was, so he tugged ferociously on Mr Grumplepumple's cloak and pleaded for them to go and investigate.

"Oh, let's go have a look. Whatever the creature is, it must be friendly or else it wouldn't be laughing. Evil things don't laugh!" Goby said with excitement.

The wise goblin was amused by the noise of the raucous laughter and agreed they should take a look, so the party quickly packed their things away and made their way down the mountain to investigate.

As they approached the bottom of the cliff, they could see the thin layer of mist that hung over the forest below; it had a pale-red hue to it, even in the evening dusk.

As they passed through the mist, the laughter was getting louder and quite contagious, so that the little group found themselves starting to chuckle.

"Haaaaaaa haaaaaa haaaaaaa," came the sound over and over again.

Elphin and Migney started to find everything hilarious and began pointing at each other and bursting out laughing over and over.

"Ohhhhh! Haaaaaaa, haaaaa, haaaaa," they screamed and started rolling about on the floor.

Goby thought they looked so funny and also started to laugh out loud.

Mr Grumplepumple tried to hush everyone up, but something had taken a hold of him too; he couldn't stop laughing!

"Shushhhh, ha ha shushhhh," he chuckled.

Suddenly, the creature stopped laughing and there was a stillness that completely changed the mood. Everyone looked at each other with trepidation.

The little group stood at the foot of the mountain in a clearing just near a dense forest, and as they looked around, there was a sense that eyes were upon them.

"Is something watching us from that forest?" said Toobah cautiously.

Goby felt very scared and tried to hide under Mr Grumplepumple's cloak, while Garvtak and Garvoid edged forward to see if they could sense anything.

Toobah and his fellow mambooas went to take a look and scour the area, then, after what seemed like a lifetime, the mambooas returned with no news.

"There's nothing to report; we can't see anything unusual within the forest," said Toobah with a military sharpness in his voice.

The popstrells had been scouring the top of the forest to see if they could make sense of this strange land, but one of them got splattered out of the sky by a spurt of water.

"Whooooshhh!" made the sound of the water as it soared into the sky.

It rose so quickly and suddenly, it knocked the little creature off course and the popstrell came crashing down into a nearby tree!

"Eeeeekkkkkkk," the little popstrell squeaked in great distress.

The others stopped abruptly and dived down to help their friend. The little bat was shaken and stunned; it had landed on a funny-looking clump of moss that had grown out of the side of a tree.

This had saved the little creature and cushioned its fall. Its little wings were soaked and heavy.

"Roll about in that moss and then flap your wings, Gok," ordered Plock.

The little bat obeyed and it did the job, and Gok was soon back up in the sky with the other popstrells.

Mr Grumplepumple took out the map that Nantah had given him, and after consultation with Toobah and the mambooas, they set a course to trek north through the forest.

Goby tried to contribute to the conversation; he was trying to practise his navigational skills and was poking his sticky little finger all over the map.

"Will you take your grubby little finger off the map; you're leaving sticky marks all over the paper, you numpty!" said Toobah with irritation in his voice. He was the one who would scold Goby because he felt Mr Grumplepumple was far too lenient.

The usual noises of the forest had returned: owls were hooting in the trees and the familiar sound of crickets chirping and frogs croaking came back.

Occasionally, they could hear the sound of water whooshing up but this had become a familiar sound and was no longing alarming to them.

It was not easy to navigate through the forest as it was dense and very dark, but now and again, they came to some clearing that opened up to the beautiful starry night sky.

All the time, Goby felt very uneasy and held on tight to Mr Grumplepumple's cloak, much to the annoyance of the wizard goblin who had to keep pulling his cloak back onto his shoulders.

"Will you stop pulling, Goby," he said with irritation in his voice.

"I think something is following us," he said in a fearful tone.

"Nonsense, dear brother. You do have such a vivid imagination," said Mr Grumplepumple in a calming voice, trying to make light of Goby's fear.

Goby turned to the impbahs to get a second opinion.

"Don't you sense something's following us, Elphin?" he whispered.

"No, I don't think so. It must be those large ears you have. You're hearing everything," Migney replied sympathetically.

Then Elphin and Migney continued their whispered conversation. Since they had met up again, they had never stopped nattering and hugging each other. It was quite sweet, actually, and a joy to see such companionship.

Goby was so pleased he had suggested that Migney came with them; his good deed of the night. He secretly wished he had a close relationship like this with a special friend but he couldn't complain. He had a loving family.

Toobah was deep in thought. He was feeling quite nervous but also excited at the prospect of meeting up with long-lost friends and family. He was hoping that, despite all this time that had gone by, the mambooas of Hanomide were still in existence and had survived the great fire of Hoot.

It was not easy navigating through the forest because it was so dense and there were many bushes which made unnerving rustling sounds, but the troop soldiered on.

After a full night of trekking, they came to a clearing; it appeared to be the end of the forest, for in front of them lay open land with a funny-shaped mountain plopped in the middle.

It looked like a crooked witch's hat and Toobah recognised it immediately.

"We have come to the Mountain of Harridan," he announced.

"It is the home of the witches of Hanomide. They live within a fortress that sits precariously on the side of the mountain and always looks like it is about to fall away," he stated with a chuckle to himself.

"The two witches who started the great fire of the Hanomide forest had once lived here but had gone into hiding after being banished from the mountain," Booma added, shaking his head, remembering the mayhem they caused.

"It brought much disgrace and dishonour to the Great Coven of Harridan," Enzo chipped in.

It was becoming lighter as the night gave way to a milky-red vanilla sky. Sunrise was on the way, and they needed to find somewhere to rest for the day.

Over to one corner lay a mound of grass with a little wood plopped on top; this was ideal and the little party made their way over to it.

Everyone settled down to eat and drink their fill before bedding down for the day, but Goby was still feeling very worried and unnerved.

He felt that eyes were upon him and asked Mr Grumplepumple if it was alright for Squiggle to sleep with him.

"Dear brother, I think I would sleep better if I had Squiggle near me; he's like my comfort blanket," Goby said, suddenly feeling very afraid. He had never been on an adventure like this before and it was turning out to be so much more than he bargained for.

Often, when Goby felt scared or nervous, he would sleep with the booquar, and Squiggle was more than happy to oblige as Goby had the softest velvety skin under his ears.

The only sound to be heard was Elphin and Migney snoring in unison under one of the trees and all was calm, then, out of nowhere, a sunbeam came flying through the sky.

"Whooooshhhhhhhh!" was the sound the sunbeam made.

They were similar to shooting stars, but these happened in daylight. They were little shafts of light that erupted from the Helia; the Sun of the Three Realms.

It whizzed through the sky at a tremendous speed making a loud whirring noise and disappeared over the horizon.

Suddenly, there was a great bang as something fell out of the tree above them.

There was a loud thud and something lay huddled up with spindly arms wrapped around its head! Everyone woke up with a start and looked at this strange creature that had suddenly appeared.

It was shaking violently and suddenly lifted its head and stared around at everyone. Its body was heavily disfigured but it somehow looked familiar.

"What in great gumstrous is that?" screamed Elphin.

And everyone gasped as it hurled itself forward and jumped onto Toobah's back.

It started pummelling and banging the mambooa and screaming with a high-pitched squeal!

"Tra-ra-ate-tah, tra-ra-ate-tah," it screamed which sounded like gobbledygook to everyone.

Goby started wagging his finger at everyone. "I told you so, I told you so, I told you that something was following us!" he said reproachfully.

Mr Grumplepumple acted quickly and pointed his staff at the demented creature whilst chanting one of his spells.

"Detachatta, detachatta rattus," he yelled and then, next thing, a bright blue spark hurtled towards the creature and hit it square on its forehead.

This had the desired effect and the creature slumped to the ground in a crumpled mess with its arms and legs splayed wide, unconscious. The enchanted spell was one of the wizard goblin's greatest achievements. It was a spell that was once used on a woolvac that had ventured up the mountain looking for a treat! It had just pounced on a goblin, but luckily, Mr Grumplepumple saw it and used the spell; it had the desired effect of leaving the woolvac comatose.

It took a few minutes for the group to take in what had happened and everyone was trying to catch their breath.

"What the blazes is that and where the Pumple has it come from?" asked Garvtak who was checking that Toobah was okay.

Toobah tilted his head to one side after he had recovered from the shock of the attack, trying to fend off an irritating goblin.

He was trying to decipher what was so familiar about this distorted thing in front of them. It was Booma, Toobah's faithful friend, who was the first to recognise this creature.

The mambooa shook his head as if in disbelief and could not speak for a moment then whispered into Toobah's ear,

"Look what it has round its neck," he said anxiously.

The mambooa looked at his friend with questioning eyes then peered down to have a good look for himself. And sure enough, there, around the creature's neck, was a chain with what looked like a coin or medallion on the end.

It looked very grubby and old but, on closer inspection, you could just make out the markings of a mountain on the round disc that was on the end of the chain. Goby was beside himself with glee at being right, and being such an impatient little goblin, was shaking Toobah's arm. He wanted to know what was going on.

"What is it, Toobah, what is it, what does it mean?" he said excitedly.

"Let me breathe, Goby. All in good time," Toobah said, trying to calm him down.

The mambooas gathered together and stared at the mangled little creature and then turned to Mr Grumplepumple to explain their thoughts.

Toobah spoke in a very concerned but calm manner.

"This pathetic little creature is the prince-goblin Harqin of Hoot, who ran off into the forest over a moolatoon ago after the mambooas would not side with him against the warlocks and witches. Booma has recognised the necklace and even the goblin, although the ravages of time have taken their toll," said Toobah, glancing at the creature with disgust.

Everybody stared at the creature for what seemed like an age until Mr Grumplepumple broke the silence.

"What are everyone's thoughts? What should we do with this creature?"

Toobah and his fellow mambooas wanted to leave the wretched goblin.

"He has obviously survived in the wilds of the forest for a long time. What's the point in having a handicap with us? Someone would likely have the burden of keeping watch over him," said Toobah, shaking his head.

They had no sympathy for the creature; he had brought about such pain and sorrow and deserved to perish in the depths of the forest.

Mr Grumplepumple then remembered the tale Nantah had passed on to him.

"There is a rumour about the goblins of Hoot and how they have been cursed. Nantah told me this while we were consulting over the map."

Mr Grumplepumple gathered everyone round and retold the story that the great warlock had told him.

"The prince-goblin had cast a spell and proclaimed it for all to hear before he fled. Harqin had set a curse upon the goblins to stop them from travelling outside of the city walls; he wanted the goblins to suffer for their disloyalty," he said, giving the creature on the floor a look of disgust.

"The prince-goblin had magical powers, the skills of which had been passed down through time from his ancestors. Unfortunately, this curse involved a connection with the gnarkull from times of old." Mr Grumplepumple checked to make sure the creature was still in a coma.

"He was said to have offered his soul to the creature once he had died, if it would honour his wish to hunt down any goblin that left the city," he finished, giving everyone an intense stare.

"It was a gnarkull that had swooped down and plucked the nishmoo from the ground so effortlessly right in front of our eyes, wasn't it?" asked Garvoid, who was keeping as far away from the creature as possible.

"Yes, it was, Garvoid," Mr Grumplepumple agreed reluctantly.

It left a terrible chill in everyone's spine as the realisation of the situation dawned on them; they had captured the evil prince-goblin.

The mambooas hung their heads low; they remembered hearing the rumour of this curse.

Goby asked, "Is this the reason why the goblins of Hanomide have not been seen for such a long time?"

Mr Grumplepumple replied with hesitation.

"The only way we can find out for sure is to make our way to the capital city and find out for ourselves."

Goby was quick to reply.

"If it's true, then surely Harqin will have to be taken back to Hootahn to lift the curse?"

It did not take long to make the decision and, reluctantly, the mambooas agreed. While the prince-goblin was sleeping, they bound his arms behind his back with the rope that Garvtak had in his back sack.

It was the same rope he had used on Goby to keep him safe from falling over the edge of the mountain.

They wrapped a large vine around the goblin's legs. It was just slack enough so that he could walk forward but not run away, and this was attached to Garvtak's waist.

Mr Grumplepumple had cast a rather large dose of his spell on Harqin, so the goblin was asleep for quite a while, but this gave the group time to study the map and plot the best course to reach the witches' mountain.

When Harqin finally awoke, his first reaction was to scream out loudly and curse at everyone, spitting and shouting some really terrible words!

He claimed he was going to make sure every single one of them would pay for this capture and imprisonment.

"I'll make sure you all die a painful death, and I'll boil your heads!" he screamed.

When he saw that it was only one little goblin that really had his attention, he went quiet and slumped into a corner.

His head was tucked between his legs in a very strange manner and what seemed to Goby like a very uncomfortable position.

Goby was fascinated with this creature. He had never seen a goblin look so terrible, his body so twisted and contorted. It was as if something had tortured the goblin to within an inch of his life and left his body crumpled and ungoblin like!

Megilonia

Chapter Eighteen

The Witches of Harridan

The moonlight was bright and the stars seemed to be sparkling much more than usual.

There were so many shooting stars whizzing through the sky as the group made their way towards the mountain of Harridan.

The forest ahead looked dense and a little spooky. Mr Grumplepumple was leading the way with his staff lit brightly to guide the way.

Garvtak kept a close eye on Harqin, and Garvoid watched his back to make sure they had no nasty surprises.

"Don't you go tripping over anything, Garvtak. You don't want that vile thing landing on you," Garvoid said and poked Harqin in the rear.

"Don't you worry about that. You're at the rear so it's the foul smell he makes that you need to watch out for," laughed Garvtak, trying to lighten the mood.

The popstrells had flown on ahead to check that all was clear but had not yet returned.

Nobody seemed too concerned as the little bats had said they might rest up for a while and meet up a little later.

As they came to another clearing, Mr Grumplepumple stopped suddenly. The ground was awash with beautiful green lights, twinkling and sparkling like precious stones.

It was a magical sight to see and the goblins and impbahs gasped in wonder and were mesmerised.

Elphin and Migney were about to rush forward and play amongst the lights when Toobah shouted at all of them abruptly.

"Stop! Don't anybody move!"

Booma quickly grabbed the little impbahs and tugged them back.

In a whisper, Toobah explained how they had come across a sight like this before and wanted to look closer at the beautiful lights.

"When we approached, we were set upon by what turned out to be a swarm of solboc flies that normally live in the bogs of the Second Realm. They began to attach themselves to our fur and started to bite!" he snapped to make an impact.

"It was only the fact that we mambooas can run fast that outwitted the flies; we managed to lose them when we climbed into the dense foliage of some nearby trees," he glanced at his friend for confirmation.

Booma explained how one had got tangled up in his fur.

"The ugly little critter was trying to bite its way out." He showed everyone the deep scar on his back.

"It was only by rubbing my back on the tree's bark that I could rid myself of the little pest," he said in a very distressed voice.

The party made a quick exit and took a little detour by going around the clearing to the right before they got back on track.

All the while, Harqin had been very quiet and sluggish.

Mr Grumplepumple was feeling slightly guilty as he had conjured up a large dose of comatose powder, which he had administered through his staff. The amount he used would normally be for a cruen or woolvac; it was obviously far too much for the little goblin.

On reaching the foot of the Harridan Mountain, Goby noticed that Harqin was becoming quite agitated and starting to mumble to himself.

The spell was now obviously wearing off; his distorted face was pale and his eyes looked wide and wild.

Garvtak also noticed this change in the goblin's manner and had to continually pull on the rope to keep Harqin moving.

"Come on, you vile excuse for a goblin," he said with disdain in his voice.

Goby wondered what was troubling the goblin. Something was wrong and he seemed to become more uncomfortable as they approached a little cottage, with smoke billowing out of the chimney, that was tucked neatly away under a clump of trees.

It looked quite inviting but the smell that hit their nostrils was not pleasant. "It smells like someone has cooked their old boots, with a hint of sweaty socks thrown in for good measure," said Garvoid, holding his nose.

Goby hid behind Mr Grumplepumple's cloak as they approached the building; everyone was feeling apprehensive.

Toobah led the way with Booma and Enzo. They decided to take a quick look and ran around the cottage to peep through the window to see if anyone was inside.

Suddenly, out of nowhere, the popstrells swooped down to join the group. They had seen their friends arrive while they were resting in some trees nearby.

Mr Grumplepumple asked his little friends if they had seen anything or anyone. The popstrells told him of the fortress they had seen on the other side of the mountain.

They had not flown inside as they did not want to bring attention to themselves, so they had sat in a nearby tree, on a large branch hanging close to one of the high windows.

Plock, the eldest and most respected popstrell, told Mr Grumplepumple how they had seen several witches inside, sitting around a large table, eating.

But the food was nothing they had seen before, and they weren't sure if it was vegetable or animal!

"It looked disgusting," Plock squeaked.

He proceeded to tell Mr Grumplepumple about the little flying objects that were hovering over the table; it was not easy to tell what they were.

As he listened to the popstrell squeak and squawk, Toobah started to laugh.

He knew of the witches of Harridan and what their diet consisted of; and told Mr Grumplepumple that the witches were carnivores.

"They mostly ate meat, but thankfully, it was mainly little animals of the forest, like voles, moles and other little critters," he said with a smirk on his face. Then the mambooa lowered his head and whispered in a deep, solemn voice, "Bats were regarded as a highly desirable treat!"

Plock was not happy with this news and gave Toobah a sharp tut and a squawk, and flew off onto a nearby tree.

Meanwhile, Goby had noticed that Harqin had buried himself under a pile of the dry leaves that were strewn across the ground as if trying to hide.

It was obvious that the little prince-goblin was scared and did not want to be heard or seen. Then, out of nowhere, came a whooshing sound from above and a haggard old witch, sitting rather precariously on a broomstick, came to land in front of the group with a thud!

Everyone was startled and taken aback by the speed that the witch had descended, but inwardly giggled at how clumsily she dismounted her broomstick.

Booma explained to the startled group in a whispered voice:

"The witches of the Third Realm call their broomsticks penadillas. Each penadilla is as individual as each witch, and they bond together as soon as a witch has graduated from her schooling."

Toobah then interjected, still in a whispered tone,

"The penadilla chooses the witch, it is not the other way round and much is decided upon by the grades of magic that the witch has achieved".

It was obvious from the dull and dishevelled look of this penadilla that the group were in the presence of a witch who had not gained straight As!!

The old hag stared at the group, moving her head from side to side trying to digest and register the creatures in front of her. Then, she spoke in a squeaky cackle that sounded like she was giggling to herself.

"Well, what do we have here, I wonder? Some of you I recognise as goblins and mambooas, but I don't recognise you, strange creatures," she said, walking forward slowly, the sound of her clothes rustling like dry leaves.

Then, as if by magic, a little creature hopped onto her shoulder and whispered something in her ear.

"Ah, yes. My little friend here tells me you are impbahs. I've never seen one before, so this is a real treat!"

The little creature on her shoulder looked like a cross between a frog and a newt and with eyes too big for its head. Its arms were longer than its body - a very strange sight to see.

The witch introduced herself.

"I am Makoleena, one of the witches of Harridan, and my friend here is called Bossum," she said in a gleeful voice.

She explained that they lived in the cottage and had just been out to collect some herbs to add to their stew that was bubbling away inside.

Goby started to giggle as he was thinking about the stew; it didn't matter what you added to the stew, it would still smell dreadful!

Mr Grumplepumple walked forward; he wanted to extend a warm welcome and thought this gesture would help to create the right atmosphere.

But as soon as he did this, the witch recoiled and stared at the ground behind the wizard goblin.

"What, what, what is that?!" she exclaimed in a loud shrill voice.

Behind Mr Grumplepumple, the ground was shaking and leaves were flicking up and down. The witch cast forth her wand and chanted a spell.

"Spickytorty," she yelled.

The leaves were whipped up into the air and exposed Harqin, who was trembling with fear!

"What is this vile thing," she cried, "and why was it hiding?" she asked.

Everyone was rooted to the spot. Goby looked at Mr Grumplepumple with panic in his eyes, but his brother gently shook his head and made a shush gesture from the corner of his mouth.

The witch was glaring down at the pathetic goblin, trying to work out what it was, and she turned to Mr Grumplepumple for an explanation.

"Explain yourself," she cried.

Fortunately for Harqin, Mr Grumplepumple had acted quickly and cast a spell on Harqin to cover his body in green fur which hid the medallion and chain as well.

This was the only way they would be able to smuggle the goblin through Harridan without the witches recognising him as the prince-goblin of Hoot. Harqin had not realised the wizard goblin had done this to him as they had approached the cottage.

He had been too busy mumbling to himself, completely self-absorbed in fear, and trying to hide himself in the dry leaves strewn on the ground.

Fortunately for Mr Grumplepumple, Makoleena was not the brightest witch of the Third Realm and accepted the wizard goblin's explanation.

Mr Grumplepumple cleared his throat and spoke in a quiet voice.

"Makoleena, please do not be alarmed, this goblin has gone a little crazy after being bitten by a Solboc fly. We are keeping him safe with a rope to stop him from running away and getting lost."

Harqin was both relieved and grateful to Mr Grumplepumple and gave him a pathetic look of thanks.

Unbeknown to the group, Makoleena had alerted the witches of Harridan before she swooped down to greet everyone.

Suddenly, there was a great whooshing sound as one, two, three, four witches appeared out of nowhere in a spurt of thick green mist!

"Whoooshhhhhh," was the sound as they landed.

They surrounded the little group and stared silently for what seemed like a long time before one of them stepped forward and extended her hand to greet Mr Grumplepumple.

The wizard goblin was highly delighted to see this witch as he recognised her immediately from previous travels with his father, Mr Gravenpumple.

"Megilonia, the Ivory Witch, how do you do?" Mr Grumplepumple said in a grateful tone.

She had attended many conventions of magic, wizardry and witchery with the great old wizard goblin of Pumple Mountain.

She tilted her head at the wizard goblin and then smiled. She recognised Mr Grumplepumple from his travels with his father; she had bumped into them several times.

Mr Gravenpumple used to take his son on journeys and teach the young goblin how to make potions and lotions and to know what ingredients were required and how to acquire them.

Mr Grumplepumple remembered that, on one occasion, he had unintentionally cast a spell on Megilonia's owl that made it grow huge ears.

This made the poor thing topple off its branch and it fell to the floor with an almighty thud!

This greatly amused the Ivory Witch and, after calming herself down from minutes of raucous laughter, she gave the small young goblin a good luck charm. She said it was to help keep him safe, just in case another one of his spells went wrong, and the recipient was not so forgiving.

"May I ask, how is your owl?" Mr Grumplepumple asked with a wry grin on his face. Then, delving deep into his cloak, he pulled out the lucky charm to show Megilonia.

He wanted her to know that he still had it and she squealed with delight and gave Mr Grumplepumple a big hug.

"Oooh! You've kept it all this time," she said with an incredulous look.

As she did this, there was a loud clicking noise coming from his cloak and out popped Squiggle.

He didn't want to be crushed in the process of the hug.

Megilonia and the other witches were surprised to see the little creature.

Goby was sure he saw one of the witches lick her lips as if sizing up the little booquar for tea!

This disturbed Goby and made him feel uneasy, but his brother seemed to be enjoying this reunion, so he kept quiet.

Mr Grumplepumple started to explain that they were here because they wanted to see if the goblins of Hoot still lived in Hootahn since no one had heard from them for over a moolatoon.

Toobah chipped in with his reason for the journey and asked the witches whether they had seen any mambooas on their travels.

"We are hopeful you can give us some good news," he said in a desperate manner.

"I'm afraid we have not seen a mambooa for a very long time, but we wish you the best of luck in your quest," said the Ivory Witch with a kind tone to her voice.

The witches had not visited the city for over a moolatoon. Whether they were feeling guilty or just being kind-hearted, no one knew, but Megilonia announced that they would like to help.

She invited the little group to join them up at the fortress to rest before they set off again.

"Come and be our guests and together we can formulate a plan," she said with a jovial grin.

"But we will need to take you on our penadillas up to the fortress as it is a steep climb, otherwise, it will take you a day and a night to get up there," she said in a very commanding yet genteel way.

Megilonia instructed each of the witches, including Makoleena, to take a couple of passengers each on their penadillas up to the fortress.

Mr Grumplepumple and Goby straddled themselves onto Megilonia's penadilla, feeling very uneasy and apprehensive.

The Ivory Witch shouted authoritatively, "Hold on tight to my ivory robe!" and they whooshed up into the air and were up and away into the clouds.

Goby kept his eyes tightly shut. He felt terrified and did not look down. All he could feel was the icy cold wind whipping his face and making his long floppy ears flap like crazy.

He could hear Squiggle clicking like mad in Mr Grumplepumple's pocket.

It was not long before they arrived at the fortress; much quicker than expected, they landed within a huge courtyard.

The other witches arrived soon after; Makoleena was screeching with laughter as she dismounted.

"Haaaa Haaaa Whaaa Whaaa!" she screamed.

She had Elphin and Migney as passengers and the fact that the impbahs were so terrified and screamed all the way, highly amused the witch.

Megilonia had to give her a hard glare and a clip of her wand to quieten her.

Garvtak and Garvoid

Chapter Nineteen

The True Identity

The fortress was huge and formidable. It had very high walls all the way round with tall turrets every few feet.

There was a sinister look to the place with many dark corners and an array of strange objects festooned across many of the walls.

Goby was sure he saw something move in a dark corner which made his heart skip a beat.

But there were also many candles and glimmering lights that added warmth and a gentle glow.

The little group were led into the great hall and asked to sit at the end of a huge table. Megilonia took her position on an oversized chair made up of many twisted and entangled pieces of wood intricately woven together to make it look like a tree sprouting upwards.

Elphin was mightily impressed and made a mental note of the design; he was going to try and replicate the chair when he got back home.

He thought he would be able to carve the wood within his room inside the Graven Tree, to make something similar. Elphin was always making something; it was just in his nature.

The other witches had disappeared; Mr Grumplepumple was hoping that they had not gone to prepare food.

If it was anything like Makoleena had been preparing, then this was going to be a very awkward situation.

Megilonia clapped her hands and the doors opened. In flew the strangest group of little creatures you would ever see. Goby's eyes widened in surprise as the creatures came forth with plates of fruits and berries, and what looked like buns, which they placed down in front of them; they looked delicious!

The creatures reminded Mr Grumplepumple of Tissamarr's little friend, Nitnac, but they were twice the size, with two sets of wings and two protruding horns on their heads. Their eyes were small and black, like little buttons sunk in their faces, and they had wide mouths that stretched from ear to ear. They had long arms and two bandy-looking legs that just hung down like they didn't belong.

They were very strange to look at and the group couldn't take their eyes off them as they landed on the table.

"That one's staring at me," said Goby to Mr Grumplepumple. His brother nudged him in the ribs and told him to just smile. The little creatures arranged the plates of food in front of them. One pushed a plate in front of Goby and gave the biggest grin from ear to ear, as it twitched its ears at him.

He wasn't sure if the creature was making fun of Goby's own ears or just had an itch and was flicking them, but either way, he wasn't best pleased.

In any case, as soon as they had come, they were gone.

Megilonia started to cackle as she found the reaction of the group highly amusing. She explained that these creatures were ebogs.

"They are indigenous to the mountain and the witches protect and care for them. The ebogs serve my witches well, and to show our gratitude, we protect them," she explained.

Mr Grumplepumple was highly relieved with the food that was presented and thanked the Ivory Witch.

"We are most grateful for your kindness and willingness to help us," he said in a grateful and relieved tone.

She leant over to the wizard goblin and whispered something in his ear, at which Mr Grumplepumple laughed out loud and then proceeded to delve into the food.

Everyone enjoyed the feast; they hadn't realised how hungry they had become. Megilonia chatted intensely with Mr Grumplepumple for what seemed like ages.

All the while, Toobah was keeping a close eye on Harqin who was sat in between Garvtak and Garvoid.

The prince-goblin looked ridiculous with his green fur but it was starting to fade and the medallion around his neck was starting to reappear!

The mambooa tried to get Mr Grumplepumple's attention but he was too engrossed in conversation with the witch.

Everyone else started to notice too, and Garvtak was trying to push the goblin under the table.

"Get your ugly, flea-infested body under the table, you stupid goblin," Garvtak muttered under his breath.

Unfortunately, the prince-goblin was desperately trying to eat everything in sight and was oblivious to what was happening to him, and was having none of it. Booma quickly ran round to the side of Harqin and pulled him under the table so quickly that it went unnoticed.

Suddenly, there was a loud screech from under the table as Harqin realised that Mr Grumplepumple's spell was fading and he was returning to his normal skin. He knew that as soon as the witches saw him, they would recognise him and kill him!

But he could not stop himself from screaming!

"Aghhh, arghhh! What am I going to do? Help me," said Harqin panicking.

Megilonia looked under the table to see what all the noise was about and the other witches came in to see what was going on.

Booma was trying to shut Harqin up by putting his hands over his mouth but the goblin had gone into a mass panic.

Megilonia flicked her wand and said something that made no sense to anyone but seemed to do the trick.

"Flickumpicktium," she shouted.

The spell produced an invisible force that whipped Harqin out of Booma's grip, hauled him from under the table and raised him up so that he was floating in mid-air over the tabletop.

All eyes were on the little goblin who seemed to have frozen with fear.

He just hung there looking rather pathetic and limp with a gormless look on his face.

But what was worse was that the medallion, on its gold chain, was hanging from his neck, exposed for all to see!

Megilonia and the other witches, who had grown rapidly in number, looked quizzically at the goblin.

Then, one of them screamed in horror and said, in a low crackle, the one word that everyone was dreading......

"Harqin! It's that vile prince-goblin, Harqin. Look at his medallion. Only the mad prince-goblin wore this!"

All the witches were cackling loudly amongst themselves and waving their wands at the goblin, spinning him round to take a better look.

It was a frightening spectacle to see, one that would be permanently etched on Goby's mind.

Suddenly, all eyes were on Mr Grumplepumple and the rest of the group. Megilonia glared at the wizard goblin; her eyes narrowed and she hissed at him.

"What is the meaning of this? Why is this vile creature with you? How did you find him and where were you taking him?"

So many questions were being hurled at Mr Grumplepumple. He was desperately trying to stay calm and in control of his emotions.

He had to stand still and be defiant. He had to give himself time to think. Everything had happened so quickly; it took everyone by surprise.

Goby, without hesitation, jumped up in front of his brother and started to waft his arms about.

"Well, let me tell you what happened," Goby started.

He was about to go into one of his fantasy stories (he had a vivid imagination) but Mr Grumplepumple quickly stopped him in his tracks.

He sent a spark from his staff that hit the little goblin on his backside and made Goby jump.

"Owww!" he yelped.

Mr Grumplepumple knew he had to tell the truth. He also knew Goby was going to tell some elaborate story that would make no sense and get them into deeper trouble.

Megilonia and the witches were silent; they were waiting for an explanation. Mr Grumplepumple took a deep breath and then related everything that had happened since first seeing the goblin playing in the fountains.

They had not realised at the time that this was Harqin, but, on reflection, it made sense now. No other creature would dare venture near the ferocious spurts of water unless they were insane!

It was all becoming clear and as Mr Grumplepumple spoke, he realised that the prince-goblin had recognised Toobah and the other mambooas, and could not resist the urge to follow them.

While the wizard goblin was talking, a couple of the ebogs were prodding and poking Harqin to make sure he was still alive.

Goby was actually feeling slightly sorry for the goblin.

Mr Grumplepumple finished his tale and stated that their intention was to take Harqin back to Hootahn to release the city from the curse of the gnarkull. Mr Grumplepumple had spoken with conviction.

The witches were very still and quiet as if trying to digest all that had been said.

It was Makoleena who broke the silence and rustled forward from the back of the room. She cleared her throat and spoke in a squeaky, cracked voice.

"It was thought that this vile creature had disappeared forever and everyone thought he was dead!"

She rested further on her gnarled, worn-out walking stick.

"We should be grateful that Mr Grumplepumple and his little troop have been able to capture this vile creature. They should take him back to the capital city and, if the rumours are true, Harqin should be made to undo the curse that has entrapped the goblins of Hanomide for too long."

The witches were now whispering amongst themselves with excitement and Megilonia looked at the little dishevelled hag who was always regarded as an insignificant witch, hence her posting to the gate of Harridan.

She looked on her with a new respect and admiration and replied,

"You are right, Makoleena. This makes good sense. We can only hope if it is true, then this wretched creature can lift the curse and call off the gnarkull".

Everyone heaved a sigh of relief and the tense atmosphere lightened to one of hope.

Megilonia released Harqin from the air and instructed a couple of witches to take Harqin away to a secure lockup and keep him sedated, as they could do without that terrible screaming again.

"No, no, please, you mustn't believe them. It's not true. I'm not Harqin," he cried, kicking and screaming as he was dragged out of the room.

The Ivory Witch asked Mr Grumplepumple and the rest of the group to follow her to the west wing of the fortress.

They could rest up for the remainder of the day.

They were shown to a long dormitory with rows of beds positioned on either side of the room. The beds were like nothing they had seen before and looked amazingly comfortable; they were raised off the ground on wooden legs.

This made them too high to just roll onto, so everyone had to help each other up onto the mattresses.

This was a real treat as a goblin's bed usually consisted of feather down and twigs intertwined, but these mattresses felt so soft and comfortable.

Before he fell into a deep sleep, Mr Grumplepumple made a note to ask Megilonia what they were made out of.

It was only the prodding and poking of Squiggle that woke him up as Helia was setting.

Everyone awoke feeling refreshed with great hope in their hearts. Toobah, Booma and the other mambooas were keen to depart as soon as possible but Mr Grumplepumple wanted to make sure they knew where they were going.

He consulted with Megilonia in the great hall while everyone ate some buns that had been provided. He showed her the map that Nantah had given him.

She scrutinised it carefully and beckoned over a couple of witches, and after much consultation, she came to sit down again.

"We have decided that I and a handful of witches will transport you and your group on our penadillas," said Megilonia in a tone that was not to be questioned.

"There are a couple of dangerous forests in your path where fierce creatures live, and you will definitely not want to encounter them," the witch said in a cautionary tone.

Mr Grumplepumple thought to himself that the witches did not trust him fully and wanted to make sure that Harqin did not escape.

Megilonia turned directly to the wizard goblin and reiterated the need to hold Harqin accountable; she emphasized this point vehemently.

"This evil goblin needs to be brought before the goblins of Hootahn. He must pay for his actions; he must lift the curse and call off the gnarkull," she said loudly.

But how this was to be done was a real dilemma, thought Mr Grumplepumple. As far as the witches were concerned, Harqin would have to offer himself as a sacrifice.

The witches knew of the gnarkull and believed they would want payment, whether it was his soul or some other prize!

Toobah and the other mambooas wanted justice, but being gentle creatures, they would prefer to find another way to lift the curse and spare Harqin.

"It was madness that had possessed the prince-goblin in the first place; he was not of sound mind," Toobah told Mr Grumplepumple in a surprisingly sympathetic tone.

What to do with Harqin was going to turn into a major problem.

Mr Grumplepumple sat quietly, contemplating the options, when he felt a little hand slip into his and he looked down at Goby who was sat beside him.

The wizard goblin loved his little brother with all his heart and sometimes he felt overwhelmed with love.

He wanted to wrap him up in feather down; the thought of any harm coming to him haunted his thoughts. He could not bear to lose Goby.

He could hardly cope with the pain he felt when he lost his father.

Goby realised his brother's dilemma. He knew him well and knew this was what he was thinking.

He wanted to offer support and come up with a brilliant solution but there weren't many options available.

"It is always you, dear brother, who bears the weight of everyone's problems, and this isn't fair, and I worry you take on too much," he said in a sombre tone. "All this worrying has aged you and is not doing you any good!"

Mr Grumplepumple gave his brother a comforting squeeze and replied with a sense of pride in his voice.

"We will have to wait and see what sort of reception we get when we deliver Harqin to the goblins of Hootahn."

Megilonia took Mr Grumplepumple and Goby on her penadilla, which was made out of a strange ivory-like wood, with intricate carvings all the way down the broom.

It had a mass of white branches bound on the end with a thick, shimmering silver twine.

Makoleena took Elphin and Migney; she was fascinated by the impbahs and seemed to want to spend as much time as possible with them, probably due to their cuteness. She had earned her place on the trip with her new-found respect.

A younger witch called Maddelarcha, who had flaming red hair and eyes to match, took Garvtak and Harqin. Garvoid and the mambooas went with the other witches, who seemed just as strange.

Megilonia told everyone to hold on tight and not move about too much on the penadillas.

"You must remain as still and calm as possible. There will be no wriggling and swaying unless you want to fall," said the Ivory Witch in a stern tone.

The witches did not take passengers very often, so, any sudden movement could be disastrous.

One by one, they soared off into the sky, where Helia had set behind the mountain after a beautiful sunset.

There was still enough light for the witches to navigate and you could see the witches and their passengers clearly silhouetted by the moon as they travelled across Hanomide.

It was a clear night with many twinkling stars and the occasional shooting star whooshed across the sky like brushstrokes on a canvas.

Garvtak had hold of Harqin tightly, even though the goblin did not try to move. He was absolutely frozen to the penadilla and had his eyes tightly shut as they travelled in the cool night air.

Megilonia pointed out a landmark below to Mr Grumplepumple; it was a long winding river that meandered through the forests, and it shimmered in the moonlight. It was the great Crimstone River that ran through all of the Three Realms.

She explained that if they followed the river, it would take them to Hootahn; it was the best guide to use in order to get them there.

They would land near the Great Forest of Hanomide which was not too far away from the city.

They had been travelling for several hours before they came across a very large clearing. After miles and miles of dense forest, it was strange to see this large expanse of open land.

As the group were flying over the land, Toobah recognised the old ruined castle where they had rested for the day and seen the goblins pass through. Those goblins had probably not come from Hootahn; they were roaming the land freely, and, reflecting back on his encounter, they did seem slightly different in appearance. They had darker skin and were taller than the goblins he knew. They must have come from another part of Hanomide, or perhaps the Second Realm.

Just as Toobah was contemplating this, the witches abruptly changed direction and started to descend.

The witches were shouting to hold on tight as they swooped down to land in the clearing on the edge of the vast forest.

Toobah felt a heavy throb in his heart; he knew he had returned home to the Great Forest of Hanomide.

Booma was squeezing Toobah's arm a little too tightly and it was starting to hurt. The mambooas had not enjoyed the ride on the penadillas; they were terrified of being so high up. But the excitement that they felt at the prospect of meeting their long-lost relatives compensated for this anxiety. Nonetheless, they felt relieved as they dismounted.

Elowen

Chapter Twenty

Elowen

Megilonia made a quick check to make sure everyone was here, especially Maddelarcha, who was carrying the vital cargo, Harqin.

Mr Grumplepumple rearranged his cloak and checked that Squiggle was okay, then walked over with Goby to where the rest of the group had congregated.

It was getting lighter; the night was coming to an end, and it would not be long before Helia was bright in the sky, so they needed to get into the forest as soon as possible.

Garvtak had to prise Harqin off the penadilla, which was not an easy task as the goblin had gone into a paralysed state of shock. Garvoid ran over to help.

"Take your ruddy fingers off the stick, you irritating nitwit!" said Garvtak.

Harqin was riddled with fear and his fingers would not let go of the broomstick.

"Tranformtillatah, slithertuss," said Maddelarcha assertively.

As she tapped the penadilla, it made a loud hissing noise and started to twist and bend as it turned into a snake.

"Hisssssss, hisssssss!" came the sound from the penadilla.

"Well, that definitely did the trick," said Garvoid, giving Maddelarcha a wide smile. Harqin almost jumped out of his skin and let go!

Goby thought the Ivory Witch had a formidable presence; she had obviously earned huge respect from her witches, who grouped, forming their coven quickly at the click of her fingers.

They huddled together for a committee meeting. Seeing all the witches together like this, with their brightly coloured hair flapping in the gentle breeze, was quite a spectacle.

It was not long before Megilonia lifted her head and beckoned Mr Grumplepumple and the others over and they all sat in a circle; except Harqin of course.

Garvoid had offered to keep an eye on him while the others joined the group.

"I'll make sure this slimy bug doesn't run off," he said, giving Harqin a clip across the ear as a warning.

Megilonia turned her head towards Mr Grumplepumple with a quizzical look in her eyes and then asked, "What are your thoughts on how we should proceed with Harqin?"

This was the question the wizard goblin had been dreading. He had thought of nothing else while they had been travelling through the skies and his heart was pulling in many directions.

But he had come up with a plan and told the group.

"I instructed the popstrells to go on ahead and see if they could fly into the capital city. They should be able to find out what the situation is and whether the goblins are still there, and whether the curse is true," said Mr Grumplepumple to an eager audience who were listening intently.

Plock had been very hesitant to comply with Mr Grumplepumple's wishes because of the gnarkull threat, but knew he had to do this.

The wizard goblin had discussed this plan with Plock long before they started on their journey from the fortress.

The popstrell knew he would be leading his troop into danger, but it was the only way they could know what was happening, so he had reluctantly agreed. They were to fly back and find the group once they had some news. Plock knew that the group would be landing near the Great Forest, so it should not be too hard to find them.

"So, patience is the order of the night. We need to wait for the popstrells to return before we can decide on the right course of action," he said, clearing his throat.

Mr Grumplepumple knew this was a delaying tactic, but how could they form a plan when they didn't have all the facts?

The witches seemed happy with this answer, much to Mr Grumplepumple's surprise, and so attention was focused on finding shelter for the day.

Megilonia turned to Mr Grumplepumple and flicked back her long hair.

"My witches and I are going to fly off and visit our fellow sisterhood who live north of the forest in the enchanted wood of Heptonstall. We haven't set eyes on them for nearly a moolatoon, so this will be an ideal opportunity for us to catch up and rekindle our friendship."

Megilonia also wanted to glean as much information as she could about the capital city and what was happening there.

"We'll catch up with you near the city walls in two night's time, as the moon is rising," she said in a matter-of-fact sort of way.

But just before Megilonia left, she whispered into Mr Grumplepumple's ear, "You must not let Harqin escape. If all this is true, he must pay for his crime, so the onus is on you to deliver!"

She gave him a cold, stern stare and then mounted her penadilla and whooshed off into the sunrise, followed by a line of cackling witches.

This left the wizard goblin cold with fear and it felt like the greatest of burdens had been laid at his feet.

He realised Harqin was the key to everything right now and needed to be kept closely guarded, and Megilonia had faith in him to do this.

Mr Grumplepumple thought to himself that the prince-goblin would try anything to escape and would use any form of trickery to fool them.

Although the prince-goblin was weak, Mr Grumplepumple wondered if Harqin still had any magical powers left in him. He hadn't shown his hand yet. Was the prince-goblin waiting for the right moment?

Mr Grumplepumple instructed Garvtak and Garvoid to bind Harqin with ropes and keep a very close eye on him.

"We'll guard him with our lives," said Garvtak, puffing his chest out.

"Speak for yourself. My life is worth more than that ugly evil goblin's life!" retorted Garvoid.

The two goblins started to squabble which was a regular occurrence, so Goby volunteered to keep first watch. He was so hyped up with adrenaline that he could not sleep even if he wanted to.

He knew how important it was for his brother to get some sleep; he was looking very grey and old, as if he had the weight of the Three Realms on his shoulders.

Toobah and the other mambooas were keen to press on and see if they could seek out their relatives.

"We'll make haste and hope to find our lost tribe," said Toobah with excitement in his voice.

"Mambooas travel quickly. Our main purpose for this journey is to find our lost family; you understand, don't you?" asked Toobah with a determined look on his face.

Mr Grumplepumple could not argue with him. He asked the mambooas to meet up with them at Hootahn in a couple of night's time. Toobah acknowledged this request with a bow and then the mambooas sped off into the forest without further hesitation.

The wizard goblin really hoped Toobah would be successful. It meant so much to him. He wanted his dear friend to find the rest of his kin and be happy, even if it meant Toobah wanted to stay in the Third Realm for good.

The group needed to find somewhere to settle for the day, so they made their way into the forest; it was not safe to stay out in the open. They needed to find somewhere safe from predators.

The forest was dark and foreboding and the little group felt nervous, but a large tree soon presented itself as the safest option. It had many huge, thick branches sprouting out not far from the trunk, so the little impbahs and goblins scrambled up and made temporary beds out of the thick foliage.

And, with a little magic, Mr Grumplepumple conjured up some feather down for the group to place on the makeshift beds for extra comfort. The wizard goblin remembered the deep sleep he had experienced in the witches' fortress and promised himself that on their return home, he would make a couple of these beds for himself and Goby.

Harqin was tied to a large branch and Goby settled down nearby in a perfect-sized nook in the trunk of the tree and everyone else went to sleep.

No feather down for Goby, though, as this would have definitely made him fall asleep.

Garvtak said he would take over after a couple of hours and then Garvoid, not to be outdone, offered to take the following watch. Goby loved his uncles, for this is how he saw them. They had helped raise him from being a little mite, and he had the greatest respect for both of them. Everyone was soon asleep and the comforting snores from Elphin and Migney helped ease the tension.

Goby was feeling a little uneasy as Harqin still had one eye open and was staring at him, but he soon realised that he must have fallen asleep as he was snoring in unison with the impbahs.

Goby looked up through the trees and could see glimmers of daylight as the leaves rustled in the breeze, but because the forest was so dense, it provided enough darkness to help the little group sleep.

Goby took out his little round Pumplestone and started cleaning it against the bark of the tree; it was like his comfort blanket, along with Squiggle, of course.

When he was feeling frightened or worried, he would play with the stone and rub it to keep it clean.

As he rubbed the stone against a nearby branch, it started to move and shifted slightly.

No, surely not! He must be more tired than he thought and his mind was playing tricks on him.

But again, as soon as he started to rub the stone against the branch, it moved! Goby was paralysed with fear as he watched something detach itself from the branch, but he was also taken aback with awe and wonder.

A creature materialised in front of him and sat up and stared at Goby.

The goblin was dumbstruck; he couldn't move or say anything, and it felt like something had taken hold of his tongue.

The creature was beautiful, like nothing he had seen before, with soft, pale-brown tree bark covering its small, slight and willowy body.

The face was heart-shaped, with the most beautiful green eyes that sparkled like precious jewels.

The creature had a mass of hair on its head that shimmered as it moved and trailed down its shoulders and back.

It looked like the stars that twinkled in the night sky.

A calmness came over Goby and he felt completely at ease. He was mesmerized by this beauty, and couldn't comprehend the feeling of adoration he had for this creature.

It sat there staring at Goby with a quizzical look on its face and then looked at Goby's ears, and its beautiful little face broke into a smile that was so wonderful it made his heart flutter. The creature suddenly spoke; it was a whisper as soft as a gentle breeze. "My name is Elowen and I can see by your face that you do not know what I am," she giggled softly.

Goby just shook his head, totally mesmerised by this enchanting vision.

"I am a wood nymph and we live here in the Great Forest of Hanomide. This is our home."

Goby wanted to keep this encounter totally to himself. He didn't want anyone to wake up, and he didn't want to share this beautiful moment.

It took him quite a while to open his mouth and say anything.

The wood nymph could see Goby was dumbfounded so she continued to talk. "I recognised that you are a goblin. We help the goblins of Hootahn, but you look different from the ones we know."

Elowen tilted her head in bewilderment and pointed to Goby's ears.

"Our goblins are tall and not as green as you, and their ears are smaller and pointed. I take it you are a goblin?"

Goby finally plucked up the courage to speak, even though it was squeaky. "Yes, I'm a goblin. I come from Pumple Mountain in the Galamides," he squeaked.

Elowen smiled sweetly at Goby and ushered him over to another branch nearby.

He glanced at Harqin, who was still snoring contently, and then moved slowly away to sit near this magnificent creature.

Elowen began to tell Goby about her family and how they helped the goblins. Goby asked if it was true that a curse had been put upon the goblins of Hootahn. She confirmed this with a firm nod.

"The wood nymphs help hide the goblins if a gnarkull comes near," she whispered. Goby was confused because he thought the goblins would not be able to escape and would be trapped within the city walls.

He asked in a squeaky voice, "If they left, then the gnarkull would find them and kill them, surely?" Elowen giggled at this and explained how some of the goblins had dug underground tunnels out of Hootahn, that brought them to the forest.

She said that if a gnarkull picked up the scent of a goblin, they would come searching, but the wood nymphs would lie across them to disguise them as trees.

She giggled again and said in a soft voice, "You saw how I was camouflaged on the tree?"

Goby nodded; he thought this was brilliant and was about to ask when the last goblin had been in the forest, when Garvtak started to stir.

Goby did not realise how long he had been speaking to Elowen.

Garvtak must have set his prickly alarm to make sure he woke up on time.

This was a little round nut that suddenly grew into a prickly ball when the time was right. You tapped the nut the number of hours you wanted to sleep. Then, it was placed in the pocket so it would prick you awake. It was a very clever nut; Mr Gravenpumple had discovered one on his travels and introduced it to the Pumple goblins.

Goby cast a glance at Garvtak, and when he turned back to look at Elowen, there was no sign of her. She must have merged into the tree again or disappeared completely.

He felt a sudden sense of loss but felt in his heart he would see her again soon. Goby was so excited to tell Garvtak what he had found out, he had to be calmed down so as not to wake everyone up!

"You won't believe what I have found out, who I have just seen! I don't believe it myself. I'm not sure if I have just dreamed it. No, surely not!" he stuttered.

Garvtak looked at Goby with dismay and told him to get some sleep.

"Tell me again at dusk when everyone is awake, then it will probably make more sense," said Garvtak with a hint of doubt in his voice.

Between yawns, Goby agreed, as all of a sudden, he felt very tired. It was probably because of all the excitement at meeting Elowen, and he soon fell into a deep sleep.

Goby was awoken suddenly by high-pitched screams that came from Harqin. The goblin had woken up and realised the danger he was in.

He wanted to bring attention to the group and alert the gnarkull, because this was the only way he was going to survive and escape.

"Aghhh, aghhhhhhhhhhh, come to my aid, oh great gnarkull, come to my aid," he yelled.

He had to alert the beast by screaming; he had no magical powers left to summon it, as his magic had left him over his long period of isolation. Harqin had forgotten how to conjure up a spell or make a potion.

But he knew the group did not know this and he had kept quiet about it, but they were getting too close to the city now, and he had no other way of escape.

Unfortunately, the screaming had alarmed Elphin and Migney who had been in a deep sleep; their immediate reaction was to scream too.

"Eeeeeekkkkkkkkkkkk!" they screeched.

When an impbah screamed, you knew about it and had to cover your ears. This was not a good situation; Garvoid was trying to put his hand over the demented goblin's mouth to shut him up.

But Harqin was having none of it and continued to wriggle about and kept screaming.

Mr Grumplepumple was desperately trying to come up with a spell that would shut them all up, but it was too late!

They could hear great wings flapping above, and then there was that spine-chilling screech.

"Eeeeeeeekkkkkk, eeecheeeeeeeeee! was the sound, the same terrible sound they had heard back in Quazboo. You could never forget that noise; it was enough to make a goblin's whole body recoil in terror. Garvtak and Garvoid managed to jump on top of Harqin and gag his mouth; with this, the impbahs' screams also came to an abrupt stop.

Everyone was staring up at the top of the tree as the gnarkull circled round in search of the noise........nobody dared move!

Suddenly, out of the corner of Goby's eye, he saw Elowen and some other wood nymphs who had joined her; he was so pleased to see her.

Goby whispered to his brother and quickly explained what they were; the whole group were staring in awe at the creatures.

"They are wood nymphs, brother. I had a wonderful conversation with one of them while I was on guard. I actually thought I was dreaming, but obviously not!" said Goby with excitement in his voice.

They moved quickly and threw out their hands to make a circle round the group and then brought their heads together.

There must have been about twenty wood nymphs; they stood crouched over everyone, very still and very calm.

Not a word was said; no one dared move, except for Harqin, who was wriggling like crazy.

Garvtak and Garvoid were sat on him and were smothering his mouth. Goby thought they were going to suffocate him at one point; the goblin was starting to turn blue.

The gnarkull circled above one more time and then disappeared over the horizon.

The wood nymphs broke the circle and retreated back to the surrounding trees.

Elowen sat by two other nymphs who looked much older than her but who were just as graceful. It was one of these nymphs that spoke first.

"That was a close call. You're very lucky that our daughter had met Goby first, otherwise, we would not have come to your aid," said the wood nymph, glancing at Goby.

With this, Goby straightened his back and lifted his head up high and started nodding in a very self-assured way, beaming from ear to ear.

The elder nymph spoke again, "We believe you have the lost prince-goblin, Harqin, in your keeping. Is this true?"

Mr Grumplepumple sat forward and tried not to seem alarmed by this question. He spoke in a calm and friendly manner. "Yes, we do," he replied, but first he wanted to thank the wood nymphs for rescuing them from the claws of the gnarkull.

"Thank you for coming to our aid. I have heard about your kind and it is an absolute pleasure to meet you."

The wood nymphs bowed their heads in recognition of the compliment.

Garvtak and Garvoid stood up and Harqin lay in a crumpled mess on the branch, his chest heaving up and down, trying to catch his breath.

He glared at the wood nymphs with hatred in his eyes.

It took Goby by surprise as he had not seen Harqin look so evil before. His eyes were scrunched up and he was hissing at everyone.

All eyes were on Harqin so that, in the end, he felt very intimidated and fell silent. He recoiled back into the tree branch to try and find some comfort.

It seemed a long time before anyone spoke again.

The wood nymphs gathered together and were whispering to each other, while Mr Grumplepumple and the others sat silently, waiting for the nymphs to speak.

It was Elowen's father who spoke next. The nymphs had obviously been devising a plan for what to do with Harqin.

He came and sat closer to Mr Grumplepumple, and, in a deep but calm voice, explained their idea.

"The goblins of Hootahn have made secret tunnels that lead out of the city and into the Great Forest; it is the only way they can move around without detection from the gnarkull."

All eyes were on the wood nymph who Goby thought looked very commanding as he held his audience.

"But only a handful of goblins can use the tunnels. They aren't very sturdy and are quite narrow. One of these goblins is called Hebden."

The wood nymph paused for a moment as if to pay homage to this goblin. "He is only young but he's very brave and agile and has been a frequent visitor to the wood; he fetches and carries for the goblins without any thought for his own safety."

The wood nymph paused again, as if reflecting on the goblin's bravery, and then carried on.

"We will inform him of the capture of the prince-goblin and ask him to report this to the High Council of Hootahn."

Mr Grumplepumple was the next to speak.

"Thank you. This seems like the best plan. We shall wait to hear back from you and look forward to meeting Hebden."

With this, the wood nymphs disappeared, melting into the trees. One minute they were there, and the next they were gone!

Hebden

Chapter Twenty-One

Hebden

The first thing Mr Grumplepumple did was cast another spell on Harqin; he could not afford for the goblin to raise his voice again.

It was now obvious that the prince-goblin had no magical powers left, otherwise, he would have used them to escape.

Mr Grumplepumple bound Harqin up from head to toe in the silk-like thread that came from the Aranemos, the Blue Spiders of Pumple Mountain. He always carried a small supply of this thread; it had come in useful on many occasions. All he needed was a small piece that he could magic into a large length of yarn.

"Spidderus, continerus," he chanted a couple of times.

Goby was so pumped up with mixed emotions of excitement and trepidation that he couldn't keep still. Mr Grumplepumple had to calm him down with some of the goblin's favourite sweets.

They were made from Glabra root and tasted like liquorice.

"Young goblin, you need to calm down. Let's see what I have in my pocket!" he said with a chuckle.

As Mr Grumplepumple delved into his pocket, Squiggle hung onto the sweet wrapper, which was made out of a thick leaf.

The little booquar plopped himself onto Goby's shoulder, hoping for a nibble - it was Squiggle's favourite sweet, too.

Mr Grumplepumple chuckled to himself again.

Goby and Squiggle were munching away and giggling at each other while Mr Grumplepumple settled down by a large branch.

He was feeling very nervous and wondered if the journey had been the right thing to do. He had put his family and friends in grave danger.

He was wondering how Toobah and the mambooas were getting on. Had they found their lost relatives? He truly hoped so.

His thoughts then moved to the witches' reunion with their sisters. They had been very helpful in steering the group away from danger. He wondered what delights would be on their menu since they did not have to cater for goblins this time. He shuddered at the thought, remembering the smell of Makoleena's stew.

Suddenly, he realised the popstrells had not returned. Where were they? They were supposed to have met up with them by the Great Forest; this sent a shiver down Mr Grumplepumple's spine.

Had the gnarkull got them, or had something else as dreadful happened?

He could not bear to think about it!

He would ask the goblin called Hebden if he had seen them. Surely, he would have seen them flying into the city? He must have come across them, surely?

The minutes turned into hours and the night turned into day, with no sign of the wood nymphs or any goblins.

Mr Grumplepumple asked everyone to bed down for the day. They were to meet up with Toobah and the witches the following night at dusk, outside the city walls, and it was so important that they were not late.

If the wood nymphs did not turn up, then they must press on with their original plan.

Helia was high in the sky, emanating her resplendent rays of sunshine, and there was a gentle breeze in the air.

The only sound in the forest was coming from the thick canopy of leaves on the top of the trees; they were rustling and dancing in the wind.

And, of course, the snoring coming from the little impbahs.

Goby was positioned next to Mr Grumplepumple. He never liked to sleep too far away, and Squiggle was asleep under his ears. Suddenly, he felt something on his feet.

He jerked one foot quickly to try and shake it off. He didn't want to open his eyes and be disturbed.

But this movement pushed Squiggle forward and woke the booquar up. Squiggle sat upright and tried to find his bearings, then took in a sharp intake of breath because there, sat by Goby's feet, was a little goblin.

He didn't recognise the goblin; it had darker skin than Goby and small pointy ears with huge round green eyes.

It just sat there with a twig in its hands and was tickling Goby's feet.

The booquar couldn't register what he was seeing; he was frozen to the spot. The strange goblin gave a cheeky snigger and put his bony finger up to his mouth and whispered, "Shush".

Squiggle was not sure what to do, whether to wake Goby up or let the little goblin have his fun.

But the tickling must have been too much for Goby who jerked his feet again and it woke him up.

He bolted upright, thinking something horrible had touched him, when suddenly, he was confronted by a little goblin laughing his head off, and Squiggle was joining in.

"Ha ha ha, hee hee, click click coo," they laughed in unison.

The little goblin soon composed himself. He offered out his little bony hand and said in a chirpy voice,

"Hello, I'm Hebden".

Goby didn't know whether to laugh or cry; why was a goblin tickling his feet?

He looked at Squiggle, who just raised his arms into the air in a gesture that indicated he was not sure what to do.

Goby looked at the unusual goblin, who was sat next to him, with a rather funny expression on its face.

Hebden explained, "I received the message from Elowen, my dear friend, and so I came immediately to see how I could help, but Elowen was nowhere to be seen. So, being the impatient little goblin that I am, curiosity got the better of me," he said, shrugging his shoulders.

"So, I went in search to find the mysterious group that had arrived in the Great Forest." Hebden finished his explanation with another broad smile.

Goby immediately felt a kinship with this fellow goblin; he liked his happy face with its laughing eyes.

Hebden started firing all sorts of questions at Goby;

"Where have you come from?" and "What are you doing here?" "Why have you come?"

And then, unexpectedly, "Why are your ears so long?"

Goby didn't feel offended by this question as Hebden said it in a very endearing way.

He explained to Hebden where they came from and the reason for their journey. Hebden listened attentively as he didn't want to miss anything.

He would need to relay all this back to the goblins of Hootahn.

By this time, everyone was waking up and Mr Grumplepumple raised his eyebrows in joy when he saw the goblin.

He realised immediately that it was Hebden and came over to shake his little hand.

"Very pleased to meet you, Hebden. We have heard a lot about you," he said with a broad smile on his face. Hebden seemed very pleased by this and gave Mr Grumplepumple a big hug, much to the wizard goblin's surprise.

Elphin and Migney shook the goblin's hand and Garvtak and Garvoid nodded and welcomed Hebden.

The only one who sat silent and still was Harqin, who couldn't say or do anything anyway.

Hebden looked over to where Harqin sat and he glared at him with a stern look on his face.

"So, this is Harqin. You don't look much like a prince-goblin. You don't look like a goblin at all!" he said in a mocking voice.

Hebden couldn't believe he was staring at the whole reason he risked his life every time he went through the tunnels and left the city.

Harqin lowered his eyes. Goby hoped it was in shame but you could never tell. Then, as if by magic, Elowen appeared with several other wood nymphs. Hebden jumped up and bounded over to greet her with a huge hug, and she giggled with delight.

"Hello, my dear, dear friend! How are you today?" she asked.

Goby felt a pang of jealousy as he saw how happy Elowen was to see the little goblin. He didn't like this feeling; such envy was alien to him, so he gave himself a silent telling off!

Everyone gathered together to listen to what Hebden had to say; they needed to know the best form of action to take.

The group were hoping the little goblin could come up with a suggestion.

"The first thing I have to do is report back to Hatnal and the great council to confirm that the prince-goblin has been captured," he said.

"Then, a small group of goblins will come and fetch Harqin and take him back to the city, to be brought before the great council." Hebden glanced at Harqin again with a look of total disgust.

Mr Grumplepumple explained that they were due to meet up with their colleagues on the outskirts of the city at dusk and if they did not turn up, then they would be worried.

Hebden advised that they stay put for now; he would get someone to meet up with the rest of their party to explain what was happening.

He explained that they would be escorted back to the Great Forest.

"It's not safe to stay on the outskirts of the city; it's too exposed," he said in a voice that seemed so mature for his age.

"The Great Forest provides good cover, especially with the protection from the wood nymphs. If the gnarkull detect goblins ....they will hunt them down!" he emphasised in a serious tone.

This sent a cold chill down everyone's spine; there were no complaints or protests.

Hebden was much wiser than his years.

Mr Grumplepumple was starting to gain a lot of respect for this little fellow and he noticed how Goby really enjoyed his company.

Everyone was in agreement as Hebden disappeared quickly into the forest, but Elowen and a few other wood nymphs stayed to chat awhile.

Mr Grumplepumple felt the wood nymphs weren't here just to keep them company; they had been asked to keep an eye on everyone and to make sure they all stayed put, especially Harqin!

Goby, Elphin and Migney chatted with the wood nymphs and Goby made sure he sat next to Elowen. He was mesmerised and would have preferred to be alone with her but knew that this was selfish; he did not want those negative sorts of thoughts. Mr Grumplepumple had taught him well.

Garvtak and Garvoid kept an eye on Harqin, who was fidgeting and mumbling to himself. You would have felt quite sorry for him if you didn't know him better. He looked helpless with the thick silk thread wrapped around him, but there was no way he was going anywhere.

Before Hebden left, Mr Grumplepumple quickly asked if he had seen the popstrells, but the little goblin shook his head.

"No, I'm sorry, there have been no visitors for a very long time; no one comes to visit," he said in a solemn voice.

This left the wizard goblin very worried but he did not want to alarm anyone just yet. He would wait to see if Toobah and the other mambooas had seen them.

Hebden came back after several hours, accompanied by four other goblins. They presented themselves with open arms and welcoming smiles.

They were quite tall for goblins with small pointed ears, and their skin was much darker than any they had seen on a goblin before.

The goblins wore strange clothing that looked like pieces of cloth sewn together in a very clever way to fit their bodies; they looked very smart and respectable.

This was not like the goblins from Pumple Mountain, who wore cloaks that draped across their bodies and were held in place by pins made from Pumplestone.

The eldest goblin spoke to Mr Grumplepumple; you could tell he was the oldest by his thick white eyebrows that hung heavy and low.

"We are indebted to you for capturing the prince-goblin. We've been living under his curse for too long."

The goblin shook his head and then glared at Harqin before he could speak again.

"Do we have your permission to take this wretched creature before our leader, Hatnal? The Great Council are very keen to meet Harqin. We need to see if we can force this evil goblin to lift the curse."

Everyone stood in silence and all eyes were on Mr Grumplepumple, when suddenly, there was a whooshing sound from above. "Whoooooooshhhhhhh" came the sound as the witches landed close by.

Megilonia and the others quickly dismounted their penadillas and joined the group.

The goblins of Hootahn recognised the Ivory Witch of Harridan immediately and nodded their heads in respect, then returned their gaze towards Mr Grumplepumple, but before he could speak, he was interrupted by a voice from the forest, and everyone turned their heads to listen.

It was Toobah. "Greetings from the mambooas of Hootahn. We've been away far too long. We are so pleased to see you, goblins of Hootahn," he said in a very respectful tone.

The goblins were taken aback by the sight of the mambooas as they had not set eyes on one for over a moolatoon.

They seemed very pleased to see them. Toobah came over and bowed his head to the eldest goblin and then shook his hand and they started to laugh! "The goblins of Hootahn have always lived in harmony with the mambooas. It was Harqin who drove a wedge between us," he replied.

Goby could see this was a very special meeting, bringing together old friends, all with the same goal.

This had been too much for Harqin and he keeled over and fainted. Everyone looked at the pathetic goblin on the floor and shook their heads in disgust. Toobah seemed to take over the situation and gave his agreement to the goblins to take Harqin.

"We wish you much luck in getting the curse lifted," he said with sincerity in his voice. "May we accompany you through the tunnels?" he asked.

"You may, but we will not be able to take everyone," said the elder goblin.

Mr Grumplepumple was so relieved that the responsibility had shifted and Harqin was no longer under their guard.

He released the silk threads that had bound the goblin and Garvtak and Garvoid quickly helped the other goblins tie Harqin up in a large sack.

One of the goblins must have brought the sack with them, obviously thinking ahead about how to transport Harqin.

They grabbed him quickly and lifted him up with a look of total disgust on their faces; you could see it was turning their stomachs.

Hatnal

Chapter Twenty-Two

Hootahn

Mr Grumplepumple got Toobah's attention and the mambooa came to sit beside him.

He asked in a concerned voice, "Toobah, have you had any luck in finding your relations?"

The mambooa lowered his head and his shoulders sank; there was sadness in his eyes.

"We have not had any luck. We've scoured the Great Forest of Hanomide and even went up Mount Hoot, but to no avail," he said.

"The few creatures we encountered had not seen a mambooa for a very long time and were very surprised to see us," he said, shaking his head in disappointment.

Mr Grumplepumple gave his dear friend a gentle hug and told Toobah not to give up hope.

"Once we've finished our business in Hootahn, maybe we could venture further north to see if the mambooas have settled near the Calder Sea," the wizard goblin said with encouragement in his voice.

This cheered Toobah up immediately. A broad smile crossed his face, which was unusual for him as he was quite a serious character, but Mr Grumplepumple knew him well.

Toobah could be quite funny when he put his mind to it and the two of them had had many belly laughs together over time.

Then he asked, "Toobah, have you seen Plock and the other popstrells? They haven't returned from Hootahn." Mr Grumplepumple looked at the mambooa with hope in his eyes.

The mambooa shook his head; he had not seen them since they met up with the witches of Harridan.

This was not what Mr Grumplepumple wanted to hear. Where were they? What had happened to them?

It was time for the goblins to take Harqin through the tunnel to avoid detection and the mambooas got ready to follow suit.

The goblins explained that the tunnel could not accommodate witches; they were too big and Megilonia nodded in agreement.

The mambooas opted to join the goblins as the thought of travelling on a broomstick again was not even a consideration!

The trees were the only heights they ever wanted to climb and Garvtak and Garvoid volunteered to go with them too.

Again, the flight with the witches had made them feel sick and they did not want to repeat the experience.

But they also wanted to get to know the goblins of Hootahn a little better.

The tunnels were not made to cater for many travellers; they were fragile and narrow so the numbers needed to be kept to a minimum.

The witches agreed they would fly into Hootahn and offered to take the back sacks that Elphin had made.

They were bulky and would need someone to hold them while they were flying.

Mr Grumplepumple offered to go with the witches and, of course, Goby was not going to leave his brother's side.

He volunteered too, and on hearing this, Hebden jumped up with joy.

"I have never been on a penadilla and would love the experience. Could I be included, please?" he said with much emphasis on 'please'!

Makoleena asked Elphin and Migney if they would like to go with her. They seemed pleased to oblige, and they were forging a great friendship with this witch, which was lovely to see.

They had to be careful because the gnarkull would be on guard and no one had visited the city for nearly a moolatoon.

Mr Grumplepumple pulled Megilonia to one side and showed her his Dagger of Pumplestone and explained the special protection it gave.

"I have been gifted this special dagger that will give me great protection. I want you to know you can rely on me if need be," he said with conviction.

He wanted to reassure her that he would deal with the gnarkull if they came close, and she seemed reassured by this.

Secretly, Mr Grumplepumple was not so confident, but he had to hide his fears and be strong.

The goblins of Hootahn, Garvtak, Garvoid and the mambooas bid the others farewell and disappeared into the forest with the limp body of Harqin. Elowen and the other wood nymphs wished everyone a safe journey and melted back into the wood, as if by magic.

Goby was going to miss Elowen and he hoped that he would see her again.

Hebden was so excited to be climbing onto a penadilla that he was beaming from ear to ear across his smiley face.

He was not worried about the threat of the gnarkull; he seemed oblivious to this.

The witches had a quick discussion on tactics and what to do if a gnarkull appeared, and how they would manoeuvre through any danger.

Megilonia said in an assertive voice, "Now, sisters, keep in tight formation. We need to look like there's more of us than there are."

The witches all agreed and nodded their heads in unison.

They did not seem too concerned, as they felt their magic could cope with a gnarkull or two, but this made Mr Grumplepumple very uneasy.

But there was no choice and he climbed reluctantly onto Megilonia's penadilla. He told Goby and Hebden to hold on tight as they mounted Maddelarcha's penadilla. He was uncomfortable with Goby riding on another broomstick, but with having to take the back sacks as well, they had to distribute the weight evenly.

They waited until the night came so that they would not be as easy to spot and then off they climbed into the sky.

The moon had appeared over the horizon in all its usual glory and was filling the sky with a shimmering hue.

They did not have too far to go, just over the tops of the Great Forest, and then they would follow the mountain ridge till they came to the other side of Mount Hoot. Then they could swoop down into the city of Hootahn.

The witches flew closely together to give the appearance that there were many of them; this, they thought, should keep the gnarkull at bay.

It seemed to be doing the trick; they saw nothing as they flew through the night sky towards the city.

But suddenly, there was a loud screech as a gnarkull came out of nowhere. It swooped past Makoleena, who was carrying Elphin and Migney.

"Eeeeekkkkkkkkk, eeeeeeekkkkkkk," it screeched.

It was Elphin who started to scream first as the gnarkull's wing brushed past his arm. He could see the bat's horrible face lit up against the moonlight.

Its eyes were the blackest of black and were sunk deep into its ugly face. It had a large upturned nose and sharp white fangs protruding from its gaping mouth.

Its huge wings caused a sudden wind current that flipped Makoleena's penadilla upside down and she yelled at the two impbahs.

"Hold on tight and don't move. I'll flip us back up the right way but you must keep still!"

Two of the other witches broke rank and followed the gnarkull, chasing its wing and pointed their wands at the creature.

Bright green flashes of light hurtled forward but the gnarkull was too quick and easily avoided the witches' sparks. Megilonia shouted to the other witches to press on and get to the city, while she turned her penadilla in the direction of the gnarkull, following the two witches that were on its trail.

Mr Grumplepumple took a deep breath and pressed his hand against his pocket to give Squiggle a reassuring pat, but the booquar was reaching for the Dagger of Pumplestone. He wanted to help the wizard goblin release it from its holder. Mr Grumplepumple knew now that this was one of those moments when he needed to be strong; he realised that the dagger was required and he had to face the consequences of ageing again!

Megilonia was gaining on the other witches and the gnarkull, when, out of nowhere came another one!

"Eeeeeeeeeekkkkkkkk," it screeched in a high-pitched scream.

It swooped down from above and tore Mr Grumplepumple's cloak that was flapping like crazy in the wind. The sharp claws sliced through the cloak easily. The screech from the bat was ear-splitting. Megilonia was quick to react and flicked her wand at the gnarkull's wings.

"Flitteratus, blassssstimartus," she shouted at the top of her voice!

"Take that, vile demon. You won't be having a kill today!" she yelled.

Out flew a bright emerald-green spark that clipped its wing but this didn't seem to do much damage. It was coming around again for another pass. By now, Mr Grumplepumple had his dagger at the ready and waited for the gnarkull to swoop past again.

His heart was thumping wildly in his chest and the wind was screaming in his ear; Squiggle was holding on so tightly to his neck that he was starting to choke.

Suddenly, he heard a familiar squawking sound coming from behind. It was the popstrells! Plock whizzed past at a terrific speed, followed by the rest of them. They were screeching loudly and twisting and twirling through the air.

"Squeakkkkkkkkkkkk," they cried loudly.

They were quick and easily caught up, then they attached themselves to the back of the gnarkull's neck!

All twelve of them sank their fangs deep into its skin, sending the gnarkull crazy. The screeching was unbearable but the popstrells held on tightly as it spiralled out of the sky.

"Eeeeeeeekkkkkkkk, eeeeeeekkkkkkkk," it screeched in pain.

It plummeted down but did not crash into the ground; somehow, it recovered its flight and flew behind the mountain, and you could still hear its cries of distress as it disappeared into the distance.

Mr Grumplepumple felt helpless and distraught as he watched this horror unfold before him. What had happened to the popstrells?

He saw the other gnarkull disappear back to the forest too. It was still being chased by the witches who were attacking it with bright sparks of fire from their wands, cursing and wailing like wild banshees as they zapped their wands at the beast.

"Wahla, wahla, wahlaaaaaa," they wailed.

There was no time to waste. Megilonia had changed direction and was heading for Hootahn, and she flew over the city walls and landed in the grounds of the city park where she could see the other witches were gathered.

On seeing the park, Mr Grumplepumple's thoughts changed. This was once the home of Toobah and the mambooas, but the mad prince had ruined all that.

He had brought an evil curse upon this beautiful city. He had so much to answer for, and a fierce anger came over the wizard goblin which took him by surprise. Mr Grumplepumple had a heavy heart as he dismounted from Megilonia's penadilla; he put the Dagger of Pumplestone back in its holder and gave Squiggle a reassuring stroke on his head.

He had been so worried about the popstrells, and then suddenly they had appeared, but only for a moment, then they were gone again!

He just hoped that they had been able to escape the gnarkull and fly away. But he was so relieved to see Goby. It brought a little sparkle of joy and he gave his little brother the biggest squeeze of his life.

Squiggle was quick to move out of the way so as not to be crushed, and he jumped onto Goby's shoulder.

Hootahn stood tall and majestic in the pale moonlight; it was much bigger than Goby had imagined. Hebden was excited to show his new friends around the place. They were met by a small party of goblins who asked them to follow them through the park to the main city.

All the while, Goby and Hebden were deep in conversation, and it was lovely to see this new-found friendship starting to blossom.

Mr Grumplepumple smiled to himself; he knew they would become lifelong friends. The group entered the main city through two huge pillars that stood at the entrance to what seemed like a maze of many streets and buildings.

A large crowd of goblins and other creatures had gathered to greet and cheer, and in the middle stood Garvtak, Garvoid, Toobah and the other mambooas.

This was a welcome sight to see. Standing next to them stood a goblin of great stature. He was wearing a beautiful cloak that shimmered in the moonlight, with a wizard's hat with a large brim and a crooked top, much larger than Mr Grumplepumple's, which sat comfortably on his head.

Hebden turned to everyone and made an announcement in a loud voice so he could be heard above the crowd.

"Let me introduce you to the chief goblin of Hootahn; this is Hatnal!"

Mr Grumplepumple had heard tales of this goblin from his father, and he was a good friend to Mr Gravenpumple.

The goblin extended his arms in a gesture of welcome to everyone and then clapped his hands.

There was a moment of silence as the goblin began to kneel down on one knee, then everyone else followed suit.

It was an incredible sight to see. Goby looked at his brother in surprise but Mr Grumplepumple was quick to speak.

"We thank you for this act of gratitude but we must insist that you see us as equals because we have a common goal."

Hatnal stood up and bowed his head and then said in a quiet but firm voice, "The honour is ours; we welcome the great Mr Grumplepumple of Pumple Mountain and his family".

Hatnal had everyone's attention. "We honour your late father, Mr Gravenpumple. You know he was a close friend of mine and we made many journeys together."

The goblin adjusted his cloak, as if to present himself correctly.

"You have brought the prince-goblin to us, and we are eternally grateful. We hope to lift the curse and feel freedom again."

With this, the crowd cheered loudly and raised their hands and starting clapping.

Mr Grumplepumple suddenly remembered his father telling him a tale of Hatnal and a rather frustrated pixie; he must ask the chief goblin to retell this tale again, perhaps when they had a moment together.

Hatnal and his council beckoned Mr Grumplepumple and everyone else to follow them through the crowded winding streets.

Hebden led the way, and then Mr Grumplepumple, followed closely by Goby, who was lapping up this attention and felt like a celebrity. Squiggle was sat on his shoulder waving his large hands at everyone.

Elphin and Migney walked in silence, amazed at this scene and the witches walked behind, occasionally chatting to a goblin or two.

The centre of the city opened up, and in the middle of a large circle stood the most enormous and beautiful building Goby had ever seen.

It was dome-shaped with what looked like creatures carved into the stone all the way around the front, and it had the largest doors imaginable.

They looked slightly out of proportion to the rest of the building and were embellished with intricate carvings.

It was obvious these goblins were highly skilled architects and builders of the highest order.

Hatnal beckoned everyone to follow him into the great hall; this was even more impressive, with huge ceilings bearing intricate stone carvings. They left the cheering crowds outside and then there was silence.

Everyone was staring up in wonder and trying to recognise the creatures that were depicted. Goby recognised some immediately, but there were others that, even in his wildest imagination, he could not have conjured up.

Hebden was very excited and skipped around everyone, guiding them to the long table at the end of the hall.

Hatnal requested that everyone be seated and make themselves comfortable. He removed his cloak to reveal a very smart tunic which he straightened before he sat down at the head of the table.

He indicated to Mr Grumplepumple to sit next to him.

"Please, my dear friend, would you do me the honour of sitting next to me?" and he waited for everyone else to settle before he spoke again.

"We would like to honour you with a feast and will offer our finest food and drink to celebrate this very special occasion."

Everyone seemed very happy and relaxed, and all eyes were on the great chief goblin - they were admiring his clothes.

No one had seen anything like them before and they were amazed at the beautiful needlework.

Hatnal could see that his clothes were of great interest and proceeded to explain their invention.

"Our tailoring skills have evolved during many years of isolation, trapped in this city. We have had to adapt to a solitary way of life without interaction with anyone else. We have become very resourceful." He looked around to gauge everyone's expressions.

"We have learnt many new skills and sewing has been one of them," he said.

Hatnal explained how his tunic had been made out of the wool of the Amoucs that roamed freely through the Great Forest. These beasts moult terribly and leave great clumps of wool everywhere, so they are put to good use.

Everyone nodded in admiration, and then Goby piped up from the seat next to Mr Grumplepumple,

"Please, Mr Hatnal, what will happen to Harqin? Can he lift the curse?" Everyone went silent and turned to the chief goblin, who seemed to ponder the question for an uncomfortable length of time.

Then, a smile crossed his face as he spoke. "Little goblin, you do not need to call me Mister Hatnal. The goblins of Hootahn do not have this custom; I am merely the chief guardian of the city." Answering thus, he cleverly avoided Goby's question and took off his hat to relax the atmosphere.

Just as he was about to speak again, the doors opened wide at the side of the hall and a line of goblins came through with every type of food you could imagine.

There were colourful quinct grain buns, cakes that looked similar to Pip cakes but with much more fruit and berries, and bowls of nuts of every description, and of course, berry wine. This was going to be a wonderful feast!

The goblins had even catered for the witches and brought to the table a large pot of broth that actually smelt quite good, but obviously had some form of meat included, so it was probably best not to ask what was in it.

The feast went on for what seemed like hours and hours and the sun was rising from the east when Hatnal showed everyone where they could sleep.

It was a domed house not far from the Great Hall. It had many rooms, with blankets of fur laid on the floor to provide comfortable sleeping areas.

Mr Grumplepumple found a room near the front of the house and settled down with Goby and Squiggle; he had a heavy stomach and an even heavier heart. He was desperate to know what had happened to the popstrells.

They drifted off to sleep quickly, exhausted from all that had happened.

They were awoken by the sound of owls - "Twit Twoooooo, Twit Twooooo," was the sound they heard, very loud and close by.

Then they heard Hebden; he was banging on the door to wake everyone up. He explained that there was to be a big gathering in the Great Hall and everyone was invited, so they must make their way there immediately.

Anthonus

Chapter Twenty-Three

The Containment

Goby was surprised to see so many witches and warlocks in one place, not to mention strange goblins, the like of which he had never seen before. Toobah whispered into Goby's ear, "They are hobgoblins, cheeky and mischievous, so watch your back. They will pick your pockets just for the fun of it, and wager bets on who can steal the most".

Toobah chuckled, then continued, "They will hand back your goods after they have had their fun, but not always in the same condition as before."

Goby was checking his pockets to make sure nothing was missing.

All round the hall, high up on the ornate pillars, sat owls of every shape, colour and size. Goby was mesmerised by them. Hebden told him the owls lived in the gardens of the Great Hall, but they usually congregated when there was a meeting.

"The owls are nosy creatures. They like to know what's going on and contribute with the occasional squawk to show either approval or discord on the matter at hand," said Hebden with a chuckle to himself.

Hatnal was standing by a large chair in one corner and banged his staff on the floor several times to command silence and so that he had everyone's attention.

"It is with great joy that I speak to you today. The prince-goblin has been found and is under lock and key in the dungeons."

With this news, there was a raucous cheer from the crowd.

Hatnal turned to Mr Grumplepumple, tipped his hat and then continued to speak; "This is great news, but we do have a problem. Harqin has lost his magic and cannot remember how to lift the curse".

As everyone was trying to digest this worrying news, the room went silent, except for several squawks from the owls up on the pillars, who seemed to be having their own little debate. Hatnal surveyed the room full of faces that had turned solemn. He seemed to be looking for answers, but no one spoke.

Then, one of the witches made her way through the crowd to stand near Hatnal. It was the Ivory Witch, Megilonia. She turned to the other witches in the room and said,

"We will try to help Harqin recall the curse. We'll make up a brew that will kickstart his memory." With this, there was a loud cackling from the witches. Then one of the local warlock's came forward and spoke.

"I am Anthonus. Most of you know of me. I have many spells that might work and I would like to give them a try."

This made the whole place erupt into a mass of chatter, and Hatnal had to bang his staff again to regain the silence.

"We must try all methods possible to make Harqin remember but we must be careful. If he regains his memory, then he will regain his magic!"

With this, everyone was shuffling nervously. This was not the news everyone wanted to hear; it was a high risk and needed to be handled very carefully. From the back of the room, another creature moved forward slowly, with much presence and dignity.

It was an elven lady; she was very slender with a beautifully chiselled face and long white hair that nearly touched the floor. She walked with grace and beauty, and when she spoke, her voice was as soft as silk.

All eyes turned towards this vision of beauty and the room fell quiet.

"I represent the elves of Hanomide. I am Biancala, Princess of Shalatarh, and we heard of the capture of the mad prince-goblin. We want to offer our help."

Nobody moved; elves had this effect on goblins. They were held in such high esteem, and were elusive creatures; you would never find an elven kind, they would find you.

Goby's heart melted. She looked so beautiful and mystical that she moved him spiritually. He felt her eyes bore into his very soul; he was sure she held her stare a little longer on him than anyone else. Mr Grumplepumple had met elves before in Clanomide but none as beautiful as this one.

She was quite enchanting and he felt unworthy of her gaze.

She continued, "We can cast a spell to create a cage of mist that will keep the prince-goblin contained once you have offered him the brew. It will stop the goblin using his magic once his memory is restored, but it will not last long." She surveyed the room to make sure she had everyone's attention, and again, seemed to pause a little longer in Goby's and Mr Grumplepumple's direction. It was quite unnerving!

"You will have a few hours before the cage loses its power."

With this, Hatnal clasped his hands together and thanked the beautiful elven princess for her contribution. One of the council goblins suddenly piped up,

"May I ask how you managed to get into the city and past the gnarkull unharmed?" Biancala smiled and suddenly disappeared into thin air. Everyone gasped in amazement, and then suddenly, she was back!

"I have a cloak that makes me invisible but it only lasts for a relatively short period of time, so I have to be careful how I use it," she replied.

Goby thought this was incredible and Hebden had to close his jaw, as it was nearly touching the floor.

They looked at each other and knew immediately what they were both thinking - to have a cloak like this, what fun they would have!

It looked like there was enough talent in this room to tackle the almost impossible task; the mood had changed and everyone's spirits were lifted.

Hatnal concluded the meeting with a positive and encouraging speech and thanked everyone for attending.

He asked Megilonia, Anthonus and Biancala to stay behind so that they could chat awhile longer and he asked Mr Grumplepumple if he would like to remain, too.

Hatnal knew of the wizard goblin's magic and thought he would be a great asset to the group.

"This plan might just work," Hatnal said with confidence to the little group still in attendance.

"Megilonia, if you and your coven of witches can make the memory brew to kick start Harqin's memory, then hopefully, he will remember how he made the curse," said Hatnal in an encouraging tone.

Anthonus then spoke in a commanding voice, "I believe I can conjure up a spell strong enough to render the goblin harmless if he tries to use his magic. I will consult with my fellow warlocks."

Biancala tilted her beautiful face towards Anthonus and smiled, then spoke in a tone of pure, serene calmness.

"My elves will make the cage of mist to trap Harqin. It will stop him from escaping prison while his magic returns, but once the mist is exposed to the outside, it will lose its potency and weaken quickly," she warned.

The plan seemed promising and everyone went away with new-found confidence in their hearts.

But Mr Grumplepumple was feeling slightly useless. What was the purpose of him staying in the meeting?

Hatnal said goodbye to everyone but held on to Mr Grumplepumple's arm as they left; he wanted him to stay.

The great hall had emptied and only the two goblins remained. Hatnal turned to his fellow goblin and stared at him with such intensity; it was quite unnerving and made Mr Grumplepumple feel uneasy.

Then, Hatnal put his arm on Mr Grumplepumple's shoulder and heaved a great sigh, as he spoke in a serious and deep voice.

"You know this task is fraught with danger. Harqin is full of anger and bitterness, and I cannot see any of the old prince left inside him."

With this, he shook his head slowly and then continued.

"The goblin has been away too long and has obviously suffered greatly. His body is torn and broken. Because of his madness, a deep evil has taken over his very core. I fear we will never be able to cure him."

Hatnal went silent and looked at the floor. He seemed to be questioning himself as to whether he should continue with the conversation but something spurred him on.

"Mr Grumplepumple, I know of your great wisdom and your courage. You were tutored by your great father who was revered by every goblin throughout the Realms. I, therefore, need to ask a great favour."

The goblin moved his chair slightly with a nervous jerk and then said in a sombre tone,

"Harqin cannot be controlled. I need you to use the Dagger of Pumplestone to kill him. I know you have this weapon in your possession. I believe it has the Spell of Resurrection bestowed upon it, am I right?"

Hearing this, Mr Grumplepumple felt his heart sink like a lead weight to the pit of his stomach. He did not realise Hatnal knew of the dagger, but there again, he was a very close friend of his father. So, he would be aware of its existence but how did he know about Nantah's protection spell?

Hatnal continued to speak.

"Even though we goblins have been imprisoned in Hootahn, we still hear what is happening throughout the Realms," he said with a wry expression on his face.

He knew what Mr Grumplepumple was thinking.

"I honestly believe the only way the curse can be lifted is by the gnarkull taking Harqin's soul. We believe this was the promise he made, and they will not accept anything else."

Hatnal was wringing his hands; he seemed very uncomfortable and kept shuffling nervously. He dabbed his brow with a very delicate piece of cloth and continued.

"We must let Harqin think he is going to live. He must believe that we will protect him from the gnarkull."

Hatnal lowered his voice to emphasise the seriousness of the situation.

"Once Harqin has lifted the curse, he must die. It is the only way."

It was a while before Mr Grumplepumple spoke, and when he did, it was with great sadness in his voice.

"My mind has been troubled for many days with how the curse can be lifted. Unfortunately, I have not been able to come up with a solution."

Mr Grumplepumple was shaking his head and his shoulders were slumped. "We could try different potions and magic spells, but I fear you may be right. The gnarkull won't go away unless they have his soul."

The two goblins sat very still, contemplating, and after much further discussion, agreed that it was the only way.

Of all the magic in all the Realms, the best defence would be the Dagger of Pumplestone!

It would protect Mr Grumplepumple against the evil that Harqin would unleash once he had his memory and his ancestors' magical powers back.

The two goblins thought it best not to breathe a word of this plan to anyone. They could not afford for anything to go wrong, and both left the Great Hall with heavy hearts.

Over the next few nights, Megilonia and her sister witches gathered to make witchcraft and prepare the brew. Witches flew in and out of the city to find the ingredients they required.

The gnarkull appeared on several occasions, checking to see if they were carrying any goblins.

They made close swoops as a way of warning, but the witches pressed on and the occasional flick of a wand seemed to keep the beasts at bay.

Anthonus had good reason to offer his services. He was the young intrepid warlock whom Harqin had fallen out with over a moolatoon ago.

They had a terrible fight over the favour of a beautiful elven creature. Harqin had desired to marry her, but the warlock had other plans; he wanted to run away with her.

Neither option was going to happen. Elves could never betroth themselves to any other kind of creature, but the two of them were so enchanted by her beauty that they became consumed and blinded to reason.

The prince-goblin was enraged when the beautiful creature fled, never to be seen again.

Harqin not only blamed Anthonus, but he also became hostile and built great resentment towards all warlocks and witches; they were not goblins and he wanted rid of them!

Hence, the warlock remained within the city when the curse was cast; he could have left but felt too guilty.

This was his home and his fondness for the goblins made him feel obligated to stay and help protect them.

Anthonus went to work quickly and researched his book of spells and the Great Book of Incantations, an ancient book written many, many cenatoons ago.

It had stood the test of time and was revered by warlocks. Every warlock had a copy that was used as a code of practice; it held many spells from how to zip up a mouth, to turning a creature into a statue.

The spells did not last forever, just a short period of time, but enough to hopefully aid or hinder a situation.

Warlocks were generally caring and kind but could be unpredictable and sometimes headstrong. It was necessary for them to consult the Great Book of Incantations as often as possible to keep them following the right path. Each warlock protected their book with their lives; if it was to fall into the wrong hands, it could have devastating results.

The warlock felt he might need more than one spell; he wanted enough ammunition to deal with whatever the prince-goblin threw at him.

He spent the next few days and nights making list upon list of spells that might help. Anthonus felt a great weight upon his shoulders. The guilt of their quarrel had been the beginning of Harqin's anger and resentment, and he had to make things right and this was his opportunity.

He was a foolish, young, arrogant warlock, blinded by beauty. He knew in his heart he could never have the beautiful creature for she was elven.

To see Biancala appear was heart-wrenching. He wondered if she might know of his lost love, Aubree, and he hoped he would have the opportunity to ask her what had happened to her.

While everyone was preparing to help lift the curse, Hebden was showing Goby the sights of the city and introducing him to many of the goblins who lived in Hootahn.

It was lovely to see such a community spirit; it reminded Goby of home and all who lived within the Graven Tree.

"Hello, Hebden," said a rather plump goblin who was sat on top of a pile of stone, chipping away at a rather large piece.

"Are you going to introduce me to your new friend?" he said in a jovial manner.

"Oh, yes. Hubble, this is Goby. He comes from Pumple Mountain," Hebden said with a hint of pride in his voice.

"Well, you goblins know how to mine for stone. I wouldn't mind visiting sometime to see how you work. The Pumple is a beautiful stone. I would love to bring some back with me and make my wife something nice out of it," said Hubble, tilting his head with a whimsical look on his face.

Goby was very pleased to hear Hubble's compliment of their beloved Pumplestone and duly invited him to visit as soon as possible.

While they were sat under a large tree that looked more like a small mountain, Goby asked Hebden why he hadn't introduced him to his family yet. He felt he had met everyone else but questioned why not his nearest and dearest?

"Where do your parents live, Hebden? I can't wait to meet them," said Goby.

Hebden went silent and hung his head low. He didn't say anything for quite a while and Goby was starting to regret the question.

Then Hebden spoke in an unsteady voice, "I do not have any family. I am an orphan; my mother and father were killed by a gnarkull as they tried to escape with me." Goby was horrified and gave Hebden a huge hug. Hebden was shocked by Goby's reaction but very pleased. He was not used to anyone hugging him; it was always Hebden who gave out the hugs.

Then he explained, "It was a terrible experience and not one that I like to talk about. It's too painful; that's why I risk the tunnels to fetch and carry for the goblins of Hootahn".

Hebden looked at Goby with determination in his eyes.

"I'm not afraid and I don't care if the gnarkull gets me because then I would be with my family again."

With this, Hebden stood up quickly and started to walk away. Goby shouted after him saying he was so sorry but Hebden had gone.

Goby sat under the tree for a long time thinking how similar his circumstances were to Hebden's. The difference was that Goby had Mr Grumplepumple, his dear brother, and his 'uncles', who he knew loved him very much.

This made Goby so sad; surely Hebden had someone who looked out for him?

Goby went to find Mr Grumplepumple, who was sat in the Great Hall flicking through books; he had a large pile by his side.

They were spell books that he had found stacked on the shelves around the hall. There were books of every size and colour crammed into deep shelves on the surrounding walls.

Mr Grumplepumple was desperately trying to find a spell that would stop Harqin from having to die, but he knew in his heart it was a futile attempt. The end result would have to be the death of Harqin.

Goby asked what his brother was doing and he batted him off with an excuse that he was looking for a spell to make glue.

"Glue? Why would you need glue, dear brother?" asked Goby in a very surprised tone.

"I need it to mend my cloak after it was torn by the gnarkull," said Mr Grumplepumple in a sheepish manner, realising what he had just said.

"What? You saw a gnarkull? Oh, fiddlesticks! Why didn't you tell me?" Goby yelled in an alarmed voice.

Mr Grumplepumple replied in a sarcastic tone, "Because I knew you would react like this and be all dramatic!"

Goby wanted to know every single detail; he was so upset that his brother had not mentioned this attempt on his life!

The wizard goblin kept the tale brief and didn't mention the popstrells; he didn't want to upset Goby who thought they were hiding out somewhere safe. He told a little white lie and said one of the witches zapped the gnarkull and it flew away.

Goby seemed to accept this and calmed down so there was a sense of normality again.

Goby told his brother about the goblans - the wives and daughters who could sew; they were very clever and made all the clothes that the goblins of Hootahn wore.

"Gorrita would love to be able to make these clothes. I'll take one of the beautiful tunics back for her. What do you think, brother?" said Goby with glee.

Mr Grumplepumple agreed. Gorrita loved Goby; she was the wife of Gorun, one of the elders from the great council back home, and would fuss over the little goblin like he was one of her own.

"I'll ask one of the goblans to mend your cloak. They'll make it as good as new," Goby said with conviction.

Goby then proceeded to tell his brother about Hebden and the fact that he had no family because of the gnarkull. This news was very upsetting and, if anything, Mr Grumplepumple realised more than ever that he must end this dreadful curse; it was his duty!

There was an ominous black cloud that hung over Hootahn; it was a constant reminder of the dreaded curse that Harqin had inflicted on the city.

It wasn't often that the goblins saw the stars or the moon; they lived in a permanent fog.

A new Junamoon was the only time when the skies looked brighter and broke through the darkness with a magnificent blood-orange glow, but this only happened once a yulatoon.

However, it just so happened that a new Junamoon was due within a couple of weeks, hence, the date was set to have everything ready.

The witches' brew would be fermented enough, in time to be administered to Harqin. Biancala had brought several elves with her to help form the cage of mist.

Anthonus had been conferring with the other warlocks on magical spells and deliberated long and hard over which spells to use. Many long and arduous hours were spent poring over the Book of Incantations. They must stop the prince-goblin from using his magic once his memory was restored, for he would unleash such terrible carnage if allowed!

Toobah went to see Harqin in the dungeons, but not to gloat, even though he had experienced the dungeons himself by order of the prince-goblin at one time.

He wanted to ask Harqin if he had seen any mambooas on his travels. Toobah was hoping the prince-goblin might have some information, now he was not so heavily drugged by spells and potions.

He was desperate to know if his relatives were alive and was willing to confront Harqin and be subjected to his ridicule.

But, as he had expected, it was not a pleasant meeting; he had been foolish to think it would be otherwise.

Harqin was in no mood to help a mambooa and especially Toobah. He just started to laugh loudly at him, teasing him, and then he said in a low hissing voice,

"I might have seen them, but then again, I might not. Only I know, and you won't ever find out!" The evil goblin stared at Toobah with his eyes bulging.

"You stupid, weird creatures, what are you supposed to be? You are not of any use or importance. In fact, you're a poor excuse for a creature and should never have been born!" Harqin yelled loudly and spat at Toobah.

Toobah was taken aback by Harqin's answer, but he persevered.

"Harqin, you must know how much trouble you have caused. Surely now you want to help and make amends?" Toobah said in an assertive voice.

Harqin continued to spit and curse at the little mambooa.

He was making no sense and Toobah was not going to show the goblin how upset it was making him. He turned on his heels and left the prince-goblin chuckling to himself; he was mocking the mambooa which left Toobah frustrated and angry.

He wished he hadn't made the visit. Harqin knew now of his sadness and frustration in the search for his kin. He would use this weakness if the opportunity arose. It was obvious this wretched creature was beyond help!

Biancala

Chapter Twenty-Four

The Deception

The night finally came and the new Junamoon had risen into the inky black sky. A bright orange glow appeared high above the ominous black cloud that shrouded the city.

It was time to fetch Harqin from the dungeon. Garvtak and Garvoid, along with four other goblins, had offered to guard him.

The witches' brew had been added to Harqin's meal an hour before so that it had time to take effect. They had fed him a rich stew, made from many pungent vegetables that had a very strong flavour, to disguise the witches' brew that had been added to the stock.

When the goblins came back to see if the brew had taken effect, Harqin was pacing the floor of his prison. He seemed very distracted and was muttering to himself.

But as Biancala and the other elves arrived, Harqin stopped abruptly in his tracks and stared at the princess in wonder and awe.

No, surely not; it couldn't be Aubree, could it?

Was this the long-lost elven beauty that he had wanted so desperately to marry?

Biancala was disturbed by Harqin's stare but she broke the spell as she spoke. "Harqin, you don't know me. I am the princess of the elves of Shalatarh."

With this, she came further forward so that Harqin could see her clearly.

"But you did know one of our kind before. Aubree is no longer with us; she has passed over to Elvaradon, the kingdom of our elders, and she now lives in peace and harmony amongst our ancestors," she said calmly.

Harqin was rooted to the spot and, while Biancala held his attention, the other elves were working their magic and moving the cage of mist towards the goblin.

The cage was the palest shade of yellow, with shimmering sparkles of light that glistened and glowed brightly.

It appeared like a mist and floated towards Harqin and wrapped itself around him, but the goblin was oblivious to what was happening.

He was mesmerised by Biancala's beauty and enthralled by her every word. The news that Harqin would never see Aubree again finally broke the spell, but it was too late - he was contained by the cage of mist.

"Arghhhh! What have you done, you treacherous demon?" Harqin yelled at Biancala. Memories had started flooding back into Harqin's mind. He was remembering everything: The love he felt for Aubree and the quarrel with Anthonus, the bitterness and anger that had crept into his heart and consumed his soul, and, of course, the curse that he had cast upon the goblins of Hootahn!

Then he suddenly remembered the conditions of the curse and the price he had to pay for the services of the gnarkull!

A deep sense of anger was building in the pit of his stomach; his blood was starting to boil.

He had started to pace his cell and could feel his fingertips burning with a tingling sensation; he knew that his magic was returning!

Harqin was trying to process everything in his mind. It was happening so fast; one minute, he was eating his meal feeling vulnerable, frightened and alone, and then, this dramatic transformation. What trickery was this?

The magic was returning; he could feel it race through his veins, but it was so much stronger than he had ever experienced before. This was incredible, he thought.

He would use this magic to escape and then he would burn Hootahn to the ground and everyone in it!

The prince-goblin was enraged and furiously tried to escape the cage of mist, but it held firm.

The goblins quickly grabbed Harqin and took him to the meeting point in the great park by the statue of Hootnam, who was the first great wizard goblin of the Third Realm, and Harqin's ancestor.

Mount Hoot and the city of Hootahn had been named in honour of this great goblin who built the city.

The sky was ablaze with a bright orange glow that shone high above.

The new Junamoon had risen, and it was breath-taking.

The rejuvenation of life across the Realms was always a sight to behold. Even the presence of the cloud hanging menacingly over Hootahn could not mask this glorious sight.

The invited party assembled by the statue: the witches of Harridan and several members of the great council of Hootahn, along with Anthonus and two other warlocks.

Mr Grumplepumple and his entourage were nervously waiting by the statue. Toobah looked disdainfully at the prince-goblin as he was brought forward.

Harqin was brought to stand by his ancestor's statue. Hatnal had hoped it would inspire compassion and patriotism in the prince, but it did not.

The goblin seemed possessed, and, to everyone's disgust, spat at the statue. Hatnal spoke in a clear and purposeful voice.

"Harqin, you have been brought here to lift the curse you have put upon this city. You have been given your memory back so you can remember the spell." Hatnal took a deep breath then continued,

"We know there was a risk in doing this as it gives you back your magic, but you must now use it to end the curse and send the gnarkull away for good!"

Harqin was glaring at Hatnal with an evil sneer on his face; there was no empathy, no loyalty or love in his eyes, just sheer evil.

Harqin spoke with a hiss, "What makes you think I would undo this curse? Why would I want to help you pathetic creatures?"

Harqin glanced over at Biancala and his eyes softened for a moment, but he then swung round and hissed louder when he suddenly spotted Anthonus in the crowd.

This sent the goblin crazy. He was screaming at the top of his voice and it seemed like something had possessed his entire body; he writhed about as if in pain. He was demented and the cloud above the city seemed to darken.

"You! How dare you cast your eyes on me, you vile excuse for a warlock? You are nothing but a pathetic, weak old fool, who was not worthy of your mother's love!" yelled Harqin as he glared at Anthonus.

There was a rumble of thunder and then an ear-splitting crack from above. It seemed like the mother of all storms was brewing and the heavens were about to open!

Anthonus braced himself and his warlock friend gave him a reassuring squeeze on his shoulder.

As he waited for Hatnal's signal, Mr Grumplepumple was starting to tremble with the thought of what he must do.

He must get close enough to use the dagger. He realised that this act would not only kill Harqin, but would quickly age him again, but it was a sacrifice he was willing to make.

He must now be strong and true to his word and rid this Realm of the evil goblin for good.

Goby stood by his brother with Squiggle on his shoulder, looking very worried. Squiggle kept ducking under Goby's ear every time there was a clap of thunder; it made the little booquar very frightened.

Mr Grumplepumple had asked Goby to keep the booquar with him. The young goblin did not understand why this was necessary, but was happy to oblige, and Squiggle never complained when he was with Goby.

Toobah, Booma and the other two mambooas were close by watching intently. Toobah thought for one moment that he could hear a familiar sound in the trees. He was sure he could hear the sound of mambooas chattering but soon realised it was just a memory and probably just the howling wind.

The mambooas had not lived here for a long time and he realised it was just wishful thinking. Toobah was willing Harqin to do as he was asked, but knew in his heart this was futile and the prince-goblin would not help in any way.

This was a very dangerous situation that could go terribly wrong. Toobah had instructed his fellow mambooas that if anything bad happened, they must protect Goby and Mr Grumplepumple.

"You must not hesitate. Any danger and we must grab our friends and run," Toobah said to the mambooas with determination in his voice.

Booma offered to grab Elphin and Migney and run with them.

Everyone was terrified. The thunder was getting louder but Harqin was still not willing to comply. He starting muttering to himself under his breath. Then his voice got louder as if he was....

"Oh no, he's trying to conjure up a spell!" yelled Hatnal.

With this, Anthonus leapt towards Harqin and thrust his staff forward with such force it nearly dislocated his shoulder.

He shouted some words that sounded very important and impressive.

"Disarmadic, Protecilama, Spontraptadum." This unleashed a burst of sparks from his staff that looked like lightning.

The light struck Harqin square in the chest and made the goblin fold over in pain, then another warlock joined in from behind Anthonus and another zap of lightning hit the prince-goblin.

Harqin was stunned and fell silent, his eyes wide with fear, and he was rooted to the spot.

The warlocks had disabled him and given him a warning to behave and obey Hatnal's request.

The cage of mist was still holding, but the yellow mist was beginning to fade. The elves were starting to lose their power to keep the cage in place. The goblin's magic was growing stronger; you could feel its presence and Harqin was becoming more confident and defiant.

Hatnal repeated his request for the prince-goblin to lift the curse and to repent and save the city.

"If not for yourself, do it to save the reputation of your ancestors. You must release the curse and dismiss the gnarkull!" yelled Hatnal.

The chief guardian of the city was wasting his time; he glanced over to Mr Grumplepumple for reassurance and to warn him to be ready to pounce.

Hatnal's words were being completely ignored, and all the time, Harqin was growing in strength.

A new-found energy was racing through him and suddenly, a more ferocious wind was howling through the great park.

Megilonia was nervously pacing back and forth; had the witches' brew been too strong and given the goblin the ability to tap into a stronger source of magic?

The witches were conversing with each other; they seemed very preoccupied and started to bicker amongst themselves. A couple of rogue sparks flew from their wands up into the sky.

"You put too much bluckpluck berry in the potion, you stupid old hag," said one of the witches to Makoleena.

She was always the first one to get an earful when something went wrong.

As she watched her sisters squabbling, Megilonia wondered what they had done.

But it was too late now to change anything. They had underestimated the goblin's ancestral powers that Harqin was drawing upon now!

The huge ominous black cloud that hung menacingly over the city started to grow bigger and darker. There were lightning streaks cracking across the sky and the loudest clap of thunder the goblins had ever heard.

It seemed like Harqin was calling upon the demons from hell!

The yellow mist was disappearing fast, and the elves had to release their grip on the cage as they could no longer hold the magic. Suddenly, the elves were gone. They disappeared into the night as quickly as they had come.

GnarKull

Chapter Twenty-Five

The Gnarkull

The gnarkull appeared out of the dark clouds and the screeching was ear-piercing as they swooped down and across the city.

"Eeeeekkkkkkkk, eeeeeekkkkkkkk!" they screeched in a high-pitched tone.

At the sight of these beasts, the prince-goblin started to laugh mockingly, but Hatnal, with Mr Grumplepumple by his side, stood his ground.

Garvtak and Garvoid were ordered to take Goby and the impbahs to the safety of the trees. The mambooas were ordered to follow, but they wouldn't move. They weren't going anywhere; they ignored the wizard goblin's demands.

"You must go. Do as I say; find shelter under the trees. Go now!" commanded Mr Grumplepumple.

But they would not leave Mr Grumplepumple. It was only right to support the goblins and fight to the end.

"I'm sorry, Mr Grumplepumple, but we aren't going anywhere. We're ready to fight, and to the bitter end, if need be," said Garvtak, looking round at everyone for reassurance and agreement.

Everyone was nodding their heads and patting each other.

Toobah winked at his kin and the mambooas stood ready.

Hatnal continued to demand that Harqin lift the curse but his words fell on deaf ears.

His cloak was flapping wildly, and his hat was whipped off his head into the air and whisked away out of sight.

Megilonia commanded the witches to take flight and attack the gnarkull in the air. Makoleena gave the impbahs a big hug, then climbed onto her penadilla. Elphin and Migney had grown very fond of this witch and tears had formed in their eyes. This was all so very upsetting.

Up and away they went, as swift as the wind, their long hair and cloaks flapping violently as the storm grew, wands at the ready as they fought to keep the gnarkull at bay!

Harqin saw this and suddenly threw back his head and lifted up his arms high into the sky as if conducting an orchestra.

He was going to attack the witches as they climbed. Anthonus could see what was happening and shot a bolt of lightning at Harqin.

This didn't seem to affect the goblin; it was as if he had grown a thicker skin and the bolts of lightning ricocheted off.

The warlocks and Mr Grumplepumple threw everything they had at him but it was futile. The prince-goblin had taken on a new form; he seemed bigger and even more grotesque than before. He turned on the group, full of malice; he was not going to show any mercy!

A bright red bolt of lightning shot out of Harqin's fingertips, aimed directly at Anthonus, who just managed to deflect the bolt in time.

It was relentless; sparks were flying everywhere and the warlocks magic was having no effect.

Hatnal kept on shouting at Harqin to stop, but he had tired of these demands and sent a bolt of lightning at him!

Everyone gasped in horror as it hit Hatnal square in the chest. This threw the goblin back with such force that he crumpled onto the floor.

Mr Grumplepumple was horrified and lunged forward, but Garvtak and Garvoid held him back.

This must have amused Harqin as he started to laugh out loud and dance on the spot, mocking the wizard goblin.

Before anyone could react, a little goblin sprinted forward through the crowd and raced towards Harqin, but the prince-goblin was too quick!

Harqin turned round quickly and sent a bolt of lightning towards the goblin, but just as the bolt was about to hit its target, another little goblin hurled himself in front of the first goblin and took the full force of the blast!

"No!" screamed Mr Grumplepumple and he hurled himself forward, breaking free from Garvtak and Garvoid.

He threw himself on top of Harqin in order to plunge the Dagger of Pumplestone deep into his chest!

Toobah and Booma raced forward at great speed and pushed past the goblins that had been grouped round Hatnal.

They quickly picked up the two brave little goblins that were slumped on the floor beside Hatnal and ran back to the protection of the trees.

However, a gnarkull had spotted the mambooas and turned to swoop down across the clearing towards them.

It nearly caught the goblin that Booma was carrying; it had its claws ready to snatch the little goblin from his back.

But Megilonia had been chasing the creature and shot a bolt of lightning at its wing. It screeched with pain and veered off and away above the trees.

More gnarkulls came; everyone was surprised at how many there were, and it looked like the witches were starting to lose the battle.

Garvoid and Garvtak were about to run towards Mr Grumplepumple when another gnarkull attacked. They could see its black evil face bearing down on them. They raised their pointy sticks; they had to protect their leader. The other goblins had gathered round Harqin and Mr Grumplepumple to prevent Harqin from getting away and to protect Mr Grumplepumple.

The gnarkull was close, its ear-piercing screeching terrifying, but Garvtak and Garvoid stood their ground.

Just as it was about to pounce, something came hurtling from the trees above, and whatever it was hit the gnarkull's head with great force.

This startled the beast and it had to swerve to miss the ground.

What followed then was a storm of stones, one after the other, aimed at the gnarkulls.

"Zoom, zoom, zoom," whizzed the stones.

Whatever or whoever was firing these objects was greeted with a big cheer from everyone in the park.

Toobah looked up into the trees with sheer delight and excitement; he knew he had heard that familiar sound before.

It wasn't wishful thinking; it was indeed his long-lost relatives, the mambooas of Hootahn. They had returned and were up in the trees yelling at the top of their voices.

"Yala yala yalaaaaaaaaa, wooooooohooooooooo," they shouted together.

"They must have been waiting up in the trees for the right moment to help and gathered many Canoti nuts to shoot at the gnarkulls when needed!" yelled Enzo.

Toobah remembered the clever slingshot devices made out of leather that they used to propel nuts at high speed.

Booma shouted to Toobah, "Well, that's definitely doing the trick".

The nuts were being shot through the air at such a high velocity, pounding the gnarkulls and making the bats career off course.

Booma explained to Garvtak and Garvoid that Canoti nuts had extremely hard shells and were not easy to open, but the labouring to get to the nut itself was worth it, as the nut was so sweet and delicious.

The mambooas we're chattering loudly and hurling everything they had. The witches had to retreat for fear of being bombarded by the nuts themselves!

Elphin and Migney rejoiced at what they were seeing and joined in.

"Eeeeekkkkkkkk eeeekkkkk," they screamed like true impbahs, from under the trees near to the mambooas. This frightened Squiggle who had been sitting on Elphin's shoulder, as Goby had asked the impbah to mind the booquar.

The cacophony of sound was incredible. The goblins had to cover their ears; the intense noise made the gnarkull nervous. The bombardment from the mambooas, combined with the lightning bolts from the warlocks below and the witches from above, forced the gnarkull back behind Mount Hoot.

Everyone was trying to catch their breath and digest what had happened as the witches came down from the skies and landed.

They looked battered and worn out, their hair matted from the wind and their cloaks dishevelled and torn.

Makoleena was trying to untangle her hair from her penadilla and not having much luck.

The goblins of Hootahn, along with Garvtak and Garvoid, looked down on the floor where the two bodies lay motionless on the ground in the middle of the circle they had created.

There was no movement from either of the bodies. Everyone gathered round - the goblins, the witches and the warlocks.

The mambooas had climbed down from the trees above and were greeted by Toobah, Booma and the other mambooas. It was a wonderful sight to see, and they were all embracing and hugging and dancing.

But the joyous meeting stopped abruptly when Toobah realised what had happened and they ran over quickly to join the others.

Elphin and Migney stayed with the two little goblins, now propped up against a tree trunk, still dazed and in shock.

Squiggle had run as fast as his little legs could carry him. He ran through the legs of the goblins and jumped onto Mr Grumplepumple. He was pulling his beard and clicking loudly in his ear.

There was a sudden movement and the wizard goblin lifted his shoulders and shook his head. Surprisingly, his hat was still in place.

Everyone heaved a sigh of relief as Mr Grumplepumple lifted himself off Harqin, which was not easy with a booquar kissing his face all over!

The prince-goblin lay very still on his side, not moving. Was he dead?

Mr Grumplepumple had leapt forward when he saw Goby struck by the bolt of lightning from Harqin. He was enraged and had his dagger ready. He could feel an intense heat from the handle; it was burning as he thrust it into the prince-goblin. The dagger cut through Harqin's grotesque scaly skin with ease. His scream was smothered and silenced by Mr Grumplepumple being on top of him. The effort of plunging the dagger took its toll and the wizard goblin felt his blood freeze; it felt like life itself was draining away and leaving him. Then, he fainted from exhaustion.

Mr Grumplepumple got up and was shaking the dust off his cloak with Squiggle slapping his shoulders to try and help.

The booquar was deliriously happy, and perhaps a little too excited, so Mr Grumplepumple had to pluck him off his back. He stroked his head and put him back in his pocket.

Everyone was chatting loudly amongst themselves. This had been a momentous night but there was also great sadness as Hatnal lay crumpled on the floor.

The goblins were just about to lift their chief guardian's body when Harqin suddenly moved and swung his grotesque body round to reveal a dagger sticking out of his chest.

There was a gasp of horror and everyone froze as the prince-goblin staggered to his feet. His face was distorted and twisted with rage like a devil!

He let out a blood-curdling scream as he tried to pull the dagger out of his body.

"Arghhhhhhhh, arghhhhh!" he screamed.

Then suddenly, there was a flash of green and someone, out of nowhere, threw themselves onto him and thrust the dagger further into his heart.

It was Hebden! A fierce rage and anger had consumed the little goblin and he was going to finish Harqin off once and for all!

Harqin let out a horrific scream and staggered back, his eyes black with evil. His body was contorted with pain and he slumped to the ground with a heavy thump.

Hebden was panting heavily and then pulled the heavy dagger out of Harqin and dragged it back to offer it to Mr Grumplepumple.

No one spoke; no one did anything. They just looked down upon the little goblin standing there with the weapon that was nearly as big as him.

He lifted it up to give it back to Mr Grumplepumple who was still completely shocked by what had just happened.

Suddenly, there was a clap of thunder so loud that it took everyone by surprise, and out of the night sky appeared a gnarkull.

It circled up above, screeching loudly. It was much larger than the others that had come before, with a much greater wingspan.

There was a whirling sound coming from Harqin's body which lay motionless on the floor; it was an eerie sound like a mini-tornado that seem to be growing underneath his body.

You could hear it building and the noise was getting louder and louder, then suddenly, there was an eruption and the body started to whirl around in the air. A dark violet vapour was floating out of the goblin's body and all of a sudden, it swirled round violently. There was a loud whoosh and it went soaring up into the black sky.

The gnarkull saw this and swooped towards it screeching loudly, flying through the vapour, but then a dark mass formed in the middle of the vapour.

The gnarkull grabbed it with its fierce claws and let out another ear-piercing screech before it flew off into the distance.

It had claimed Harqin's soul!

The dark black cloud, which had hung over the city of Hootahn for so long, began to split apart and melt away.

In its place was the magnificent Junamoon that shone in all its glory.

Goby and Hebden

Chapter Twenty-Six

Unity of the Three Realms

The curse was lifted! Hootahn was saved and could now return to being a happy place, where creatures could live in peace and harmony together.

Anthonus explained to Mr Grumplepumple that the gnarkull had been summoned from the land of Grackinium, which lay on the other side of the Great Calder Sea, but now they had Harqin's soul, they would return to their homeland, hopefully, never to be seen again.

The goblins of Hootahn came out of their homes and made their way to the park, although they had been given strict instructions from Hatnal and his council to stay indoors.

Everyone was cheering and praising the brave group that had defeated the prince-goblin, but of course, there was also great sadness for they had lost their beloved leader, their wise and fearless chief guardian.

They all became solemn and quiet when they saw Hatnal lying on the floor and some of the lady goblans rushed forward with flowers and fruit to cover the body.

Mr Grumplepumple was curious and asked why the goblans were doing this strange thing to Hatnal.

It was Hoolanoc who answered; "This is a tradition in Hootahn; we believe that when a goblin leaves this Realm, they will enter the next Realm in another form," he said in a solemn voice.

"Provisions are needed for their journey; they must be placed on the body as soon as possible to make sure the food goes with the spirit, the goblin's soul."

Goby noticed this gesture was not extended to Harqin's body as it lay cold and grey like a solitary stone.

Hoolanoc, the chief goblin's right-hand goblin, climbed up onto the feet of the statue of Hootnam. He raised Hatnal's staff as high as he could and everyone recognised it immediately. The park fell silent as the goblin spoke in a nervous but clear voice,

"It has been a glorious night. We have won the battle and lifted the curse, and we are so grateful to many of you ."

Hoolanoc surveyed the crowd and tilted his head in the direction of Mr Grumplepumple, who had his arms wrapped around Goby.

"But first, we must pay our respects to our chief guardian who has lost his life in this Realm. We must make sure he has a smooth passage into the next and honour his death."

There was a deep murmuring from the crowd and a number of goblins came forward with what looked like a giant golden leaf on which they gingerly placed Hatnal and carried him away to lie in state in the halls of the elders.

Another leaf was brought for Harqin's body, but this one was dull and brown, with no beauty or importance.

Hoolanoc surveyed the crowd. He wanted to lift their spirits. This was a new era, so he declared that there would be a huge celebration to pay thanks. He announced, "It is time to prepare; there is much to do and organise".

The crowd dispersed quickly, full of excitement. There was a feeling of great joy and gratitude and they wanted to make sure that the celebration would go down in history as the biggest party ever held in Hootahn!

Toobah and the other mambooas were engrossed in conversation with their new-found family; Mr Grumplepumple was so glad to see this reunion. It had made the whole journey worthwhile to see his dear friend's face. He made a mental note to visit the north shores of the Calder Sea when next on his travels.

But that might not be for some time. The use of the Dagger of Pumplestone had taken its toll and he could feel the effects of the ageing that came with it. Mr Grumplepumple looked at his brother and his heart filled with pride.

He asked Goby, "What happened? Why did you put your life at risk?"

Goby was happy to explain, and Elphin and Migney settled down to listen, along with Garvtak and Garvoid.

Goby explained, "I saw Hebden run forward when Hatnal had been struck, and I knew exactly what he was going to do, but I couldn't let this happen; I couldn't lose my new friend who I had become so very fond of."

Everyone was looking at the little goblin with pride in their hearts and tears in their eyes.

"So, I instinctively ran after Hebden and just managed to hurl myself in front of him in time!" said Goby as if it wasn't a big thing.

Mr Grumplepumple looked at Goby with a broad smile.

"You took the full force of the bolt of lightning that Harqin unleashed, so how did you manage to survive this blow?" he asked.

"Well, luckily for me, the buckle on my back sack took the brunt of the hit; it stunned me, but it saved my life!" Goby said with astonishment.

All eyes turned to the little impbah. Elphin had done well. His little invention had a greater importance than first thought. Everyone patted Elphin on the back and gave a big cheer of gratitude.

This embarrassed Elphin and his face immediately turned bright red as everyone praised him.

It made the little impbah very proud and Migney was bowing to him in a gesture of jest but also great pride.

The witches then said their goodbyes. They were going to stay with their sisters in Heptonstall Wood. The food of the goblins did not suit their palate, but they said they would be back for the celebrations.

Makoleena gave Elphin an enormous hug. The news of Elphin's buckle saving the night travelled fast.

"In a roundabout way, little Elphin, you saved Goby's life and you should be very proud of yourself. I'm very proud of you," she said in a choked-up crackle. Then she hugged Migney too, as she didn't want him to feel left out.

Megilonia looked at Mr Grumplepumple with sadness in her eyes; she heard about the consequences of using the Dagger of Pumplestone from Garvtak when she questioned why the wizard goblin had aged dramatically. Mr Grumplepumple looked tired and frail but still wore an air of authority and command, and was organising his group to go back to the city.

Hebden had returned from helping to convey Hatnal's body to the Great Hall and was now stood by Hoolanoc.

He was staring at Goby, huddled in the comfort of his family circle. He felt a stabbing pang of jealousy, but it did not last long.

The little goblin had become very close to Goby and was happy for him. Hebden was reflecting on what had happened and how he had been by Goby's side after the mambooas had retrieved them after Harqin's blow.

The little goblin was still dazed from Goby falling on top of him with all his body weight, but it had saved his life.

The little goblin from Pumple Mountain in the First Realm had saved him.

Mr Grumplepumple looked over and spotted Hebden, so he beckoned him over to come and join them.

Hebden was happy to oblige and ran over to join the family circle.

"We owe a great debt of gratitude to you, young Hebden," said Mr Grumplepumple.

He asked the little goblin, "How did you know Harqin was still alive?"

"I never took my eyes off him and, when he rolled over, a great fire roared inside me and I just bolted over towards him. Harqin was not going to survive. It was he who had killed my family and he was not going to kill my new friends as well," he said, panting heavily as the emotions were getting the better of him.

"I didn't care if I lived or died and I was willing to sacrifice my life, so I hurled myself onto Harqin to bury the dagger further into him." He finished speaking and glanced over at Goby. Goby reached over and gave Hebden a huge hug and thanked him again.

Mr Grumplepumple saw so much of Goby in Hebden. They had formed such a deep bond of friendship that he knew it would last a lifetime.

They were all about to walk off when they heard the fluttering of tiny wings and out of the woods flew the popstrells, led by Plock and all of them squeaking loudly.

They came to land on the statue; everyone was so pleased to see them.

Goby felt a pang of guilt because he hadn't given them much thought. Plock flew over to land on Mr Grumplepumple's shoulder. The wizard goblin was so glad to see them; he thought they had not survived their gallant action when attacking the gnarkull.

"Oh, my dear Plock, I cannot tell you how much pleasure it gives me to see you are alive," Mr Grumplepumple said with great joy in his heart.

Plock explained how they all managed to escape but many of the popstrells had torn wings, so they had to hide in the Great Forest until they had healed. On seeing so many gnarkulls in the skies, they were frustrated that they were unable to help, but they couldn't fly, so they had to stay put.

Mr Grumplepumple stroked the little bat and told him not to fret; they had performed above and beyond the call of duty. They had saved his life and he was forever grateful.

With this, the little bat fluffed up his chest and flew off back to the statue of Hootnam.

The celebrations in Hootahn went on for days and, as word spread, goblins, witches, warlocks and many other creatures came to join in the festivities. They wanted to celebrate, but also pay homage to Hatnal, the chief guardian. There was music, laughter and many tales and songs to be heard.

Mr Grumplepumple, Goby, Garvtak and Garvoid were presented with the most beautiful tunics you could imagine, which had been made especially for them.

They were resplendent in their finery and there was even a little hat for Squiggle, which suited him well, and made the little booquar smile from ear to ear.

The impbahs and mambooas were not for having these strange clothes made for them, as they were happy in their own skin. However, Elphin asked for some colourful tags to put on the back sacks.

Carboot and some other members from the Second Realm came to attend the celebrations, much to Mr Grumplepumple's delight.

It seemed the Three Realms had finally come together again in unity and harmony. Hoolanoc, Carboot and Mr Grumplepumple sat at a table together; they drank berry wine and feasted upon the bounty of food available.

They retold tales from times gone by and shared their experiences, some bringing laughter and some sadness, but they were happy in each other's company. They swore to each other that they would never let anything or anyone come between the Three Realms again.

This was sealed with a vow and the honorary salute of their staffs.

***

Toobah had found his long-lost relatives, which, of course, was the main reason for the quest in the first place.

There were not as many mambooas as he would have liked; the ones that returned to Hootahn had come from the north of the Third Realm.

They had settled near the shores of Hardcastle, at the most northerly point of the land, where many forests lined the shores of the great Calder Sea. Hardcastle provided a safe haven for them and they had settled well.

Sarhoo, the head of the tribe, received news that mambooas had entered the land.

One of the creatures they traded with had paid a visit to Sarhoo; he explained that mambooas had been asking after them and had entered Hootahn. They could not believe this; they thought they were the only mambooas to have survived the great fire!

They wanted to return to Hootahn as soon as possible but they knew of the curse on the city, and the trader explained how Harqin had been found alive and captured, but that was all he knew.

They could not just rush in as the situation could be dangerous.

It was Barboo, the young mambooa warrior, who came up with the cunning plan. He had gone with another scout to survey the city in secret.

From the darkness of the trees in the great park, he had seen Toobah and Booma in conversation. He was so excited and desperately wanted to jump down and make his presence known but stopped when he heard Toobah telling Booma he had visited Harqin in the dungeons. Toobah was telling Booma how evil the prince-goblin had become and how worried he was about the plan failing.

"I fear giving Harqin back his magic to lift the curse will not work. I think he will summon the gnarkull immediately!" said Toobah in a sombre voice.

Barboo knew then that he had to keep their presence secret; they had the advantage of surprise and so the plan was hatched.

Barboo reported back to Sarhoo, who was very proud of his son.

A small group of mambooa warriors, who were masters of the slingshot, were gathered, and, led by Barboo, they travelled undercover to the city.

They positioned themselves in the trees and waited for the right moment to attack the gnarkull.

***

Sarhoo and Barboo gave Toobah and the mambooas a warrior's salute and promised they would visit Pumple Mountain someday soon.

The two tribes of mambooas shook hands and gave embarrassed pats on the back; they were warriors, so hugs were not considered appropriate.

Toobah was insistent that they should not leave it too long, however, Sarhoo hesitated before he answered.

"We need to rekindle our bond; will you not consider coming back with us to Hardcastle and living amongst your own kind again?"

Toobah had given this much thought and there was a great temptation to go, but after a lengthy discussion with Booma and the others, it was decided their home was with the Pumple goblins.

"My dear cousin, we have found each other again and that is good, but we must make sure our kind prosper and grow, therefore, we need to live across the length and breadth of the Three Realms," said Toobah with conviction.

Sarhoo understood what Toobah was trying to say, so he hugged his cousin and they said their goodbyes.

The witches of Harridan had returned for the celebrations but did not indulge in the food, although, the wine was most acceptable and Makoleena indulged a little bit too much.

She nearly squeezed the life out of Elphin and Migney with her hugs and kisses; even her little toad was very obliging with its adoration.

Megilonia and her sisters were to take Mr Grumplepumple and the others back with them to the Harridan Mountains and then the group would travel back to Quazboo to drop off Migney.

Goby and Hebden had become even closer after Goby's brave act to save his friend. The little goblin had never experienced anyone showing him so much affection before.

He had been a loner since his parents died and he preferred it that way. He did not want anyone to go through the hurt and pain he had experienced.

So, living on his own, fetching and carrying through the tunnels had become a way of life, and the constant threat of the gnarkulls hadn't perturbed him in the least. Hebden did not value his life very highly, but Goby had changed that.

This little goblin had been willing to sacrifice his life to save him, and this was such an unusual act of kindness and bravery, that Hebden felt such a deep respect and adoration for Goby.

The time had come for the little group to make their way home. It had been quite an adventure and their tales would be told for many moolatoons.

It was time to say goodbye, and the creatures of Hootahn had all gathered near the statue of Hootnam.

Even Biancala and her elves had graced the occasion and wanted to give thanks to Mr Grumplepumple and his little group.

Anthonus came forward and pressed something into Goby's hand. He whispered into his ear,

"A little something I was given to pass on to you in honour of the bravery and courage you have shown".

Goby looked down at his hand and saw a wonderful wood carving; it looked like a wood nymph.

It was beautiful and had the look of Elowen; he was so in awe of this gift, he was speechless.

Anthonus explained that the wood nymph had asked if he would give Goby this gift. She wanted him to remember her and hoped that, one day, they would meet again.

Goby placed it in his new tunic in the pocket next to his heart, where it would remain for all time.

Megilonia was keen to be gone so everyone made their way to the penadillas. Mr Grumplepumple and Goby were to ride with Megilonia, as before. Squiggle made sure he was deep inside Mr Grumplepumple's cloak pocket. Elphin and Migney went with Makoleena, of course, and Garvtak and Garvoid went with Maddelarcha.

Toobah and the mambooas politely declined to be transported by anything that flew in the sky; their first experience was to be their last.

They thought it would be safer and quicker to travel by land, guided, of course, by the popstrells.

This made Plock and his fellow kin feel very important and they squeaked with pride.

Goby was feeling very sad. His heart felt so heavy with sorrow as he was leaving his dear friend.

The little goblin was so torn. He wanted to stay with Hebden but, of course, he could not. His home was in Kracklewood with Mr Grumplepumple.

He would miss Hebden so much, but they promised each other that they would visit as often as they could.

The two little goblins parted with a strong embrace which lasted for a long time.

Mr Grumplepumple turned to Hoolanoc and nodded in respect and winked; the crowds cheered and clapped very loudly.

Hoolanoc had presented Mr Grumplepumple with a multicoloured cloak of the finest Amoucs wool; it was magnificent and he was wearing it with pride.

It was to replace his battered and worn-out cloak that had been torn by the gnarkull and he felt very humble accepting it, but that was typical of Mr Grumplepumple. Hoolanoc had also taken the opportunity to have a private word with Mr Grumplepumple as he wanted to discuss Hebden.

"Our little Hebden seems to have grown very fond of Goby; they are like two berries in a pod! Would be a terrible shame to split them up, don't you think?" he said in a quizzical manner.

Mr Grumplepumple knew exactly what Hoolanoc was trying to say.

Mr Grumplepumple turned to the little goblin who was stood by his side. He smiled with such warmth of kindness and said,

"You'd better not dither, young goblin, it's time to go!"

Hebden's eyes lit up. He was stunned and immediately looked up at Hoolanoc. The new chief guardian of Hootahn turned to the little goblin and said with a heavy but happy heart,

"We think you may have found your new family, Hebden. Would you like to go with them and live in Kracklewood?"

The little goblin burst into tears. He could not help himself, and Goby was beside himself with joy. Goby turned to his brother and gave him the biggest smile his little face could muster. Hebden did not hesitate; with tear-stained eyes, he hugged Hoolanoc and then wrapped his arms around his new family.

Megilonia said she could manage two small goblins and a bigger one, so Goby, Hebden and Mr Grumplepumple all jumped onto Megilonia's penadilla and off they flew.

Elphin stayed in Quazboo for a little while with Migney and the other impbahs before he returned home to Kracklewood.

Toobah had found his long-lost family so the quest had been successful and life in the Graven Tree had returned to its normal, peaceful state.

A little refurbishment was required in Mr Grumplepumple's home to accommodate a new family member; rather a lot of wood was collected to make up some comfortable beds, and a wardrobe for their new clothes!

The End